IN HIS ARMS

"I am perfectly fine, Mr. Butler," Rachel answered briskly. "And quite accustomed to taking care of myself."

But when she struggled to stand once more, her troubled ankle yielded beneath the pressure of her weight. With a slight cry, she sagged earthward just as Jonah Butler's strong arm encircled her waist.

"My dear, I am a man of honor," Butler boasted with a crooked grin. His sly tone made a complete mockery of his words. "My conscience would never allow me to abandon you in the face of this encroaching peril."

Rachel's cheeks warmed before Jonah Butler's unflinching scrutiny. In her twenty-two years, she had endured countless storms and survived perfectly well. The real peril she faced here was not the huffing weather. It was, she knew most assuredly, lingering in the arms of this muscular stranger. . . .

Dear Romance Readers,

In July 2000, we launched the Ballad line with four new series, and each month since then we've presented both new and continuing stories set everywhere from medieval England to the American West—the kind of passionate, romantic stories you love best, written by the most gifted authors. At the back of each book, we'll tell you when you can find subsequent books in the series that have captured your heart.

First up this month is Pam McCutcheon, with the first installment of the charming new series *The Graces.* A fairy godmother is a very good thing for three sisters who need a little help when it comes to romance—and the women who pitch in, beginning with the **Belle of the Ball,** have quite a few ancient, and highly effective, secrets up their sleeves! Next, Golden Heart finalist Laurie Brown presents *Masquerade,* as a British operative meets the woman who steals his life story for her potboilers—and captures his heart in the process. Will he learn **The Truth About Cassandra?**

Talented newcomer Caroline Clemmons takes us to the sweeping Texas plains as she begins the story of *The Kincaids,* and introduces us to a man determined to find **The Most Unsuitable Wife**—who soon discovers a passion he can't resist. Finally, Marilyn Herr explores the paths taken *In Love and War* as a hard-headed man and an equally spirited woman caught up in the dramatic French and Indian conflict decide to follow **Where the Heart Leads.** Enjoy.

Kate Duffy
Editorial Director

In Love and War

WHERE THE HEART LEADS

Marilyn Herr

ZEBRA BOOKS
Kensington Publishing Corp.
http://www.kensingtonbooks.com

For Barbara, Ginny, and Marion
—wise, wonderful, longtime friends

Prologue

Venango, Pennsylvania, 1753

No! She would not peek! No matter how devilishly handsome the man's . . .

Clutching a worn wooden paddle, Rachel Whitfield furiously resumed battling her soiled laundry. May breezes rippled the linens, unfurled on a flat boulder rising from the Allegheny River.

Plump servant woman Mary Hutchings paused to rest her weary arms. "Ah, breathe in, Rachel, luv! Nothing warms the soul more than a spring afternoon. Only smell those heavenly locust blossoms, I beg of you. They flutter through the air like a thousand angel wings. Rachel? Deary? You seem . . . unduly absorbed in thought."

Despite her earlier vow, Rachel peered once more through thickset hickory branches at the dusky stranger.

"Mercy! He . . . disrobes!" she murmured. A slow, sensual tug brought the man's fringed buckskin shirt above his chest, then up over his head. Watching those naked burly shoulders, Rachel felt her lips part.

"What did Pa say about the man, Mary?" she begged, inquiring about the brash stranger who had arrived at her father's Venango trading post that same morning.

"Let me see." Mary scratched her silver-white hair a moment, then gathered up her laundry burden. "Your pa first met him years ago back in Lancaster. Said his name was Jonah Butler. He's just fetched a pack train in from Philadelphia," Mary called over her shoulder as she shuffled toward Eli Whitfield's trading post.

Sweat-stained and muddied from his arduous journey west across the Alleghenies, Jonah Butler's bold, beseeching gaze that morning had made Rachel instinctively snag her homespun skirt close against her thighs. She knew what brutish urges lay behind that brazen male stare. Thankfully Old Eliza, a trader's wife who'd moved farther west into the Ohio wilderness, had educated Rachel on *that* score.

Men were harsh necessities on this mountainous frontier. But they brought no real pleasure to a woman, according to Old Eliza's admonitions.

"Men are thoughtless creatures, my dear. Entirely absorbed in their own gratification," Old Eliza had once warned Rachel. "In their rough haste, when they throw up your skirt, they plunge in and cause pain. Expect not to enjoy it, child. A bit of advice—just close your eyes and think of England. Mercifully, 'tis over in the wink of an eye."

Hesitating over her laundry now, Rachel blinked. Pain and rough handling? Why would any rational woman endure such nonsense? In defense, Rachel vowed to keep her skirts properly in place and avoid any man's touch. Forever!

Her gaze returned to the glistening bulge of Jonah Butler's naked shoulders. He . . . he seemed about to remove more clothing. Shielded from Butler's view by a dense viburnum thicket, Rachel felt her mouth parch.

Beneath whispering hemlocks at river's edge, Butler appeared unaware of feminine scrutiny. He stepped out of his moccasins. After several firm-handed tugs, the ebony-haired trader slipped off his fringed leather breeches. Nothing remained except a breechclout, which he wore Indian fashion.

Peeking at Butler between interwoven branches, Rachel swallowed hard.

Had she not often seen her brothers, Zeb and Gabriel, stripped to the waist? Well, yes, but their physical attributes scarcely interested her.

To Rachel, Jonah Butler seemed profoundly . . . different. He gave new definition to the word *man*. And when he bathed in the river, and his breech-clout shifted as he bent over, virginal Rachel stirred with a restless, unfamiliar longing that near terri-fied her.

Her tongue involuntarily moistened her lips.

Puzzled by this sighing response to the muscular trader's near naked appearance, Rachel clenched her fists.

"Men are thoughtless!" she remembered Old Eliza warn. "They cause pain."

Rachel tucked her skirt tighter around her knees to ward off any possible male intrusion. She patted the prim blond plait inside her mobcap and pulled her neck scarf even higher around her throat.

Suddenly blue jays upriver squawked a frenzied alarm.

Searching in vain for Mary Hutchings, Rachel heard a tumult of desperate sounds. Men's shouts, abrupt clatter, thrashing tree limbs. More outcries, this time in French. Metal crashing against metal

. . . a man's frantic scream. Crouched in fear beneath an overhanging hemlock limb, Rachel saw the glint of a metal ax head in sunlight and the flash of a red cap.

"Renard? Is that you?" one Frenchman yelled to another through tangled laurel thickets.

In stunned terror, Rachel tore blindly through the underbrush. Aimless running, faster than her legs had ever carried her.

"Rachel! Rachel . . . my God!" A man's voice echoed through the trees as Rachel's frantic gulps for air slowed her mad dash. Someone was chasing her, shouting her name! A thick male hand abruptly clawed at her arm.

Rachel whirled at the touch.

"Pa!" she screamed, staring at Eli Whitfield's terror-stricken expression. Clinging to her father, she felt him tremble. "Wha . . . what in God's name just happened? Blood spatters your face and shirt!"

A shocked Eli Whitfield stuttered to form his words. "'Tis Zeb, Rachel!" he cried, referring to his eldest son. "The villains seized him! M-maybe even killed him. And Lord Almighty, I could not save him!"

"Who, Pa?" she shouted, her voice quavering. "Why would anyone hurt Zeb?"

"Frenchmen from up north, Rachel. They want us out of here. Zeb tried to stop them from putting a French flag on the cabin. They struck at him with a hatchet, then carried off his poor body. Surely he could not survive those wounds . . . only a m-miracle . . ."

Rachel seized her stunned father by the shoulders. "Pa, what about Gabriel?" she asked of her younger brother.

Whitfield gestured a blood-soaked forefinger. "Back in the cabin, with Mary."

"Then let us go after them—the three of us! And that trader who came here this morning! We shall . . ."

Eli shook his head dismally. "Gabriel's bleeding. And the scoundrels carried off Jonah Butler along with poor Zeb."

"Oh, Eli! How can we possibly do as you say?" Mary Hutchings demanded as she helped Rachel bandage Gabriel's knife wounds.

"There can be no debate, Mary. Tomorrow we raft south on the Allegheny . . . maybe all the way to the Monongahela," Eli advised his servant and two remaining children. "If the French find us here again, they intend to kill us."

Rachel clenched her jaw defiantly as she wrapped a piece of torn muslin around Gabriel's arm.

She had failed Zeb today. Her hesitation might have cost her older brother his life. Crouched in cowardly terror, she had allowed him to be butchered by some depraved Frenchman nicknamed Renard—the Fox.

And what of Jonah Butler, that swarthy trader who curiously appeared on the Whitfield doorstep the very same day Zeb was attacked—then just as mysteriously vanished after the assault?

Never again, Rachel vowed, tossing a basin of bloody water into the dooryard, would she shrink in shocked cowardice before the evil intentions of any man. Somehow she would locate the Frenchman called the Fox and mete out her own form of justice to him.

And, just as surely, she meant to purge the dangerous image of robust Jonah Butler—the roguishly handsome fur trader who troubled her thoughts—forever from her mind.

One

Perspiration beads dampened Rachel Whitfield's forehead and trickled between the soft cleavage of her breasts. Surely no one would notice, under scorching August heat out here in the wilderness, if she took the liberty of . . .

With one cautious backward glance at the Monongahela River, Rachel loosened the large kerchief tucked firmly inside her bodice. Fanning herself with one hand, she fought off the attentions of a fat black fly.

As she'd done nearly every day for the past three months, Rachel glared north—toward the meandering Allegheny River and Canada—with a determined oath. "One day I shall find you, Zeb Whitfield. And the man who stole you? Oh, that wretched Fox shall pay dearly for his treachery!"

Rachel returned to the task of digging snakeroot, to be sold at her father's new trading post. Knee-high stands of the herb brushed against Rachel's long striped apron and coarse homespun skirt.

Far in the distance from the grassy meadow where she labored, a cloud of dust signaled approaching horses and men. Rachel's skin tingled, as if she sensed her life was about to change forever.

"Nonsense!" she muttered. "Only another pack train, likely." Fanning herself, Rachel clutched her root-filled rye basket and studied this apparition from the east.

Dim sounds reached her ears. The creak of leather straining from the warm press of horseflesh. Low guttural male voices passing comments to one another.

"Headed for Pa's trading post," she whispered on a guess, referring to Eli's new cabin perched in the valley where Turtle Creek joined the Monongahela.

The lead drover's appearance seized Rachel's attention. A man strangely familiar. Tall, broad-chested, he rode his Conestoga horse with the arrogant confidence of a fierce backwoodsman unaccustomed to accepting no for an answer—to any demand.

Watching him, Rachel shivered despite the August heat.

The lead man's teeth gleamed white in the afternoon sun as he laughed. His shining, coarse black hair whipped about from the onslaught of mounting winds. Clad in a fringed buckskin hunting shirt, leggings, and moccasins, he seemed to Rachel a dangerous sort of man who surely lived on the edge of decency. A man not to be trifled with.

A man who . . . who might not properly respect women.

Whistling summer gusts whipped Rachel's skirt flat against the back of her knees.

Nearly within range of recognition now, the stranger focused on her with an enigmatic smile before gesturing at the sky. A hostile storm, massive in its proportions, raged east from the Ohio River Valley toward Rachel. Dark roiling clouds seized the heavens. Distant thunder vibrated soil beneath Rachel's bare feet.

"Mercy!" she exclaimed, sensing the storm would surely overtake her before she could reach her father's post, a half-mile away.

In barefoot haste, Rachel attempted a fast trot toward Turtle Creek. A mistake, she quickly learned.

Lush blue-green meadow grasses, swaying beneath urgent winds, concealed the mouth of a rabbit hole just large enough to snare Rachel's foot and twist her ankle. With a sudden cry of pain, she sprawled headfirst onto the ground. Her basket shot into the air. Harvested snakeroot flew in every direction.

Forlornly massaging her offending ankle, Rachel missed the lead drover's silent approach.

His baritone greeting sounded harsh. "You need a man, m'lady."

Trapped by her infirmity on a grassy tussock, she glared at him. "I need no one, sir!" she shot back.

Her glance swept up the arrogant stranger's leather-clad muscular frame, from his moccasined feet to his open-necked shirt. A sprinkle of black chest hair peeped between the buckskin thongs lacing his shirt-front together. The bearded man's buckskins did little to conceal his taut-framed, swaggering body.

Like some wild bear in search of game, Rachel decided with a painful swallow.

It was Jonah Butler.

And close up, he appeared to Rachel the very sort of brusque, dangerous man about whom Old Eliza had oft warned her.

He smirked at her disarray—the loose honey-colored tendrils escaping her mobcap, long skirts billowing in the aggressive wind, her partially undone throat scarf.

"My scarf!" Rachel cried in red-faced embarrassment.

Her hand fluttered to her bosom in a defensive effort to retuck the loosened kerchief. Struggling to compose herself, which only seemed to expose her ample cleavage further, she discovered that pain prevented her from standing unassisted.

"Jonah Butler at your service, ma'am," the man said, bowing with mock civility. "I could not help but notice your plight, miss . . . miss?"

Rachel sensed hawklike predation in his leering gaze. His handsome ruggedness made her decidedly uneasy. She had no intention of telling him her name. Clearly he was an untrustworthy man. A lecher who had questions to answer about Zeb Whitfield's wretched disappearance.

And Rachel's earlier fascination with Butler's near-naked masculinity? Oh, never could he be permitted to learn of that personal weakness!

"I am perfectly fine, Mr. Butler," she answered briskly. "And quite accustomed to taking care of myself."

But when she struggled to stand once more, Rachel's troubled ankle yielded beneath the pressure of her weight. With a slight cry, she sagged earthward just as Jonah Butler's strong arm encircled her waist.

"My dear Miss No-name, I am a man of honor," Butler boasted with a crooked grin. His sly tone made a complete mockery of his words. "My conscience would never allow me to abandon you in the face of this encroaching peril."

Rachel's cheeks warmed before Jonah Butler's unflinching scrutiny. In her twenty-two years, she had endured countless storms and survived perfectly well. The real peril she faced here was not the huffing weather. It was, she knew most assuredly, lingering in the arms of this muscular stranger.

Fierce winds clawed at Rachel's long skirt and striped apron as raindrops speckled her bodice. She wedged her palms against Butler's chest. Try though she might, she could not bring herself to push him away. His supportive clasp became . . . an embrace.

When he lowered his head for a kiss Rachel did not—could not—resist. The searing arousal of his brief full-mouthed kiss rendered Rachel's knees weaker even than her ankle.

Jagged lightning bolts pierced fast-moving navy clouds. Rachel felt the ground tremble beneath her bare feet from pounding thunder.

Butler's voice rumbled softer now. "I may be a cad, little Miss No-name, but even I cannot abandon you, lame. We seek Eli Whitfield's Turtle Creek post. May I take you there?"

Sullenly, she nodded. "I am Rachel Whitfield, sir. Eli's daughter."

Butler hoisted Rachel bareback atop his bay-colored Conestoga horse, then eased himself into the saddle. Lacing Rachel's arms around his waist, the tanned trader gave a hand signal to his assistant who rode the rear-most horse.

"Hang on to me for safety, m'dear," Butler called back to her with an ironic wink as he led the pack horses on a slow half-mile walk to Turtle Creek.

Silver raindrops escalated to a downpour. Pelted by rain, Rachel silently clung to Butler's muscular mid-section and pondered how she had gotten into this dilemma. And what in Heaven's name would Pa say if he discovered she had allowed a bearded stranger to kiss her?

She could feel this arrogant trader's warm strength through his deerskin shirt. A man to whom she'd never even been properly introduced. His pounding heartbeat echoed through her fingers and naked arms till she felt it was her own. The tingle of his kiss still teased her lips.

Foolish thoughts, so uncharacteristic for a prim, sensible sort like herself, crowded Rachel's mind. She felt an urgent need to cling to this powerful frontiersman and . . . and never let go.

Shamefaced, she sought the busy refuge of her father's walk-in fireplace after they reached the sprawling post. And peeked through the window at an animated conversation between her father and Butler.

"Your cheeks are right rosy red," widowed Mary Hutchings commented on seeing Rachel. Stepping carefully to avoid brushing hot coals with her hem, Mary stirred a cauldron of rabbit stew. "I do believe riding with Mr. Butler has given you a beneficial glow, Rachel."

"Nonsense!" Rachel responded, welcoming the fire's penetrating warmth along her bodice and skirt. She coiled her strawberry-blond plait into a tight bun at her nape.

The flame in her cheeks?

Modest, compared to the surge of heat in her lips, her arms, the soft flesh atop her thighs from the very thought of Jonah Butler. She could still feel his shameless touch echo through every part of her body.

"Then why are you staring out the window at him, my girl, eh?" Mary laughed good-heartedly.

"Not so a'tall, Mary! I . . . I was merely curious to

see what sort of merchandise those horses brought from Philadelphia."

The amiable white-haired servant smiled slyly. "Well, my dear, you could always go out and help your father unpack everything, same as you usually do."

"No! That is, I mean, Pa will call me when he wants me to organize the accounts. The men must be dreadfully hungry, Mary. 'Tis best if I help you get food ready."

A tidy excuse to compose herself, Rachel figured. No man had ever affected her in this same hotly disturbing way. As if he had gently massaged his callused masculine hands over all of Rachel's sensitive flesh. Even remote and craving regions she never knew she possessed.

Old Eliza's admonition pricked Rachel's memory: "In their rough haste . . . men cause pain."

"Besides, Mary, Mr. Butler has troubling questions to answer. What part, I wonder, did he play in Zeb's disappearance?"

"While you wonder, luv, you might want to check the apple pie. Mind the coals, lest they tumble into the pie. Rachel, dear, I have been meaning to speak to you about . . . about Zeb."

Reaching with a pothook, Rachel lifted the Dutch oven from the fire. Gingerly she removed hot coals from the lid before inspecting a fragrant pie baking inside. " 'Tis no use, Mary. You cannot change my convictions. And mind! Not a word of it to Pa."

Hands on hips, Mary frowned at the young woman she'd mothered for the ten years since Eli Whitfield's wife died. "Oh, luv! Promise you will tell me before you . . . before you do anything rash."

" 'Tis not rash, Mary, wanting to rescue one's own falsely imprisoned brother."

"Rachel, dear child, that's merely a dream you nurture. You well know we've been told Zeb is likely dead."

"Or in some Montreal prison!"

"Can you possibly expect that you—one lone woman—could travel all the way north to Canada and . . ."

Shaking her head solemnly, Mary tossed chopped green onions into a casserole of turnips and potatoes.

"And single-handedly look for Zeb? I must try, Mary! If no one else shall, I must."

"But you be a mere slip of a woman."

" 'Tis a known fact I can shoot as good as any man."

Mary scowled in response.

"Well, all right, Mary, if you must be precise. On a good day, with the wind blowing just right, I can shoot almost as well as . . . well, a good many men. Even so, Mary, what if Zeb still lives? How can I just let my brother rot in some vile French prison? 'Tis not right. They seized him simply because he was an English trader on the Allegheny River—Zeb's only sin."

"Along with a half dozen other British traders."

"And who knows? Next month they might decide to drive off Pa again. Or some other trader. We must fight back at the French, Mary!"

" 'Tis not safe for a woman to do as you scheme, luv. Should you not be contemplating marriage instead?"

"Marriage! Indeed not. I shall never forget Old Eliza's words about men's brutish ways."

"Take into consideration, luv, that Eliza was persistently beaten by two drunken husbands. Not all men are cruel such as they."

Suddenly Mary's expression changed from alarm to a bemused grin that Rachel could not fathom. She followed the servant woman's glance to a doorway. There, Jonah Butler leaned against the wooden frame. Regrettably, Rachel felt her gaze wander over his lank body and explore the inviting curves of his shoulders, the brawny muscles of his neck, the carefree toss to his long dark hair that seemed in defiance of any comb. Rachel's stare fixed on the thick black beard that parted to reveal Butler's full-lipped carmine mouth.

She knew, all too well, how that mouth could erode her cherished sense of decency and good judgment.

"Eli sent me in for a jug of cider," he drawled. His insolent stare raked Rachel's body.

In his eyes she saw an uneasy mix of red hot coals and black ice—a wild spirit akin to what she'd observed in the eyes of passion-swollen buck deer in hot pursuit of a doe.

Rachel swallowed hard.

"Come warm yourself by the fire, Mr. Butler," Mary insisted. "Your clothes are still soaked."

"Thank you, ma'am. Eli and I have more unpacking to do, but a short spell of drying out would . . . feel good."

Rachel resented the way he drew out those last two words. Feeling good? 'Twas not moral. Or decent. Furiously, she labored over assembling a corn pudding. But Jonah Butler's large shoulder came dangerously near her own slender frame as she worked at a rough-hewn table near the fire. For one brief moment Rachel's sharp-edged concept of what was moral . . . and decent . . . came unraveled.

"Miss Whitfield, your ankle seems improved," Butler commented, eyeing Rachel's skirt with profound concentration. "Much improved, I might add with a great sense of relief."

His scrutiny of her ankle—was that of purely medicinal interest? Hot circles flamed Rachel's cheeks. She refused to face him. 'Twould be most unwise, standing close to the ill-mannered drover as he contemplated her in that disturbing manner of his.

"I am obliged to you, Mr. Butler," she replied brusquely. "For your kind rescue, that is. My ankle seems to have restored itself."

"Heartily glad I happened on the scene, Miss Whitfield. As a fair turnabout, your fire has restored my comfort. So if I might trouble you for that jug of cider your father requested . . ."

Rachel led Butler through the kitchen to a cramped corner pantry where the jug was stored.

Somehow when she gazed up into Butler's tanned face, as she was doing now to hand him the jug, she felt as though all the world had fallen away. As if Butler were alone with her on some magical island and nothing else mattered but the two of them being together, staring into one another's eyes.

Butler's work-roughened hands swept over Rachel's as he slid the heavy jug from her grasp.

"I . . . hope I have the honor of rescuing you again in the near future, Miss Whitfield," he said, in a raw, chest-deep voice. "Many times, in fact."

She heard the sultry unspoken invitation in his tone.

Nervously she fingered an etched silver locket that dangled on a rawhide string around her throat. A gift from Old Eliza, the tarnished pendant purportedly brought good fortune to its wearer. Abruptly recalling

Eliza's admonition about men's carnal lust and rough haste, Rachel turned aside.

"Kind of you, Mr. Butler. But I make a habit of rescuing myself."

She whisked past him and returned to the kitchen fireplace before she might accidentally betray her true agitation. Decent women, after all, did not allow strange, wild-looking frontiersmen to hug and kiss them . . . full on the mouth, of all things. Unfortunately, Rachel had done just that.

And loved every minute of it.

She coughed quietly. She was a decent woman. Wary of men's passions and grasping hands. And determined, too, not to permit such foolish lapses again. Not when there was a chance Zeb might desperately need her help.

"Good rabbit stew, ma'am," Jonah Butler commented later over supper, with a nod to Mary Hutchings.

"Caught the hares myself only this morning," nineteen-year-old Gabriel Whitfield boasted from the opposite end of the oblong kitchen table.

"Wish you could catch what else lurks hereabouts," Eli growled, before biting into a meat chunk.

Mary shook her fist. "Vile French threats! They plague us with their insinuations."

"And their evil deeds," Gabriel agreed.

Tom Blaine, Butler's young assistant, wiped his mouth with his sleeve. "Mayhap at Logstown Jonah and I can learn more about French intentions."

Listening to them all, Jonah Butler ate in stony silence.

Rachel distrusted the dark-featured stranger. What role had Butler played in Zeb's disappearance? Ah, if only she could reveal her audacious secret plan! Her father would forbid it, of course. He would sputter about personal danger and the ludicrous impossibility of success.

Rachel knew better.

One day her father would praise her for her daring initiative. And Zeb? Oh, if he still lived, Zeb would be fetched home to his family, where he belonged.

Butler swallowed a gulp of whiskey. "The French meant business when they ran you folks off the Allegheny at Venango, Eli. They scheme to connect Canada with Louisiana by a chain of French forts . . . and drive out any English trader who gets in their way."

Gabriel shot up from his wooden bench and paced the planked floor. "But Indians from Logstown told us they *want* the English to build a fort at the Ohio Forks. Even said our trade goods are better and priced cheaper than French goods."

"Pa, how many miles do you reason Logstown is from here?" Rachel asked, feigning sweet innocence.

Eli eyed his daughter suspiciously. "Why do you ask?"

She played at appearing meek. "Merely curious, Pa. Surely I can better keep your account books if I learn more of the area."

A lie, of course.

Rachel needed terrain information to assist her in her planned trek to Montreal. But Jonah Butler's sharp-eyed scrutiny unnerved her more than her father's. Almost as if Butler understood the reason for her concern.

"Logstown, Miss Whitfield? 'Tis perched on the Ohio River only a few miles west of the forks, where the Allegheny joins the Monongahela. Might you . . .

be planning a trip there?" A smile twitched one corner of Butler's mouth as he awaited her response.

Rachel bristled at his intrusive question. "I am con-
tent to remain at home, sir," she lied. "Travel does not
interest me. Not in the slightest."

Did Butler suspect her plans? She fidgeted nervously with her silver pendant.

"What should interest you, daughter, is finally securing a husband." For emphasis, Eli Whitfield
thumped the table with his fist.

"Pa!" Rachel blinked angrily at her father. " 'Tis no
matter to be discussing before strangers."

"Jonah is no stranger. I've known him for years."

"Well, I have not!"

Eli glared at his daughter. " 'Tis no secret, Rachel.
A woman your age should be married by now, with a
strong husband to watch over her. Not hiding from
marriage as if it were the plague."

"The plague?" Butler chuckled at Eli's outburst.
He lazily contemplated Rachel's rising anger. "Why,
Miss Whitfield, whatever has made you shun mar-
riage with such indelicate vehemence?"

Rachel shot up from the wooden bench where she
sat. "I will not—"

"I declare!" Mary Hutchings exclaimed, attempt-
ing to dampen the confrontation as she peered into
empty trenchers. "Hungry men certainly devour their
food in a hurry. With the afternoon storm over, I
wager this hot August evening makes you all eager to
escape outdoors, eh?"

Rachel held the cabin door open to encourage a
hasty male exit.

The humid air smelled of damp earth. Orange
wood lilies, freshly plumped from rain, glistened in
pale evening light as robins sang evening lullabies.

When the men settled down with tobacco and pipes Rachel retreated to the storeroom, where a foolscap ledger and crow-quill pen awaited her. She loved the discipline of maintaining orderly account books for her father's business.

Fresh trade goods from Europe and the West Indies intrigued her. Pungent aromas of molasses and spice, the feel of imported crockery, the heft of powder and shot.

"So . . . mice and little Miss No-name haunt the storeroom."

Rachel whirled at the sound of a man's voice.

Two

"Mr. Butler! You startled me."

Lavender blue shadows obscured Jonah's swarthy features in the early twilight. But Rachel could never mistake those wide shoulders, that broad chest for anything but the man she'd clung to this very same afternoon. The memory of that arousing horseback ride, even now, made virginal Rachel blush.

Butler leaned one thick-muscled arm against the doorjamb. "So you can write and cipher, Miss Whitfield," he said, idly contemplating her.

She bristled. "Momma taught all four of us . . . before she died. Momma was a clever woman." Recalling the woman she missed dreadfully, Rachel glanced down.

"I get the feeling you resemble her, ma'am." He moved a step closer to Rachel.

She liked hearing Jonah Butler speak, though she dared not confess it. His graveled deep voice made her feel exquisite comfort and curious excitement all in the same delicate heartbeat.

His scrutiny, however, made her uneasy.

"You must excuse me, Mr. Butler. I have work to do here."

"I see. That would doubtless be the reason why you chased the men off so quickly after supper."

"I am here, Mr. Butler, because my attention to detail helps Pa."

"And because you like to see what comes in on the pack train?"

She shuffled a ledger page, trying to ignore his gradual approach. The muslin sack! Imperative that she deflect Butler's interest from the vital bundle wedged behind a molasses barrel. "I live on the frontier, Mr. Butler. New trade goods excite most anyone."

"You mentioned four of you?"

"There's Zeb. He has Pa's knack for bartering. And he's an excellent blacksmith."

"I gather he was Eli's right-hand man before the French . . ."

She flinched.

"Sorry, Miss Whitfield. I know the mention of Zeb pains you."

Blocking Butler's path to the muslin sack, she fiddled with the cool edge of an iron bar. "There's Gabriel, my younger brother. And Sukey, my older sister. Her real name's Susannah. She lives in Lancaster with her husband. Tell me, Mr. Butler, how is it that you and Pa seem to know each other so well?"

"Eli and me? We met years ago in Lancaster, before you folks moved west to open your Venango post."

"You seem . . . warmly disposed to one another." Rachel saw a glitter of comprehension in the tall man's eyes.

"An understatement, Miss Whitfield. Eli saved my life. That day, three months ago at Venango, a Frenchman was about to sink an ax into my back when your pa disarmed him. I owe Eli a debt of thanks for that favor. One of these days I expect he'll decide to collect."

He took another step toward her.

"Miss Whitfield . . . about this afternoon. I, uh, just wanted to . . ."

Feeling her heart pound, Rachel busied herself refolding a stack of trade blankets. "I accept your apology, Mr. Butler and—"

Butler locked his hands on to his beaded Indian belt and laughed harshly. "Gracious of you, ma'am. But I was not about to apologize."

"I beg your pardon!"

"You may beg for anything you like, ma'am, any day of the week. If 'tis in my power to grant your wish, I shall most cheerfully oblige."

"Sir!" His suggestive insolence made Rachel flare with indignation.

"I only wanted to say . . . that kiss was sweeter than honey on its best day, Miss Whitfield."

"A stolen kiss, sir! And completely without merit. Decent men do not steal kisses from helpless women."

He guffawed.

"A decent man?" Butler laughed again. "Miss Whitfield, for some curious reason I suspect you are not a helpless woman. Another suspicion—you shall rejoice to learn that Tom and I are leaving for Logstown tomorrow at first light. Am I correct?"

Rachel sniffed. "Rest assured, sir, I have no preference whether you stay or leave. Though I sincerely doubt I shall miss your . . . your surly presence."

Wearing a sidewise grin, he nodded in her direction. "Well, on that cordial note of hospitality, then, Miss Whitfield, I bid you good night."

She watched him turn to exit the cramped storeroom. "Wait!" she called suddenly.

He halted.

In a casual circle, he turned to face her again, this time with his thick arms crossed over his chest. His right eyebrow peaked. "You thought better of your frigid farewell?" Butler asked, larding his voice with sarcasm.

"Indeed not!"

With a slight shiver, she contemplated this husky man who postured before her with his buckskins, bushy black beard, and uncombed shoulder-length hair. "It's just that, I . . . I guess I was not around when you told Pa your version of . . . that day in Venango."

His tone gentled. "You want to know about Zeb."

"Yes. I need to know, Mr. Butler. So badly."

"I cannot tell you."

Her head jerked up. "What? Why not?" Was wild-featured Jonah Butler actually a villain in non-too-subtle disguise? she wondered. A rogue who concealed his fiendish actions under a mantle of denial?

"Cannot tell, Miss Whitfield. Not will not tell. Your brother and I were captured by at least a half-dozen Frenchmen. I was blindfolded and led away by a rope. We marched till sundown that day. Next morning when I woke, I was alone . . . with a fierce headache. One of those devils had struck me on the head the day before."

"Incredible!" Rachel exclaimed, scarcely believing Butler's story.

"But true. My captors had abandoned me on a high ridge west of the Allegheny River. My weapons were gone. And the men who seized Zeb had stolen my packhorses, too, the bloody bastards."

She winced at his choice of words, but only briefly. Frontier men rarely couched their outbursts in delicate parlor prose.

"Then you know nothing of Zeb's fate?" she a... wistfully.

"Nothing, ma'am. I scoured those hills looking for some tracks to follow, but with my head out of sorts, I found no clues."

"What did you do then, Mr. Butler?"

"Floated down the Allegheny on a fallen log till I reached Kittanning. A Lenape healer patched me up. I struck a path east to Conestoga for more horses, then to Philadelphia for some friendly handshakes with Quaker investors who . . . Well, you know the rest."

Indeed. Her father's livelihood depended on the tenacious bravery of drovers such as Jonah Butler.

Indians from the Ohio Valley traded furs and hides for European goods at western posts like Eli Whitfield's at Turtle Creek. Pack trains of sturdy horses carried those same furs east over the Allegheny Mountains—the Endless Mountains—to Lancaster or Philadelphia. A European market greedy for American furs drove investors to finance the unbroken circle—European goods moving west; Indian-caught furs moving east.

Ever optimistic, Rachel remained hopeful about her brother.

"There might still be a chance," she murmured. "So long as no one tells me they have seen him dead, for certain, I'll keep—"

"Miss Whitfield, please understand I was not eavesdropping. But this afternoon I overheard you mention something to Mrs. Hutchings about a plan."

Rachel stiffened.

Watching Rachel's lower lip jut forward defiantly—and seductively—Butler tensed. He leaned over her. "In God's name, Miss Whitfield . . . Rachel . . . do not attempt a journey to Montreal in the misguided notion that you can save Zeb. No woman belongs alone in this wilderness. You would not be safe."

Fire erupted in her bosom. Rachel resented any man telling her *do not.* Especially a large, overpowering man who'd stolen a kiss from her at will—even if she *had* succumbed to his embrace.

She edged back from the trader's long shadow. "Thank you for your advice, Mr. Butler, but my life— and safety—are my own concern. Besides, you . . . you heard wrong."

God in His infinite mercy would surely overlook that one tiny lie, she hoped. Jonah Butler, however, with his gruff frontier manner, might not be quite so forgiving.

She retreated even further from him lest he continue to probe her schemes.

"Doubtless you and Tom Blaine will find the stable acceptable tonight, Mr. Butler. Good night. You will forgive me if I return to my accounting."

Butler apparently thought better of his intended words and turned once more to leave. "Dreams are fine, Miss Whitfield," he called gruffly over his shoulder to her. "Just do not let them interfere with harsh reality. Good night, ma'am."

Poking a scratchy pile of straw into more comfortably arranged bedding, Butler rolled onto his side in Eli Whitfield's crude stable. Two stalls away, a pair of goats bleated to one another as Butler's young assistant, Tom Blaine, settled down for the night. Through the stable's open doorway, mellow sounds of softly nickering horses pastured for the night and inquisitive owls serenaded Butler.

Nothing worked. He had trouble sleeping.

A crescent moon shone a sliver of light through the doorway. Pinpoint stars twinkled like some sort of giant celestial decoration as sighing evening breezes shifted across Butler's lanky frame.

Clenching his jaw, he rolled over again.

This exquisite August night, strangely, was like no other. He felt . . . alone. Lonely, even. He, who by choice crossed formidable mountains and stared down bears and fought men bare-handed . . . felt as though he needed someone to spend the night with him.

He knew precisely who that someone ought to be.

Butler stared in the direction of Eli Whitfield's cabin, where dimpled Rachel probably readied herself for bed. He tried to imagine what she looked like pared down to her shift. Then he tried to envision how she looked . . . without her shift.

Groaning, Butler rolled over once more.

He should never have kissed her. He knew that, of course. Grasping and pawing at that prim little honey-haired virgin like some sort of crazed bull. Lord, he must have been insane. Probably scared the daylights out of her.

Scared him, too. Where, he wondered, did all that impatient energy come from?

"Damned if I know," he muttered, half aloud.

Only certain thing was, once he set eyes on Rachel Whitfield, he wanted to make her his, in every single arousing sense of the word. He wanted . . . needed . . . to draw her inside his arms and touch every inch of her sweet body. Wanted to kiss all her exposed silken skin, then explore what lay concealed beneath her clothes.

Butler's arms ached with painful emptiness. The fire in his loins threatened to rage out of control.

Muttering a curse, Butler punched at the straw bedding again.

No woman could be allowed to disrupt his life. He had plans. And he was making headway. The lucrative fur trade between Indians in the Ohio Valley and businessmen in Philadelphia made everyone happy—except the French.

And Jonah Butler happiest of all.

An ambitious man, he planned to establish a whole string of trading posts from Lake Erie all the way out to the Illinois territory. He had big plans, all right.

And a personal vendetta against the French.

No place in those plans for a demanding, prissy little wench hobbled to his waist who'd whine for him to grow roots in one spot. Not that Rachel Whitfield seemed inclined toward marriage.

Scratching himself, Butler sat up and stared at the Whitfield cabin. Rachel was there. Smooth-skinned, sweet-smelling, velvet-voiced Rachel Whitfield. A woman who made him restless with just one look and one stolen kiss.

Butler rubbed his burning mouth with the back of his fist.

He would correct his careless mistake by making certain he never kissed prickly tempered Miss Whitfield again. But looking at her made him crazy with hopeless longing. Only one cure for that special variety of madness, he figured.

Leave Turtle Creek tomorrow with a vow never to lay eyes on Rachel Whitfield again.

Hot, sticky August afternoons stretched into the first balmy days of September with still no word of

Zeb Whitfield's fate. Tense and calculating, Rachel knew she must act soon.

Early one morning she hesitated at Turtle Creek before filling a pair of wooden water buckets. She watched, amused, as a hummingbird dipped its needlelike beak into scarlet lobelias arched in lanky stalks over the stream. Like a child, Rachel rippled her fingers through the cool water and splashed droplets across her sun-blushed brow.

Bearing the brim-full water buckets on a pole across her shoulders, she trudged back toward her father's trading post. Huge old drooping hemlocks lent a spicy tang to air still damp with morning dew. Overhead, a red-tailed hawk screamed before diving toward its prey. Distracted by the raptor's piercing cry, Rachel sauntered within fifty yards of Eli Whitfield's storehouse before she noticed two Frenchmen conversing with her father.

Her belly tightened. The sound of French accents alarmed all her senses.

Eli's two visitors had dressed with a bit more elegance than any ordinary *coureur de bois.* Linen shirts with a hint of ruffles instead of buckskin hunting shirts. Head scarves tied at jaunty angles. Glistening gold medallions dangling around their necks.

And lethal-looking belt axes suspended from their waists.

Had they come directly from Montreal? Had they news of Zeb? Would they bolt and run if she rushed up and plied them with all the questions tormenting her? Worst of all, was one of them actually Renard— the Fox—the evil man who had attacked and captured Zeb?

Men, Old Eliza had once cautioned Rachel, often

thought of women as stupid, helpless creatures with not one clever thought in their dainty heads.

Rachel would rely on that belief.

"Bonjour, messieurs!" she cheerfully greeted the two strangers, who watched from a casual distance as Eli repaired their rifles. "Care for a cup of fresh water on this warm summer day?" Her calculated smile radiated disarming politeness.

"Bonjour, Mademoiselle Whitfield," the taller of the two men addressed her. "Most kind of you. My name is Chabert Michaux. And this," he said, pointing to his hook-nosed companion, "is my brother, Philippe."

Both men drank long and deep from the cup Rachel offered. All the while their cold gray eyes scrutinized her shapely frame.

"Mademoiselle, your father . . . seems to have an active business here. Is he frequented by Shawnee and Delaware customers?"

Chabert Michaux's probing tone troubled Rachel. She needed to gain information from him without divulging any herself. She played at deception.

Rachel threw up her hands in a pretense of frustrated inadequacy. "Customers? Why, uh . . . oh mercy, kitty-cat! What have you done now? We brought you here to drive out the rats, not . . ." Rachel scooped up her playful cream-colored tabby and prattled on in a frivolous tone. "I declare, just when I think I can trust little Basil here to behave, he rips apart the . . . Oh, forgive me, Monsieur Michaux. You were saying something about . . . trade, yes, exactly. You are a trader from Montreal, did you say?"

Rachel smiled sweetly to further bewilder Chabert Michaux.

"Oui, mademoiselle. And something of a diplomat

for New France as well." Michaux's chest swelled as he boasted. His humorless eyes carefully measured Rachel.

"A diplomat, monsieur? What a busy man you must be! Why, you likely are familiar with every nook and cranny of Montreal."

"Well, most of them, Mademoiselle Whitfield. It is my home, after all. I see your storeroom has an ample supply of pelts. Tell me, mademoiselle, if you please, how many Delaware and Shawnee natives would you guess pass through your father's trading post in a week's time?"

They played at a game of cat and mouse, Rachel suspected. At times she was the cat, at others the mouse. She had a burning hunch that Chabert Michaux and his brother were not simply here to get their rifles repaired. They seemed bent on a mission of espionage.

"How many?" she mused, tapping her forehead absentmindedly with her index finger. "Let me see. Ah, you must forgive me, Monsieur Michaux. I cannot recall numbers well a'tall. But I *can* tell you this: My poor father never seems to get the amount of business he requires to prosper."

Chabert Michaux's eyes brightened. *"Non?* Tell me more, mademoiselle. I care about your father as a friend, you understand."

"Of course you do, Monsieur Michaux. Such a kind man you are, indeed, sir. No, no, Mister Basil, you must not! Oh, what a naughty cat!" she exclaimed, feigning flightiness by fluttering her eyelids. "Do tell me more about your city, monsieur. I am completely fascinated by foreign places."

"Well, mademoiselle, you are in one right now. By rights, the Belle Rivière and all of this valley are part of New France," he grumbled, referring to a French term for the Ohio River. "English territory stops at the Endless Mountains, east of here. Those mountains are a natural barrier, *ma petite.* Englishmen need to be reminded of that fact. Philippe and I intend to . . . help them with their recollection."

Rachel bit her tongue to avoid blasting this arrogant Frenchman with her opinion of his goal.

"These are, of course, manly political issues, Monsieur Michaux. Far too complex for my humble woman's brain. Family matters are what concern my poor heart. These days I yearn for news of my brother, Zeb, whom we have been told might languish in a Montreal prison. Have you any news that could alleviate my suffering, kind sir?"

Michaux's food-speckled brown mustache twitched. A hasty glitter of recognition flashed across his gray eyes.

He knows! Rachel reasoned, damning his soul for his sadistic silence. He knew something about her brother's fate and he had chosen not to tell. Perhaps Michaux was one of Zeb's captors. Or worse. Might he even be the Fox?

Stroking his soiled mustache, Chabert Michaux leaned toward her. "It pains me to observe your unhappiness, Mademoiselle Whitfield. Truly. Kind man that I am, I shall see what information I can discern about your brother. Perhaps in the future, you and I will . . . be able to assist one another even further."

"Most kind of you, indeed, monsieur."

Rachel scurried into the storeroom to avoid further conversation with a man she considered tainted.

The muslin sack!

She needed to touch it once more, to reaffirm her goal. Reaching into a cobwebbed corner, she loosened the sack's drawstring tape. Yes, everything was there in readiness for the day when—

A sudden scrape made Rachel gasp aloud. Trembling, she spun around.

"Mr. Butler!" she cried in baffled recognition.

"Still dedicated to your accounting, Miss Whitfield?" Butler asked with a quizzical leer.

She flipped an errant tendril back from her forehead before squaring her shoulders. "You appear to question my capability, Mr. Butler."

Butler snorted. "Your capability, Miss Whitfield? Not at all. Indeed, I suspect you are capable of . . . just about anything."

He infuriated her. Most assuredly. Tall and brusque and handsome, he made her heart pound in escalating frenzy. Surely the emotion she felt was nothing more than rage.

Well, was it not?

He seemed no more trustworthy than glib-voiced Chabert Michaux, out in front. Yet for some foolish reason Rachel could not define, she felt enraptured that Jonah Butler had returned. Her heart sang, her soul took wing, all from the sight of an audacious, bushy-bearded wildman who . . .

She took a second look.

Three

Butler appeared different on this, his return trip east from Logstown. His glistening black beard and mustache had been trimmed quite close to his face. The fringed buckskin shirt he wore seemed recently wiped clean. Even his dark wavy hair had been clipped and adequately combed.

Forgetting propriety, Rachel leaned closer to stare. Butler's carmine-red mouth and white teeth peeped between his groomed facial hair. With a restless stir, Rachel remembered the arousing power of that magnificent mouth, those great broad shoulders.

Decency?

For one brief moment she tossed that word out the door like a handful of crumbled bread crumbs.

At her scrutiny, he yielded to a crooked grin.

"Did you intend whispering something to me in private, Miss Whitfield?" he drawled.

Rachel recovered her dignity. "Certainly not! I . . . merely thought I saw a . . . a cut on your face."

"That?" he asked with a harsh laugh as he pointed to his cheek. "Nothing important. Just the calling card of a hot-tempered *coureur de bois* west of here who felt I had dwelt enough days on this earth."

"Jonah! I mean, Mr. Butler. Why ever did he feel that way?" she asked, struggling to cloak her anguish.

Decency? Oh, the very concept chafed at Rachel's true feelings. For some primitive reason, which she instantly despised, Rachel yearned to lean against this burly trader, to glide her hands up over his chest before kissing away his pain.

Instead, enshrouded by *decency,* she braced her hands at her sides.

He glanced out the log storeroom's open door. "After the Michaux brothers leave, Miss Whitfield, I shall tell you more. If, in fact, they do leave."

"What do you mean?"

"Have you forgotten Venango?"

"Never! Not till the day I die, Mr. Butler. But do you believe the Michaux brothers had anything to do with—?"

Butler shook his head. "Can never be certain. I missed seeing all of Zeb's captors. And the blow to my head interferes with my recollections of that day. But strange rumors are swirling around here, Miss Whitfield. The woods have eyes, you know."

He slipped out the door before she could question him further.

Rachel carefully tightened the tape drawstring of her muslin sack. Unease prickled tiny hairs along her neck. The western frontier, she knew, was a treacherous, undisciplined place where people often died young.

And under mysterious circumstances.

Tiptoeing outside the storeroom in her bare feet, Rachel glimpsed mammoth long-needled pines swaying gracefully in a western wind. Breathing in sweet hints of meadow rue and yellow lilies, she watched an orange butterfly fuss over mint-scented beebalm.

"Momma," she whispered into the summer breeze, as if that pale call might somehow reach her mother. Hannah Whitfield lay buried at Venango along with

Rachel's two infant sisters. Fifteen years earlier, Eli Whitfield had led his family west across the Endless Mountains to make his fortune as a fur trader along the Allegheny River.

"Momma!" Rachel whispered again, mourning the beautiful woman lost in childbirth soon after that exodus.

Now, a tinderbox of violence lay ready to explode in this lovely region. Men—French and English—harbored secrets that threatened Rachel's very existence. Could she rely on Jonah Butler any more than she could trust Chabert Michaux?

No.

"I shall trust no one," she murmured. And confide in no one. They all had their secrets. Rachel would have hers. The time to act neared.

Breathing easier as she watched the Michaux brothers strike a trail west toward the Monongahela, Rachel helped Mary Hutchings prepare a meal of roasted wild turkey and potatoes with boiled lima beans.

And listened intently for new information.

Eli and Gabriel Whitfield sat elbow to elbow with their hired hands, alongside Jonah Butler and his slouching servant, Tom Blaine.

"Two thousand Frenchmen?" Bellowing in alarm, Gabriel nearly choked on his cider. "Can that possibly be true?"

"A likely assessment, according to the Indian runner I met at Logstown," Butler replied, finishing off a potato swimming in turkey gravy. "He understands some French. He overheard the commander boast about troop strength. The main detachment landed at Presque Isle in June. Frenchmen have already begun building another new fort about fifteen miles south of Presque Isle. Fort Le Boeuf, they're calling it."

Rachel clenched her hands. "But that sounds like they mean to descend the Allegheny River."

"Worse than that, I fear, Miss Whitfield," Butler declared, reaching for a biscuit. "They aim straight for here . . . and the forks of the Ohio River."

"How in thunder are they surviving?" Eli raged. "Last I heard, the grain crops have been dismal in Canada these past two years. I wonder if the governor in Philadelphia knows any of this."

"He will, by God, just as quickly as I can get there," Butler announced, grim faced and determined.

Tom Blaine gestured toward Butler with his gravy-shined forefinger. "The French already tried to interfere with Jonah's mission."

"The cut!" Rachel exclaimed. "So it was not just a drunken brawl. That French trapper tried to kill you to stop you from reaching the governor in Philadelphia!"

Butler scowled. "Thank you, Miss Whitfield, for your kind assessment of my drinking habits."

She always managed, Rachel noticed, to run afoul of Butler's temper. She ignored that character trait this mild September evening when impending disaster swirled through these mountains. Jonah Butler had a dangerous mission to accomplish, all right.

And Rachel had her own as well.

Emerging from the cool stone springhouse later that evening, Rachel overheard tense voices. Male voices that made her blood run cold. Less than ten feet from where she stood, shielded by a raspberry thicket, her father and Jonah Butler smoked pipes in the open air.

"You once said, Jonah, that you felt beholden to me," Eli Whitfield began cautiously.

"Rightly so, old friend. Countless times. The last was best. You saved my life at Venango. I can never forget that." Butler drew on his pipe.

Eli nervously pawed the ground with his moc-casined foot. "Then . . . I must ask you a favor that means a great deal to me."

"Name it, Eli."

"I have a married daughter, Susannah, in Lan-caster. Sukey, we always called her."

Rachel felt her ears stretch ten feet tall as she dis-creetly eavesdropped on this exchange. What could her father possibly be asking Jonah Butler that would involve Sukey in any way?

"Jonah . . . my Rachel is in danger here."

Butler guffawed. "Damn, Eli! You *all* are in danger here."

The grizzled trader shook his head. " 'Tis far dif-ferent for Rachel. As a man, Jonah, surely you understand the manner in which those Michaux brothers eyed her this afternoon."

Butler grunted. "All too well."

"They could easily arrange to carry her off, with far less difficulty than when they hauled away Zeb."

Butler's black brows dipped low over his eyes as his crossed arms shielded his chest. "Eli, what in bloody hell are you asking me to do?"

Hunched and frowning, Eli Whitfield shuffled ner-vously in the dust. "Escort Rachel east through the Appalachian passes to her sister's home in Lan-caster."

"What?" Butler bellowed, scarcely able to believe his ears.

"Jonah, you know the mountains better than any man around here. I heard you say once that you made the journey from Turtle Creek to Philadelphia in ten days."

"Not with any damn . . . not with a *woman* along, Eli. And this time I must make speed. The governor has no notion of what those blackguard French are up to. Or how far south their army has already advanced."

"Rachel's no longer safe here, Jonah. She might not be alive when you return."

Hearing this exchange from the springhouse steps, Rachel clutched her bodice in anger. No man, French or otherwise, would carry her someplace she had no intention of going!

Safe? Her father thought she was no longer safe here with him?

"How safe does Pa think I would be out on some remote mountain pass in the clutches of a brawny wild man like Jonah Butler?" she hissed softly. Alone with him, and probably one or two of his male servants, where they might attempt to force her . . .

No! No, indeed.

No matter what arrangement Butler and her father were about to make, Rachel would have none of it. Their male deliberations had forced her hand.

"I must act this very night," she murmured. She had to launch her secret plan at once. "Pa leaves me no choice."

Tiptoeing into the storeroom, she located the muslin sack hidden behind a stack of folded blankets. With a tug on the drawstring tape, she widened the bag's mouth.

A shadow passed the doorway.

Rachel pressed her frame against the cool chinked log walls to avoid detection.

Whistling a tune, Gabriel Whitfield ambled by on his way to the stables.

Rachel stole a furtive glance out the storeroom's doorway. Dusk, enhanced by a moonless, cloud-blotted sky, shielded her movements.

She returned to her secret cache and began withdrawing its contents—each piece a discard from Gabriel's outgrown wardrobe. Battered felt brimmed hat. A fringed leather shirt. Leather leggings with fringe dangling down the sides. A worn pair of moccasins.

Fingering her carefully guarded treasures, Rachel dimpled into a sly smile. "Perfect!" she whispered. "Gabriel's outgrown clothes well suit my purposes." Though warm for this time of year, the cut of the masculine leather garments would go a long way toward disguising Rachel's feminine face and figure.

Her eyes shone as she contemplated the dusky sky. "This very night I shall set out alone for Montreal. No one shall stop me. One way or another, Zeb Whitfield, I intend to find you!"

And with the aid of a few tricks, she would be masquerading as a boy.

Well after midnight, Jonah Butler awoke to an eerie sound. It was night silence, all right, but there were all sorts of silence. Somehow this version felt wrong. He glanced over at Tom Blaine, sound asleep on a cushion of straw. No way to rouse his young assistant without alerting whatever crept around in the dark.

Butler's scruff hairs rose as if sensing danger. Silently he cupped his ears to detect any trace of sound, the way a Mingo hunter had taught him years before. Something stirred ever so slightly in an interlaced grove of hemlocks beyond the first rise. A Frenchman, maybe, come to finish off that bungled assault on him?

Butler reached for his rifle and powder horn.

Stalking noiselessly on moccasined feet in the pitch darkness, he crept toward those same hemlocks.

Now he could see a moving shape. Parting a cluster of long, swordlike sweet flag leaves, Butler raised his loaded rifle and prepared to shoot.

He studied the object in his sights while hesitating with his finger on the trigger.

Suddenly the creature turned . . . just enough for Butler to get a better look.

He cussed silently. This apparition was no animal. At least not the four-legged variety. This creature was human—with long honey-colored hair streaming down its back. Hair so lustrous it shone even on a moonless night. A woman—with a knife. She was about to slice off that splendid long hair.

"Rachel!" Butler suddenly blurted. "What the hell are you—?"

Like a trapped doe, she froze. "Who is it?" she hissed. "Show yourself!"

Butler lowered his gun and advanced toward her. "What the bloody hell are you doing out here in the middle of the night . . . dressed in a man's buckskins and about to cut off your hair, for Gawd's sake?"

She sniffed. "I might ask you the same, Mr. Butler. Why are you creeping around here in the dark? Everyone else is asleep, you know."

That thought occurred to him as well. Standing close to Rachel Whitfield alone in the dark, other disturbing thoughts struck Jonah Butler. The soft feel of her skin under his callused fingers. The sweet taste of her lips when he'd kissed her. The seductive hint of lavender that always seemed to rise from her swirling skirts and hair.

He muffled his voice to a graveled whisper. "You were preparing to run away. Dressed like a boy. Why, Miss Whitfield?"

"None of your business," she replied archly.

"Wish it were so," he replied wistfully. "Most unfortunately, Miss Whitfield, I fear you have just become my business. Your pa insists that I escort you to your sister's home in Lancaster."

"I *will not* go!" she snapped, shaking a finger at him. "You cannot make me. You have no right!"

Smart, sassy, primly beautiful . . . and unbroken. Gawd, Butler thought, he found Rachel Whitfield more excitement than most men could handle.

"Wrong again, ma'am," he replied, drawing himself up to his full height. "You have become not only my right but my responsibility. I owe Eli a debt. This is how he demands it be repaid."

"I shall not be coin for my father's debts, sir."

"I assure you, Miss Whitfield, I find this situation even more distasteful than do you. Now, maybe you will tell me why you plotted to run off."

She gnawed pensively on her lower lip. Jonah Butler was a large, rough man. He stood squarely in front of her with a loaded gun and a look of fierce determination.

"I . . . I want to find Zeb."

His eyes widened. "Meaning?"

"I . . . fully intend to reach Montreal and find news of my brother."

"Jesus!"

"Mr. Butler!"

"Pardon me, ma'am. I underestimated you. But I fear you shall have to allow someone else to discover whether Zeb's alive or dead."

He blocked her with his firm presence.

Her chin jutted out. "I intend to find my brother. And if he is alive, I will find a way to free him."

Butler glared down at her. "Dressed like a boy," he commented dryly.

"Dressed any way I please." She matched his glare with a stern one of her own.

Abruptly, she darted off into the darkness with the speed of a mountain lion in search of freedom.

Despite his size, he was faster.

He caught her by the arm, and feeling her frantic breaths, drew her close against his chest to calm her. A mistake, he sensed almost at once. Rachel Whitfield's heaving bosom pressed into the curves of his own brawn. He meant to comfort her.

Instead, his effort became something of an embrace.

For one brief moment she made no attempt to flee.

Butler felt Rachel stir and warm inside his arms, as if she craved his muscular solace. Without meaning to, he tipped up her chin into the September night and bent down to kiss her.

Till he collected his senses.

Beautiful Rachel Whitfield—impassioned, tawny, and tempting—was about to become his responsibility. She was *not,* Butler reminded himself, his hot-blooded plaything, though that intriguing concept appealed to him immeasurably.

He backed off, still holding Rachel by one arm. "Games are over for tonight, Miss Whitfield. We leave first thing in the morning."

At dawn Rachel woke to the sound of her father's call.

" 'Tis time, Rachel," Eli announced, his voice more tender than harsh.

"Pa?" She rubbed the sleep from her eyes.

After a breakfast of corn mush that seemed to lodge in her throat, Rachel stood sullenly by Butler's lead packhorse, where her father and the rangy trader commiserated.

Weeping, Mary Hutchings pressed packs of food on Rachel. "My darling child," she whispered through her tears, "these are troubled times in which we live. I shall pray for you daily till I hear you are safe in Lancaster with Sukey."

She hugged Rachel to her bosom.

"Oh, Mary! You've been like a mother to me. How I shall miss you, dear friend." Fresh tears dampened Rachel's cheeks.

Backing away, Mary focused on the necklace dangling from Rachel's throat. "The silver pendant, luv. Wear it at all times. Old Eliza said it would bring you good luck and one day save your life. Rachel, Eliza was a tormented woman beset by two abusive husbands. But her prophecy, I feel certain, is to be believed."

Eli Whitfield took his daughter by the hand. "Trust me, child, you are no longer safe here. You belong in Lancaster under Sukey's protection. I want your solemn promise that you will not try running off to Montreal . . . or anyplace else in search of Zeb."

Warm gusts filled Rachel's nostrils with the blended scent of pine and joe-pye weed. Overhead in jutting bleached sycamore limbs, a pair of wood thrushes trilled flutelike phrases.

Rachel hung her head in contemplative silence.

"I . . . cannot promise that, Pa." Tears rimmed her eyes as she gazed up at Eli. "I might never see you again. Or Gabe, or Zeb. Pa, have we not always been a close family?" She clutched at her father's coarse linen shirt. "We *must* find out if Zeb still lives. And if he does, we must find a way to free him from his dreadful French prison."

Through his daughter's veil of tears, Eli Whitfield saw the fire in her expression. Nothing short of iron-clad determination, he knew, would ever restrain impulsive Rachel. Tight-chested and sad, he reluctantly spun toward Butler.

"Jonah," he said with a nod, turning his daughter over to the drover's care.

Rachel blinked in horrified misery as gruff Jonah Butler knotted one end of a long rope around her waist, the other end around his own wrist.

Rachel jerked on the rope. "Pa!" she cried, turning back to her father. "How could you possibly believe I would be safe alone on the trail with a scoundrel like . . . like Mr. Butler?"

Eli steadied her with a stern hand to the shoulder. "Jonah is a man of honor, Rachel."

"My instincts tell me 'tis not true, Pa. Surely I would be safer here with you and Gabe and Mary!" she begged.

Acting on Eli's solemn nod, Butler hoisted Rachel atop a speckled bay mare, second in a string of pack-horses. With a signal wave to Tom Blaine, mounted on the rearmost horse, Butler swung his long legs over his own lead gelding.

A fresh spate of tears rimmed Rachel's eyes as Butler led her east. She turned in the saddle to view her father's diminishing figure.

"No, Pa! No!" she whispered, seeing Eli fade, then vanish, into the forest mists.

Four

Tied single file behind Rachel, twelve packhorses softly nickered and occasionally nipped at one another. Tom Blaine rode the last horse in order to keep watch over precious fur bundles strapped to each animal. Bundles that could slip. Or worse, fall to the ground.

As they began their journey east across Pennsylvania, Rachel glared ahead with pure hatred at Butler, her burly tormentor.

"I despise you, you smug bastard!" she muttered under her breath. "And I shall yet escape your clutches when you least expect it."

Jonah Butler rode high, bearing a Pennsylvania rifle perched across his left elbow. He wore the wary expression of a wolf on guard for enemies . . . or prey. Yellow fringe trimmed his blue homespun hunting shirt. A lethal assortment of carefully sharpened weapons dangled from his leather belt.

Rachel fingered the rope linking her to this obstinate trader. No restraint this side of hell—and *no man*—she vowed savagely, would keep her from carrying out her plan.

Butler nudged his horse into a slow, steady gait . . . vital to pace the strung-together packhorses, considering the mountain ranges that lay ahead of them.

With the wind at his back, Butler stole frequent glances over his shoulder to be certain Rachel was safe. And still with him. Her arms and legs swung free. The rope around her waist hung loose and easy . . . he'd made certain of that so she would not be uncomfortable.

"Damn! An insufferable burden," he muttered beneath his breath. Bound to a spirited woman hell-bent on marching alone to Montreal just when he needed to reach the governor in Philadelphia with all due haste. He'd have to watch her closely.

Clenching his fist, Butler felt the rope that linked his wrist to Rachel's waist.

He glanced back at her once more.

Hungry for the sight of her, greedy for her touch, Butler knew all the while that for hundreds of miles he must not touch Rachel Whitfield. Their very lives—and perhaps a thousand more in the colony—depended on it.

She returned his caring glance with a glare of stubborn ferocity.

Fire in a woman? Oh, Lord, on a more carefree occasion, he loved it. Butler tried to blot images from his mind of saucy Rachel Whitfield riding the horse behind him. The way Rachel's stockinged legs, clad in moccasins, bounced softly against her mount's barrels. The drape of her nut-brown homespun skirt cascading down over her thighs. The flash of her ankles.

Butler swallowed hard.

Ardently prim little Miss Whitfield.

As if to deflect any man's unseemly gazes, she had wrapped her scarf snug around her throat. She wore her hair pinned in a small perfect bun at her nape. A futile gesture, by Jonah Butler's reckoning. He remembered how lustrous that beautiful red-gold hair shone when it streamed down her back . . . how soft to his touch. Some unknown future day, he would unpin that long hair and twine its silken length around his fingers. He would . . .

Brushing his mouth with the back of his knuckles, Butler wiped those thoughts from his head.

He cleared his throat and spat contemptuously. Women and serious business never mixed. Like oil and water, those two were. A woman? Good now and again. Maybe for an afternoon or a night. Just enough time for a belly-filling meal and a high-spirited romp in some warm, secluded bed.

Nothing more.

Longer than that and women started to mewl about a man affixing himself to home and hearth. They whimpered of "till death us do part."

None of that figured in Jonah Butler's plans.

Born with a lust for danger and excitement, he rose every morning hell-bent on exploring what lay beyond the next mountain or river. He didn't belong in some smoke-grimed city. His natural place was out in the wilderness. He intended to become the richest trader in all of Pennsylvania, with a lucrative fur trade that would stretch all the way from Philadelphia clear out to the Illinois territory.

And no bloody Frenchman was going to stop him.

As his mount gingerly plodded along a washed-out trail, Butler scowled.

Men of New France, of course, had different ideas about which nation should benefit from the vital Indian fur trade. Alarmed by the success of English traders, France stood poised to intervene.

War.

That, Butler figured, was precisely what European powers were headed for. A gigantic war that would affect every mighty nation clawing for the fur trade. The main battleground? Not some obscure European battlefield far across the Atlantic.

"Hell, no," he muttered under his breath with a disgusted shake of his head.

It would be right here. In the backwoods of Pennsylvania.

He had to reach Philadelphia as quickly as possible. The Pennsylvania Assembly, slow as molasses on a cold January day, had no idea just how dangerous the situation had become.

Butler stole another glance at the fiercely proper form of Rachel Whitfield riding the horse just behind his own.

He only hoped turbulent Miss Whitfield had no foolish plans that might interfere with his dangerous mission.

Rachel's horse swayed gently beneath her hips as the pack train edged east of Turtle Creek. Twisting narrow hillside passes rang with a buzzing litany of late summer insects. A warm rising sun released the delicate fragrance of blue-eyed grass.

"Beware, Monsieur Fox," she whispered. "I shall hunt you down. Perhaps quite soon."

She glanced below at the rope connecting her own diminutive body to Jonah Butler's imposing bearlike frame. Her eyes narrowed. Did Butler really think he could control her with a mere rope and that smug bravado of his?

"Then let him believe it!" she muttered, biting back a half grin.

No man, regardless of how many ropes he dangled,

would ever restrain her, Rachel vowed silently. Nor stop her from locating poor imprisoned Zeb.

She feared the touch of a robust man hungering for women. Pain. Was that not what a man's devilment brought to women? Tugging her garments tighter around her body, Rachel knew she must avoid Butler's touch at all costs.

At the right moment, at the right place . . . she would outwit him. Simple as that.

Rachel smiled wickedly.

Her fingers reached for the cool metal of Old Eliza's silver pendant dangling about her throat. If ever Rachel needed the pendant's good luck, now was the time.

"You all right, Miss Whitfield?" Butler hollered back to her after they'd ridden a half-dozen miles.

"Fine, indeed, Mr. Butler," she shouted forward defiantly.

"Just beyond that next ridge up ahead there's a stream with clear cool water. Good place to rest for a bit."

Through a tight-laced canopy of giant oak and tulip poplar, Rachel guessed the sun must be nigh overhead as the three of them—Butler, Tom Blaine, and herself—stretched out beside a wide-banked creek. They ate a cold lunch of ham and potatoes sent along by teary-eyed Mary Hutchings, while the horses nibbled from a mix of corn and oats.

Afterward, Rachel fingered the rope at her waist. "Mr. Butler, I . . . I must retreat behind those laurel bushes for a moment."

Gruff, bearded, with his felt hat pulled low over his dark eyes, Butler looked straight at her. "I will accompany you."

"Certainly not!" she huffed.

"With my back turned, of course."

"How your back is turned does *not* concern me, Mr. Butler. I may be your prisoner, but you must allow me the decency to . . ."

"Miss Whitfield . . ." Butler let out a long sigh. "You are not a prisoner. I am merely escorting you east to safety. Much against my will, I hasten to add."

"Then if I am not a prisoner, Mr. Butler, untie me." She glared defiantly at him.

He studied her for a moment. Ten days of this torture, maybe eight if he was lucky, and he could deposit this troublesome wench with her sister in Lancaster. Ten days. Precious time that an encroaching French army could put to good use. He could ill afford the risk of having to spend additional days searching dense forests for a pestilential woman bent on vanishing.

Butler crossed his arms in front of his brawny chest.

"No," he growled.

Her blue-green eyes blazed in anger. "Very well," she replied, gnawing on her cheek. Her bosom rose and fell in a long, deep breath. A sudden smile softened her face. "But you shall find your suspicions completely unfounded, Mr. Butler. I deserve your trust."

He scowled down at her. "I find that most difficult to believe, Miss Whitfield. After you," he said, holding up his rope-tied wrist as he gestured toward a laurel thicket. "You have my word, ma'am, that my back will remain turned until you rejoin me."

Facing the gurgling stream, Butler felt several minor tugs on the long rope. His gut tightened with apprehension. Was this slip of a wench playing tricks with him again?

"Miss Whitfield?" he called, maintaining his bargain not to look, though concerned about her whereabouts. He felt another tug on the long rope. "Need some assistance?"

Wearing a stern expression, Rachel reappeared from behind him. "Really, Mr. Butler! You see?" she said, apparently holding a fierce scold in check as she demurely edged past him en route to the stream. "You need not concern yourself with my welfare."

Butler's eyes narrowed. "So you continually remind me, Miss Whitfield," he uttered from somewhere deep within his chest.

A smile played across his lips as he gnawed on a grass stem gripped between his teeth. He watched Rachel's determined footsteps. All wrapped up was prim Miss Rachel Whitfield, with her tightly pinned hair, shoulder scarf high up around her throat, and terse little mouth.

But he knew different.

He could never forget how smooth her pale pink skin had felt under his work-hardened hands. How her long golden hair captured fire and moon glow in its glistening tendrils. Or how sensuous Rachel's feminine body, with her gently rounded breasts and hips, felt against his own hard frame.

Bloody hell, she was a sassy woman! More than a handful for most men. But Jonah Butler was not most men. He never shrank from predatory wolves or enraged bears.

Or difficult women.

He held up his rope-tied wrist. An urge, deep and primal, made him want to jerk that lengthy rope toward him. Made him yearn to reel in strong-willed Rachel Whitfield like a wriggling prize catch bolting from some ice-cold forest stream. A devilish urge that would only complicate his life. And earn Butler the eternal enmity of his old friend, Eli Whitfield. And . . .

Butler lowered his arm.

"Wait till those folks in Philadelphia hear what French soldiers are up to, back here on the frontier!" Tom Blaine blurted out, as he finished watering the horses. "Imagine the look on their faces."

"Will they be all right, Mr. Butler? Pa and the others, I mean." Rachel could no longer conceal her fears.

Butler rechecked the bit of Rachel's speckled bay mare. "The quicker I get to Philadelphia, Miss Whitfield, the safer they shall all be."

The fate of countless people—perhaps even the destiny of European nations—rested on his ability to reach Philadelphia quickly with news of the aggressive French backwoods advance. Guns. Frontiersmen needed more guns, and some fearless English soldiers.

Butler rolled the emerald blade of grass across his lips again. On this vital journey he would have to keep his masculine impulses under rigid control.

Rachel Whitfield? She could mean no more to him than some inanimate crate of merchandise to be safely lugged across those Pennsylvania mountains. For the sake of everyone in the entire colony.

The long afternoon ride brought their pack train to a steep incline overlooking Brush Creek.

With a hand signal to Tom Blaine, Butler halted and dismounted. "Looks like a good night position," he called back to Rachel. Using a visual trick learned from the Shawnee, he studied his surroundings in an all-encompassing manner. Nothing missed his scrutiny.

"Something wrong, Mr. Butler?" Rachel inquired.

"Just being cautious."

"Grazing would have been better for the horses in the grassy lowlands we just passed." She saw his scowl as they both worked to hobble the unhitched horses with twisted grapevines. A bell around the neck of each horse alerted Butler to their whereabouts.

"Just . . . making an observation, you understand, Mr. Butler."

"An elevation makes a safer campsite than lowlands, Miss Whitfield."

"Safer?" Nervously, she peered over her left shoulder. Then her right. "From what?"

Butler finished hobbling the last horse. "From hungry animals. Downpours. And from whomever is following us."

Rachel swallowed hard. "Following us? How can you be certain?"

His beard twitched to betray a subtle smile. " 'Tis my job, Miss Whitfield. When a man lives outdoors he learns to rely on his wits. And all of his senses."

Biscuit in hand, she watched him greedily attack his allotted portion of cold ham. "Who do you think it is, Mr. Butler? Following us, I mean. An Indian party, perhaps?"

He continued chewing. "Maybe."

Butler's taciturn mood unnerved Rachel. "Sir, you are not entirely forthcoming with information."

"No?"

Something about that curious twinkle in his earth-brown eyes alerted her caution. Just how much could she trust this brawling frontier trader—never a breed to inspire trust under the best of circumstances? And how far could she push him before he might . . . ?

Rachel sighed. "Mr. Butler, you literally drag me

out into the wilderness, then you alarm me with your
talk of—"

"Ma'am, I have learned to listen. An art you ought
to consider cultivating, I might add. As for the wilderness, you've been part of it for years, ever since your
pa brought you west of the Susquehanna."

Butler resumed chewing, though he shifted uneasily as two of the horses nickered softly.

Finishing her biscuit and cold ham in disgruntled
silence, Rachel sat upright on a smooth granite boulder. "I . . . have to . . . visit behind the bushes," she
announced.

Butler jerked his head up in mid-bite. "Now?"

"Now," she acknowledged, lightly fingering the
large rope knot dangling in front of her coarse linen
apron.

He stood up with an audible groan.

Her eyelashes fluttered. "You could always . . .
untie the rope, Mr. Butler. Surely that would make
life far easier for you," she offered obligingly. And
sweetly.

A scowl creased his weathered face as he reached
for his rifle. "Never again. Not in my weakest moment. Not even if I become too drunk to stand, will I
agree to cross the mountains with a woman in tow.
Ever!" he muttered.

Rachel's eyes widened. "Is that gun necessary? I
mean, we are only . . ."

Ignoring her question, Butler followed her twenty
paces into the laurel, then turned his back. "Scream
if you need help, ma'am," he advised, scrutinizing a
ridge interwoven with tulip poplars and oaks for signs
of movement.

"Humph!" she grumbled. "Indeed, I need help.

Most *anything* would be an improvement over this captivity."

After a series of delicate tugs on the rope attached to his wrist Butler heard Rachel's footsteps return on crisp moldering brown leaves. She walked unevenly. He knew why.

"Sore from riding all day?" he asked.

She detected a hint of kindness in his manner. Impossible, she reasoned. Brutish, mocking Jonah Butler—kind? A barrel-chested lout who stole kisses from women in distress?

Perhaps, now that dusk had settled onto this tree-clad incline, Butler had his own ideas of what to do with her in the darkness. And his tough, young, slouch-hatted assistant as well. Indeed, these two males might be far more of a threat to her safety than any creature roaming out there in the bushes.

Clearing her throat nervously, Rachel neatened the mobcap under the wide-brimmed straw *bergère* hat that covered her severely pinned bun.

"I am quite resilient, Mr. Butler," she replied, waddling in a stiff-legged gait toward the blanket she'd laid out for sleeping.

He studied her uncomplaining bravado.

Setting down his rifle, Butler withdrew a long, deadly looking hunting knife from his leather belt. With a few quick strokes, he gathered a fistful of fir branches and mounded them over a moss-covered flat area.

"Your bed," he said simply.

She stared at his efforts to make her comfortable. "Thank you, Mr. Butler. And good night."

"One more thing, Miss Whitfield. Before you sleep, I suggest you cover your face and arms with mud."

"Mud? Cover myself?"

"Keeps insects at bay, ma'am. Being a foul-tempered man, especially when I crave sleep, I do not fancy being wakened by a foolish woman besieged by insects."

Reluctantly following Butler's example, Rachel dipped her fingers in soft mud lining the stream bank and smeared a thin clay coating over her exposed skin. Exhaustion claimed her weary body. Wrapping a trade blanket snug around her slender frame, she collapsed onto the bed Butler had crafted for her.

Butler was right, of course. She ached in ways too numerous to mention. Her pelvis and inner thighs tortured her with pain, her back felt broken in two, her neck . . .

Brushed by warm September breezes, Rachel addressed various parts of her anatomy, begging them to relax and give her a night of peaceful repose. In the darkness beneath tall oaks that screened out moon and stars, Rachel nestled into the soft, sweet-scented evergreen branches and closed her eyes.

Suddenly she heard the rustle of dry leaves.

Her eyes bulged. Her breaths came in shallow gulps.

"M-M-Mr. Butler?" she asked of the trader, who she thought lay less than five feet from her side in the pitch darkness.

"Ma'am?"

"The man who tried to kill you in Logstown . . . is it possible he is the one out there in the woods now?"

She waited for the reassuring sound of Butler's deep voice as cicada songs reverberated through the darkness.

She heard him slowly exhale.

"Entirely possible, ma'am. The French emphatically do not want me to reach Philadelphia. Alive, that is."

The French? Rachel digested this information with an awkward swallow. Might the man French backwoodsmen called the Fox be lurking just a few hundred yards away? Or even closer? The very same man who had captured poor Zeb?

"Mercy!" she whispered on a sigh. "I hear sounds . . . in the dark, Mr. Butler."

She heard him breathe out, more loudly this time.

"A skunk in search of grubs, Miss Whitfield. Maybe a possum hunting for bird eggs. Or deer after acorns. Good night, Miss Whitfield," he grumbled, rolling onto his side.

Just who posed the most risk to her personal welfare? she wondered with chest-tightening apprehension. French marauders? Curious Indians? Hungry animals? Or the muscular trader who controlled her with a long rope and lay with knife and gun in the dark near her side?

Five

Rachel's thin fingers stroked the mud layer covering her cheeks.

Louder than any primitive drum, her pounding heart echoed in her ears. She shrank within the nubby confines of her trade blanket. She wanted to believe the blanket and river mud would protect her from Butler's crude, grappling advances. Any moment now she expected him to greedily reach for her.

Any moment!

Men . . . *did* things to women in the night, Old Eliza had warned her. Abrupt, painful things. Men leered and boasted of these acts, which poor suffering women were forced to endure.

She would scream. Most definitely.

When he grabbed her, as he was surely about to, she would scream as if her life depended upon it. Screaming would likely do no good out here in the middle of the wilderness, where no one else could hear. Still, it would make Rachel feel better. Possibly even frighten the predatory trader away. She would . . .

Barred owls, hooting a calming velvet refrain, intruded on Rachel's anxious thoughts. Night breezes whispered through hemlock branches and shivered countless beech leaves. Faint chimes of horse bells suggested animals' swaying motions.

Wait! What was that?

Her ears alerted Rachel to a new sound. Heavens above! What malignant evil awaited her now?

The soft buzzing snores of Jonah Butler and Tom Blaine purred against her ears. They were asleep. Hallelujah! Perhaps if she lay perfectly still all night Butler would not . . . disturb her.

Gradually, Rachel allowed her own breathing to slow and deepen. Struggling to find a position that lessened the aching stiffness in her body, she listened to stream water gently tumble over myriad stones.

At last she succumbed to sleep.

"Wake up, Miss Whitfield."

Rachel struggled to open her eyes.

"We have work to do," Butler barked abruptly at first light next morning. "No time to lay about."

Kneeling at Brush Creek, Rachel splashed cool bracing water over her face before drinking from her palms. When the water stilled she noticed Butler's weathered face reflected next to hers for a brief moment in the stream. As if he had stolen a glance at her.

Abruptly he turned away.

"The black sticky loam of our night camp, with its lush grass, offered good grazing for the horses, Mr. Butler," Rachel commented later, as they finished a cold breakfast of biscuits and cheese. "How is it you know where to find these camps and trails?"

"Old Indian trails, ma'am. Some were once animal paths." Butler's mouth closed around the last of his biscuit. His eyes locked suspiciously on hers. "Why do you ask?"

She busied herself flicking imaginary dust particles from her apron. "Oh, no reason at all, sir, I assure you. How many times have you crossed these mountains?"

He doused the night's fire. "I've lost count."

She studied his expression. "Out here near alone in the wilderness, you are not afraid. I can see it in your eyes. You love this life, do you not, Mr. Butler?"

Easing up to his full height, he stretched kinks from his arms. "If I didn't, I would not be here. I sense a motive in your persistent queries, Miss Whitfield. Banish those runaway notions from your fancy at once. The mountains are no place for a woman alone. Wolves will rush to gobble you. The four-legged version immediately; the two-legged sort even quicker."

Leering, he gestured for her to rise.

Tethered to Butler by the long rope, she had no choice. She smoothed wrinkles from her pale brown linen skirt and white apron. "You are a detestable man, Mr. Butler."

He almost smiled. "Thank you, ma'am. I've been called worse."

Forced by the rope to follow at Butler's side, Rachel made herself useful as he and Blaine worked.

After removing hobbles, the men allowed the horses to drink before tying them together in a long, single-file chain. Rachel silenced each horse's bell for day travel with a stuffing of moss, while the two men heaved two-hundred-pound loads atop the animals.

Heavy labor made Butler's muscles bulge, Rachel noticed, fanning herself with a broad leaf at the observation. Watching him bend and stoop and reach as he checked each horse and examined bundled furs, she fought back an annoying urge to . . . well, *touch* him.

Absurd. An indecent urge, which she immediately bottled up.

"Pain," she whispered in a stern reminder, primly refastening her hair into a tight bun. A man's touch caused women pain and must . . . *must* be avoided by any sensible woman such as herself.

"Girth tightened, Miss Whitfield?" Butler called back to her.

Rachel nodded.

Affectionately patting Sara, the shy mare she rode, Rachel peeked over her shoulder at her captor. A collection of deadly looking weapons dangled from Butler's leather belt—a tomahawk on his right side, hunting knife on the left, along with a powder horn and leather pouch filled with homemade bullets. A snakeskin band trimmed his round felt hat, drawn low over his dark brown eyes.

Though a formidable-looking man, Jonah Butler could not be allowed to quash her furtive plans.

Even so, Rachel resumed fanning herself.

Listening to the easy clip-clop of horse hooves striking soft earth that second day, she breathed in evidence of frequent springs along the marshy trail. Large stands of giant old pines in the lowlands stood guard over sedges, pokeweed, and tall cattails. Purple asters and feathery yellow goldenrod wands signaled the approach of autumn.

The sight of vultures ripping at a softened groundhog carcass broke Rachel's mellow reverie. Riding high on the bay mare, Rachel fingered the rope knot jouncing against her belly.

"Maybe it can be loosened," she murmured with a closemouthed smile.

Butler led the pack train on a gradual ascent through massive stands of hickories and yellow poplars. Ancient trees blotted out sunlight so efficiently that undergrowth became sparse, allowing ease of travel.

Like some giant European park, Rachel mused, only far too quiet. There were no people. Even songbirds, who favored edges of clearings, were absent.

They rode the entire morning.

The silent darkness of dense shade induced a sense of gloom in Rachel. Strangely, she stole a reassuring glance ahead at Butler. Tall and commanding in the saddle, he rode with a rifle propped across the crook of his arm.

Rachel dragged her gaze from the broad-backed scoundrel.

She would break free soon and trek north through these same shade-darkened woods till she stumbled on Indian paths that would lead her to Montreal.

Quite soon.

Leaves suddenly shifted noisily.

Rachel blinked hard. What of the mysterious individuals who dogged their footsteps? Surely it was Jonah Butler they intended to harm, not her.

Butler had a mission of vital importance, without a doubt. His journey might even protect her own father. She wished Butler no harm—so long as he did not interfere with her goal of rescuing Zeb before he died confined in some vile Montreal prison.

"Exactly," Rachel whispered, nodding her head in silent affirmation of her secret plot.

An unwelcome soul-searing vision crept suddenly into Rachel's mind.

Wounded and bleeding, Jonah Butler lay spilling his life's blood in some dim forest recess . . . without her there to bind his wounds and save his life. Annoying, that vision. And a solitary image of herself sleeping alone in the dark without Butler's burly presence just five feet away to protect her.

Rachel shuddered. Would she miss Butler when she struck north alone?

Even now, weeks after his first visit to Turtle Creek, she could still recall the feel of Butler's firm chest, his enfolding arms, his searching mouth. . . .

Rachel closed her eyes, struggling to envision Zeb Whitfield's face, not the brawny figure of darkly handsome Jonah Butler.

At noon Tom Blaine wiped his mouth with a greasy handkerchief. " 'Twas the last of our cold ham and biscuits, Jonah."

Butler shook his head. "Never saw a boy eat so much, Tom. You're all appetite." He scrutinized a small opening in the forest canopy. "A storm approaches. We must ascend Chestnut Ridge before nightfall. We'll build a fire there and cook some fish before the downpour."

"Mr. Butler!" Rachel cried in disbelief as she munched the last crumbs of her biscuit. "How can you possibly tell? The sky is scarcely visible through all these trees."

With a brooding glare, he fingered the scabbard of his hunting knife. "Close your eyes, Miss Whitfield. A cautious traveler can smell a storm building. Any Indian will tell you that. You can feel it."

"Feel an approaching storm?" Tearing her gaze from Butler's weathered face, thick arms, and veined hands, somehow Rachel knew it to be true. There was little the man could not fathom.

Could he read her mind as well? Did he know just what, and when, she planned to—?

Riding east that afternoon through fern-carpeted woods, Rachel secretly rejoiced at escalating winds that strained against her mobcap and clawed at her neckerchief.

An approaching storm? Excellent! This would be the perfect night to make her escape.

At some incautious moment, while Butler and Blaine labored tending the horses, Rachel would bolt free. A corner of her mouth eased into a sly smile.

No man could tie her down. Not even brawny Jonah Butler.

A sudden, ominous whistle startled her.

Grim-faced, Butler turned sharply in his saddle to stare back at her. "You all right, Miss Whitfield?"

"Yes. But what on earth was that?"

"A hatchet . . . aimed for me. Attackers often miss their desired target, Miss Whitfield. Stay alert," he ordered as he quietly unsheathed his hunting knife.

Giant poplar branches trembled from sharp gusts shivering through slender blue-green pine needles. Rachel clutched at the thin cotton scarf embracing her shoulders as her horse plodded along behind Butler's mount. Tonight, she reminded herself, nervously brushing a fallen leaf from her striped fustian bodice. Tonight she would have to be more bold than at any other time in her life.

Late that afternoon they rode a serpentine trail ascending Chestnut Ridge.

"Such rocks!" Rachel exclaimed, marveling at mammoth round boulders littering the forest in every direction.

Squint-eyed and unsmiling, Butler studied chestnut and walnut groves on both sides for enemy signs.

When they halted for the evening alongside a laurel-rimmed slope, the two men unpacked and groomed the horses. Rachel loosened bell clappers and knelt to gently hobble each horse's front legs as a chipmunk darted into nearby wood sorrel.

Only then did Butler untie the straps linking each horse.

"I saw jumbo trout yonder in that stream, Jonah. Big fat speckled ones. I can taste 'em already," Tom Blaine declared. "I'll go fetch us some."

Butler nodded. "I'll make a fire." He held up his wrist, linked by rope to Rachel's waist. "With Miss Whitfield's assistance. Or in spite of it."

She ignored his jibe. Tonight she would be sweet. Painfully so. "I can help you gather dry wood," Rachel offered with contrived congeniality, hoping to deflect Butler's suspicions. "I saw you retrieve tobacco from your saddlebag, Mr. Butler. You crave the taste of a smoke, I can tell."

He studied her newly benign manner, a switch from Rachel's usual sulky behavior toward him. "I crave the taste of many things, ma'am," he commented, not betraying any emotion.

Still tethered to Rachel, Butler followed her high up on Chestnut Ridge, away from dampness that might spoil wood for a fire. "You seem to walk with a touch more dignity tonight, Miss Whitfield."

She sniffed. "'Tis not polite to comment on a lady's walk, sir."

Butler guffawed. His lips curled into the closest semblance of a grin he'd worn all day. "Why, Miss Whitfield!" he said, stroking his stubbled jaw. "Whatever gave you the idea I was polite?"

"Believe me, sir, nothing you ever said or did gave me that impression. I simply intended that . . . Oh, look! In front of those dogwood trees, a stand of raspberry bushes still bearing a few fragrant berries."

"We can return for them after I start a fire."

Tall, with a long reach, he stretched high overhead for dead branches. With thick vines he tethered fuel together and dragged the large travois bundle back toward their campsite.

"Hold out your apron, Miss Whitfield," he ordered.

"I beg your pardon?"

"Make a bucket of your apron for the tinder."

Together they gathered downy fluff from skeletonized milkweed and thistle plants for tinder. With both hands, Rachel held out her apron to receive the lighter-than-air bounty.

Eyeing the ominously blackened heavens, Butler sought shelter beneath a rocky overhang, high on Chestnut Ridge.

"Good place to weather out the storm," he commented with a grunt. Crouching low after removing his hat, Butler constructed a tepee-shaped arrangement of dry wood. Next to the heap, he expertly twirled a wooden bow drill to ignite a spark.

Rachel blinked back her fascination with Butler's hardened masculinity—his practiced hands, his lean body, the cascade of his black hair curving above his shoulders. She fought to avoid staring at the stretch of fabric across his broad back, his upper arms, his thighs, and . . .

Pain, she reminded herself, breathing faster than usual. Pain and suffering. Man's only legacy to woman. This was not the night for her to become inquisitive about a man's touch. Or infatuated with Jonah Butler's husky masculine appeal.

Especially not tonight.

She had to appear quietly cooperative so as not to arouse his suspicions.

"Greens, Mr. Butler," she shouted abruptly by way of distraction, pointing to clumps of lamb's-quarter and purslane. "Wonderful with fish. I shall gather some for our dinner, eh?"

Still tethered to Rachel, Butler savored his pipe as she filled her apron with fresh greens.

Tom Blaine returned with a trout of prodigious size, which he cleaned and placed over the fire. "Storm's about here," he observed, taking the greens from Rachel.

Sudden gusts wrapped Rachel's wheat-colored skirt against her thighs and tore at her straw hat.

"We best pick your raspberries right now," Butler advised her. "Tom can manage the fire." He handed the youth a bark slab to shield the fire from wind and rain.

Ready to chide Butler once more about the rope, Rachel gnawed her lip instead. Something about the way Jonah Butler said *we* . . . a flickering spark in the depths of his walnut brown eyes when he stared at her . . . made her for one foolish moment secretly glad she remained linked to the husky trader.

Picking raspberries, for Rachel, had never before seemed a sensual exercise.

It did now.

With high winds whipping butter-colored tendrils from her tightly pinned bun, she fought to keep her skirt modestly in place.

Nothing missed Jonah Butler's bushy-browed scrutiny. Silently he observed the way Rachel's wind-blown bodice and skirt defined her breasts, her arms, her hips and legs. He'd had women before. Lots of times, when he craved the comfort a woman offered. He wanted to believe Rachel Whitfield was just one more woman. Take off their clothes in the dark, he thought, and wenches were all the same.

A lie.

Since that first kiss, Butler knew that Rachel Whitfield was like no other woman. Not just a pair of inviting legs that he ached to part with his knees and moisten. She had a face, this woman. She had haunting green eyes, satin skin, hair the color of ripened grain, and a mouth that . . .

Sweat beads formed above Butler's eyebrows. Pleasurable heat, demanding relief, flooded his body. His male organ swelled with a compulsion to make Rachel Whitfield truly belong to him right here, right now, on this mountainside.

His feelings for Rachel, though, went far deeper than those of a male animal in rut. She tormented his waking thoughts and troubled his dreams. A dangerous state for a frontiersman who relied on razor-edge wits to keep him alive. He had no use in his wandering life for a full-time woman.

He had a private grudge to resolve with the French. A grudge that drove Butler to face any risk. In the process, he intended to become a wealthy trader beholden to no man. Or woman.

And yet . . .

Something about Rachel Whitfield made Butler spill over with unpleasant urges. He felt bizarre loneliness when she disappeared. He near burst with jubilation when she smiled at him—a damned rare occurrence, he had to admit.

To contain all his restless urges around tart-tongued Rachel Whitfield, he would avoid smelling her sweet lavender-scented fragrance.

And never stand close enough to touch her. No matter what.

"Mmm!" Rachel whimpered. "Does anything taste so good as a raspberry plucked fresh from the stalk? Here, Mr. Butler. You must taste."

He resisted at first. Till she parted his lips with one large ripe berry. Her body leaned dangerously close as she offered the fruit. Lavender and raspberry and sweet satin skin made Butler's head spin. His knees weakened. His life beat pounded.

A giant crack of thunder, echoing off Chestnut Ridge, forced Butler to refocus.

"Pick fast," he told her gruffly as he helped her. "Storm's here."

Savoring the last of her broiled trout portion, early that evening, Rachel huddled beneath the jutting rock ledge with Butler and Tom Blaine as they waited out the storm.

Rachel faked a protracted yawn. "A wise choice, Mr. Butler. This location, I mean. 'Twould appear, despite this storm, that we shall enjoy a long, tranquil sleep in this sheltered cove." She yawned again.

Butler eyed her suspiciously. He sucked on his pipe stem. "Faint words of praise? Mayhap being tethered to me has mellowed you, Miss Whitfield."

Watching Butler manfully appreciate his pipe with playful lips, Rachel felt a disturbing sense of . . . of need. Of longing. Brawny Jonah Butler spelled trouble for her in many ways.

She had to launch her secret plan tonight.

Dangerous? Yes, Rachel thought, glancing at the trader's red mouth. But no more dangerous than remaining in the wilderness tied up with burly Jonah Butler.

The storm, when it came, was everything Rachel could have hoped for. Crashing thunder, blinding flashes of lightning, sheets of rain that threatened to grow worse by the minute. God's own wrath assaulting the steep incline of Chestnut Ridge? Or Hell's fury?

Butler's horses whinnied nervously while jerking their heads and pawing at rock-strewn earth.

Rachel gnawed her lower lip. Escape on a night like this?

'Twas a night made to order. She had to take advantage of nature's violence. Busy calming the horses, Butler and Tom Blaine would not have the time or energy to track her down.

Or the inclination.

Rachel's jittery fingers fretted over worn apron seams. Exactly what she wanted, was it not? Then why did she feel so ill at ease?

She peered out from the sheltering limestone cove at the tumultuous weather. Perhaps it was merely a fear of the furious storm that made her apprehensive about plunging alone into the night darkness.

Zeb!

She was about to make this dangerous sacrifice for her brother, she reminded herself with a series of hasty little breaths. She owed Zeb that much because one sun-splashed June afternoon years ago he had . . .

Rachel couldn't bear to dwell on that wretched episode.

Huddled by the fire, she massaged her thin, bare arms. Butler overlooked nothing, she observed, marveling at his ingenuity with even tiny survival details. His clever placement of a fire beneath the rock overhang brought welcome reflected heat on all sides. Adroitly he'd propped bark slabs to shield low flames from penetrating rain.

She stared over at his tanned, firm-jawed profile.

"Think the rain will continue all night, Mr. Butler?" she asked anxiously, mindful of the blinding flashes and booming thunderclaps.

Butler's lips played with his pipe. "No need to fret,

Miss Whitfield. You're safe here. Tom and I will watch over you." He studied the fire as he spoke, careful that no stray flames ignited any roots or crisp leaves.

She cleared her throat with a small cough. "I appreciate that fact, sir," she replied, eager to appear compliant on this particular night. "I . . . I just wondered if you thought the storm might abate soon. You seem to have heightened intuitive skills where nature—and danger—are concerned."

He swung that lazy gaze of his in her direction.

All a crafty facade, she'd learned from past experience. Jonah Butler was a difficult man to sort out. But that seemingly innocuous expression he so often wore masked a man on guard at every moment.

Abruptly he stood up.

Six

"'Twill be one hell of a night, Miss Whitfield," Butler announced, eyeing the turbulent storm from their perch high on Chestnut Ridge. "Tom, we best calm the horses. They seem overwrought."

Rachel followed at his side. "I shall assist you, Mr. Butler."

With a short knife, Butler pried open the rope knot at his wrist linking him to Rachel. "Stay by the fire and out of trouble, Miss Whitfield. You'll be safe and warm here. Tom and I have work to do."

She watched the two men approach their terrified horses, clustered now in a fidgety huddle. Dumbstruck, Rachel stared hard at the rope dangling loose from her waist.

With one swift thrust of his knife, Jonah Butler had liberated her. Busy as he was comforting his horses, he might never notice if she vanished into the stormy night.

Now was her chance. The very moment for which she had prayed. *Now!*

Pathetic whinnying from more than a dozen frightened horses tormented her ears. A chorus of collar bells jangled as the agitated animals shifted over rocky ground. Each bell had a slightly different pitch. Rachel recognized the tone of her own horse's bell. A sweet-tempered gentle bay, Sara always responded warmly to Rachel's voice and touch.

Her conscience lurched.

Right . . . and wrong. Two clear-cut entities. Or so she had always believed. Good people did right. Bad people did wrong. Simple to work out.

Except now.

Run! a voice whispered inside Rachel's head. *Run furiously and never look back. He shan't find you in the darkness. Head north to free Zeb! Now . . . now, before 'tis too late.*

"That's my girl," Butler called low, all the while gently stroking his animals. "Steady. Steady, sweetheart. Tom and I are here with you. 'Tis all right."

Rachel listened to Butler's husky voice coo consolation to his horses as if he were comforting anxious children.

Heavy rain drenched his clothing, pressing it fast against his skin. Lightning flashes illuminated his craggy face. Undaunted, he smoothed each horse's forehead while whispering reassuring words.

A man's brave kindness to animals. To her own sweet little mare. Rachel sensed a compulsion to watch. And listen.

Ignoring the dueling commands within her head, Rachel felt her moccasined feet lead her out of the sheltered rock cove . . . through a stand of lanky poplar saplings . . . not dashing north, but instead shuffling toward Butler's side.

A giant crash of thunder exploded suddenly with earsplitting ferocity.

Rachel screamed. Squinting her eyes shut, she covered her ears.

Peering cautiously through her latticed fingers, she saw, not more than twenty feet away, a huge old maple tree split clear down the middle—a victim of lightning. Sizzling odors of burnt wood and fractured air stung Rachel's nostrils.

The horses grew frantic.

Rachel dashed to her terrified mount. "Easy. Easy, Sara, my sweet girl. Here I am," she murmured, all the while patting her mare's neck and shoulder. Accustomed to working elbow-to-elbow with her brothers, she joined Butler and Tom Blaine in the downpour as they worked to calm the whinnying, prancing, head-tossing Conestogas.

At last the storm quieted to nothing more than a steady rain, allowing the horses to relax.

Exhausted and shivering, Rachel retreated to the small campfire where Butler and Blaine soon joined her. Her soaked garments clung to her body like a second skin, she noted with weary embarrassment.

Despite his exhaustion, Butler seemed to have made the same observation. His eyes raked her form. The red flesh of his tongue traced a slow path along his lower lip.

"You . . . best move closer to the fire, Miss Whitfield, and dry out your clothes," he advised, turning aside.

The outline of Rachel Whitfield's nipples, the curve of her hips, the angle of her thighs—all barely concealed by rain-soaked cloth that pressed tight against her feminine shape—had a profound affect on Butler. Even dog-tired, he longed to peel those wet garments off prim Rachel Whitfield. One article at a time. And . . .

Butler knelt to add more fuel to the fire.

He wanted to draw her inside his arms and revive her his own special way. Gently rubbing her skin till it glowed warm and pink. Kissing her till she squirmed beseechingly against his chest. Pure mountain madness, he reasoned. Damn that old devil, mountain madness! Could strike a man on any slope at any time.

Butler cursed silently.

Only a fool traveled deep into the woods with a sultry young woman like Rachel Whitfield. Butler had no choice. Not with the favor he owed Eli Whitfield.

Any woman, he figured, would do for a man in need of quick comfort. He didn't need sassy Rachel Whitfield—a troublesome wench if ever he spied one.

He did not need her.

Any woman would do for a hasty turn in bed, Butler reminded himself, averting his gaze from Rachel. A man existing on the untamed frontier was accustomed to deprivation of a personal sort. Another eight or ten days and some likely whore in Lancaster or Philadelphia would satisfy his lust.

Till then, with brute determination he could control his masculine impulses.

Most likely.

As Rachel squatted near the fire, Butler's rope dangled from her waist.

He flexed his wrist. By his own hand she had become free of him. His hand felt unpleasantly light without Rachel attached to it.

"We need sleep now, Miss Whitfield," he said. "First thing in the morning, before we ride off, we shall discuss our . . . our *arrangement.*" Hell, maybe her spirit had finally been tamed, though that seemed a wild stretch of the imagination.

She nodded, a gleam of recognition in her eyes. "Yes. First thing in the morning, Mr. Butler, we shall definitely have a new arrangement. Good night, Tom. Good night . . . Mr. Butler."

Round-eyed with uncertainty, she watched a fatigued Jonah Butler and his assistant collapse onto their blankets.

"Sleep, Miss Whitfield," Butler ordered with drooping eyelids as he faded toward slumber. "Dawn will come in the wink of an eye."

The wink of an eye?

Somehow as Rachel nudged her hips into a more comfortable position on her earthen bed, that phrase called to mind Old Eliza's words. "Men thrust up a woman's skirt and cause pain . . . You will not enjoy it, Rachel! Close your eyes and think of England . . . thankfully in the wink of an eye, it's over."

Lying on her side, Rachel drew her thighs close together as if to ward off any male intrusion. In a careless moment she had forgotten Old Eliza's warning. Jonah Butler's kindness toward terrified creatures on a stormy night had briefly blinded Rachel.

A foolish lowering of her defenses.

Butler was a strong, overpowering man. Had he not stolen a kiss from her in an earlier unguarded moment? Pray, what else might he decide to steal from her out here in a shadowy forest thick with hawks and wolves and copperhead snakes?

Her lips thinned to a taut line as she listened to the steady rain . . . and the snores of Jonah Butler and Tom Blaine.

Working up her courage, Rachel felt her breathing accelerate.

Now, an inner voice seemed to whisper. *Now!*

Slowly . . . noiselessly . . . an inch at a time, Rachel rose from her blanket. In that same stealthy manner—

rolling each moccasined foot warily from heel to toe the way a cautious heron moves—she edged north. Away from her captor's campfire. Through the rain-soaked forest that capped Chestnut Ridge.

Like a stalking crane in search of prey.

Jonah Butler, she knew, had the hearing of a bear and the nimble responses of a stag. She prayed his exhausted slumber would dull his hair-trigger instincts.

She carried nothing with her. Not even food. Nothing could be allowed to hinder her escape . . . and her journey north to Zeb. Her fingers traced the silhouette of a tiny flat knife that she'd stolen from Butler's saddlebag and hidden inside her stocking garter.

Rain, silken soft now in its steady persistence, drenched Rachel's exposed mobcap and face and soaked her garments.

Gaining speed, she glanced up at the cloud-blanketed night sky. Complete darkness, blacker than the fur of a skunk. No moon or stars to shine the way. Not on this storm-plagued night, she observed, as her moccasins tread softly across a carpet of broken, hay-scented ferns and pine needles.

She clutched the rope knot at her waist. That same rope, once she pried open the knot, would prove useful in her solitary flight to Canada.

A reckless grin curved Rachel's mouth, even as her heart continued to pound. Had she bested fierce Jonah Butler at his own primitive game of cat and mouse? Had she?

Lord, what exhilaration!

Rachel's breath came in deep gulps now as she began running in the drenched darkness. She must not allow herself to contemplate the hungry bears and panthers who prowled this same forest. Or the jagged terrain, with huge yawning crevices that sometimes swallowed careless hikers.

Fear?

Despite her terrors, she wouldn't yield. She ran faster now, as rain drenched her mobcap and tugged her long hair loose from its pinned moorings. Faster . . . faster through the darkness.

Suddenly two strong hands reached from the dark and seized Rachel.

She screamed as she felt her arms pinned against the trunk of a beech tree.

"Damn it, woman!" a male voice roared. "Will you show no mercy to a man in need of sleep?"

"Mr. Butler!" Rachel exclaimed in shock. "How did you . . . ? I never heard you . . ."

"Woman, do I have to tie you fast to your horse like a sack of wheat? *God's blood!* I will if I must, damn it, to get you across these mountains." Butler bellowed in rage.

Tears stung Rachel's eyes and spilled down her cheeks. Fatigue took its toll. She yearned to draw up her knee and drive it straight into Butler's groin. She wanted to flee like some weightless bird on the wing.

But she was exhausted, stunned, and shaking.

Pinned to the smooth wide beech trunk by her male captor, she shook with sobs and hated herself for the teary lapse.

He released her arms.

"Rachel . . ." Butler cleared his throat. His voice quieted to a low rasp. "I do not believe in terrifying women, Miss Whitfield," he said, plowing his fingers through his coarse dark hair. "I should like nothing better than to be rid of you and your mischief. But I owe your father a debt that I intend to repay."

"Why should I be the coin for your debts?" she raged through her tears.

Towering before Rachel, Butler nudged her chin up gently with his knuckle. "Because, Miss Whitfield, you are every bit as vexatious as a sack of gold. Though a mite more shapely, I might add. Now, will you come with me agreeably, or do I have to . . . ?"

She crossed her arms in a defiant wedge before her chest. Her lower lip jutted forward.

With Butler's sharp instincts, he noticed her right knee draw back in preparation for a painful assault. Quickly he scooped her up into his arms. "'Tis late and I'm too tired to argue, Miss Whitfield," he growled, clutching a rain-soaked Rachel against his chest as he stomped back toward the campfire.

"Let the tyrant think what he will," Rachel whispered under her breath next morning as she splashed bracing springwater across her face. Fool! No man could control her actions, or her destiny. For Zeb's sake she meant to reach Montreal one way or another. Jonah Butler's debt to her father or anyone else was no concern of hers.

She would use him.

Butler knew the passes across the Alleghenies like the back of his hand. Rachel would wait. Maybe even make a pretense at being docile to dull his razor-sharp senses. Then . . . when Butler had safely escorted her as far east as the Susquehanna River, she would bolt north. Following the river, she would no longer have to worry about getting lost.

Here was a clever new plan that well suited Rachel's purpose. After all, following the placid

Susquehanna north would place her even closer to Montreal.

She smiled.

Her morning smile faded, though, when she glanced sidewise at the ruffian Butler, stretching in crystalline early sunlight.

He walked from one horse to the next, running his hands over their coats in search of burrs or wounds. Scowling, he lifted each of their hooves to check for cast shoes. Invariably he patted each horse's soft nose as it nuzzled against his hand.

Against her better judgment, Rachel watched his burly chest and arms in motion, his large hands, his weathered face. A hidden urge drove her to moisten her lips with her tongue.

Jonah Butler was coarse, rude . . . even insolent. He harbored a casual disregard for women. He viewed her with near contempt—a sentiment she considered mutual. He was an undisciplined trader with the instincts of a wild varmint. And likely, Rachel figured, he'd never dressed or behaved like a gentleman in his entire life.

Yet . . . something about the way he had tenderly carried her close to his chest last night stirred tingling sensations in Rachel's forbidden regions.

"Don't expect to enjoy it, child!" Old Eliza had cautioned Rachel. *Enjoy what?* she wondered now as she cast about for any sign of her mobcap. What harsh acts did a man commit against a woman that so triggered Old Eliza's admonitions?

Without warning, a pair of unsmiling Lenape hunters suddenly materialized through the trees at Butler's side. "Are you certain?" she heard Butler inquire of the two men, who conversed with him in a blended mix of English and Delaware.

"Tom," she whispered, catching Butler's assistant by the sleeve as he tightened the girths of several horses. "Who are those men? Mr. Butler seems . . . familiar with them. Yet they materialized from nowhere."

She watched the trader offer his guests a breakfast of broiled fish, followed by a friendly round of pipe-smoking.

"Them? No need for you to worry, ma'am," Blaine commented, continuing his scrutiny of Butler's pack-horses. "Swift Otter is an old half-breed friend of Jonah's. In fact, I doubt many Indians live on the frontier that Jonah isn't on comfortable speaking terms with."

She eyed Swift Otter's unusual garb, apparently culled from his mixed European and Lenape heritage. Brass hoop earrings dangled from his painted face. He wore a cinnamon-colored coat, a red waistcoat, and trousers over his stockings and shoes.

Rachel read a look of concern on Butler's wind-burned face. "See how they wave their arms, Tom? 'Tis as if . . . something is about to happen. I feel certain I heard the name Michaux mentioned."

She helped Blaine unhobble the horses and tie their leads into a single file.

Butler doused the fire and confronted Rachel. "Miss Whitfield, we must set off at once," he announced brusquely.

"Sir, what news have the Lenapes brought? Have you learned more about French military advances?" she begged. Such action might impede her imminent dash to Canada.

"Nothing of interest to you, ma'am."

"I shall ride when you wish, sir."

"What? No trip behind the bushes required?" he asked.

She bit her cheek. If she offered him a saucy retort, she had no chance of learning his news. "Despite your insolence, sir, I am ready. But Mr. Butler—"

"Quite right, Miss Whitfield. I had forgotten," he said, glancing at her waist, no longer anchored to his wrist with a rope. "We have not time for lengthy discourse, ma'am." Butler pried open the rope knot at her belly, then offered her a hand up on her horse. "I promised your father I would do everything in my power to safely deposit you in Lancaster. 'Tis no longer wise—nor safe—to shackle you fast to me."

He strode toward his own mount while Rachel struggled for words.

"But Mr. Butler . . ." she began, desperate for the latest military news.

With muscular grace, Butler swung onto his own saddled horse before calling back toward Rachel. "Why, Miss Whitfield, can it be? Might you actually prefer being fettered to me?"

"Mmph!" she snorted, aggrieved by Butler's playfully suggestive tone. This would not do! Not only had she failed to pry the latest news from the secretive, arrogant trader, he now assumed she longed for his close company.

Butler rode at the lead of the meandering line of packhorses. His whimsical attitude switched at once to the lean, wary, hooded gaze of an eagle in search of prey . . . or a predator.

"He knows a tasty tidbit of information about the French," Rachel muttered under her breath. "And he chooses not to share it." *The fiend!* Somehow she had to winkle it from him.

Even a hasty glance at Butler now triggered dangerous memories for Rachel.

Far too well she remembered Butler's smoldering stolen kiss at Turtle Creek. And his broad, powerful chest. Tenderly had Butler cradled her to him last night in the wretched downpour. As if somehow he would protect her with the last ounce of his strength.

A ridiculous assumption, Rachel concluded, as the pack train gingerly descended Chestnut Ridge's rock-strewn eastern slope.

The late morning sun, searing in its intensity, edged high above mammoth ancient pine trees as Rachel caught her first glimpse of old Indian huts clustered in a shallow valley.

"Loyalhannon," Butler called back to her as he gestured at smoke ribbons rising from the Lenape village.

A clear rippling creek skirted Loyalhannon. Parched from rising trail dust, Rachel craved the taste of that cool fresh water trickling down her throat.

"Mr. Butler," she began, walking with him toward the stream, "perhaps now you will tell me what news sets you so on edge."

But when she knelt at the banks of Loyalhanna Creek, she immediately found herself engulfed by a trio of curious native women.

"Come eat with us," they insisted in unison, drawing Rachel closer to a campfire that sizzled beneath a spit of roasted venison. They offered brief introductions.

"You speak English! But . . ." Rachel watched in dismay as Butler and Blaine retreated to a circle of Lenape and Shawnee hunters. Would she never have a chance to be alone with the curt drover? Her hunger, coupled with the women's insistence, forced her to yield.

A young wide-faced woman wearing a quill-decorated leather dress giggled. "You need not worry. Your husband will return shortly. He is quite handsome." Corn Woman handed Rachel a gourd of thick corn soup.

"Oh, but he is not my husband!"

"No? Then . . . you are his servant? His cook?" A second woman, Little Squirrel, asked. Wampum beads jangled around her neck, wrists, and ankles.

At that, Rachel nearly choked on the pottage—a blend of pumpkins, beans, and ground corn flavored with chestnut meal and sweetened with juice from sugar maples.

"I travel with Jonah Butler. At the insistence of my father," she quickly added. "But 'tis against my own wishes. He seems to feel I am his captive. Once or twice I tried escaping from the rogue. And I shall do so again."

Nodding in comprehension, the Lenape women studied Rachel. "You must be his woman," they agreed.

"Jonah Butler's woman? *Never!*" Rachel shouted.

Seven

"You misunderstand, ladies. Mr. Butler is merely conducting me to my sister's home in Lancaster. You see, malicious Frenchmen captured my brother at our father's trading post in Venango. My father feared for my safety and . . ."

Eyebrows peaked on the female Lenape faces.

"Shh!" Corn Woman whispered, pressing a thin finger to her own lips in warning. "Several Frenchmen are among us right now."

"Here?" Rachel gulped. "But where? I see none. And how is it you speak such fine English?"

Rising from her haunches, Little Squirrel smoothed her leather skirt. "A Moravian missionary lived among us for a while. Till he moved west to Logstown. We . . . We were sorry when he had to leave. He taught us some words of English and German."

The ephemeral sad veil crossing Little Squirrel's face told Rachel the woman had obviously loved this Moravian missionary.

Corn Woman tugged at Rachel's hand. "Say nothing," she whispered, "and I shall show you where the Frenchmen linger."

Through a maze of slender locust trees, she led Rachel a hundred yards downstream. Gesturing for silence, she swept aside hemlock boughs to reveal a lone hut.

"The sweat lodge," she murmured, pointing straight ahead. "One of the Frenchmen—a tall, boastful man with hair above his lip—suffers with a persistent cough. My uncle is a wonderful herbalist who makes the ill well again. He works now to heal the Frenchman."

The spicy scent of crushed cedar and hemlock needles underfoot teased Rachel's nostrils. Leaning forward, she overheard deep-voiced French accents drift from the hut doorway. Bother! She clicked her lips with annoyance. The French phrases she'd gleaned from passing traders at Venango were inadequate. If only she had paid closer attention! Now she strained to listen, understanding nothing.

"Careful!" Corn Woman admonished Rachel as they approached waving grasslike plants that bore cylindrical chartreuse blossoms. "'Tis flypoison. Uncle warns us not to use it."

"Why ever not?" Rachel asked, cringing back from the treacherous leaves while hoping for a glance at the Frenchmen.

"Flypoison makes animals—and people—very sick. Causes them to become helpless with much pain."

Rachel's eyes widened. "I shall remember that. To be certain, of course, that I never use flypoison by mistake," she quickly added, committing the plant's appearance to memory.

At that moment two men, clad only in loincloths, emerged from the sweat lodge. Reddened by steam that clouded the lodge's interior, they lurched toward the Loyalhanna Creek.

To Rachel, their identity was unmistakable. The

shorter of the two had an empty eye socket. The taller Frenchman's saggy mustache underscored a twisted nose obviously broken in some long-ago fight.

"Merciful heavens!" Rachel exclaimed, clasping her hands over her mouth to stifle the outburst.

"Have you met those same Frenchmen?" Corn Woman inquired.

"Indeed! 'Tis the Michaux brothers—Chabert and Philippe. But what are they doing here?"

Corn Woman was about to respond when Chabert Michaux's sharp hearing alerted him to the women's presence. Squinting through the maze of coarse-barked locust trees, he quickly focused on Rachel's reddish-blond hair.

"Mademoiselle Whitfield? Can it be you?" he shouted to her.

She shrank back from his outburst.

But Chabert Michaux grew emboldened at the sight of her. "Mademoiselle! I must speak with you!" he bellowed, dashing toward Rachel.

Though seized with distrust, Rachel stood her ground. Was it possible that Michaux was delivering on his promise? Had he learned Zeb's whereabouts?

Snatching up a gaudy green and black trade blanket, Michaux hastily draped it around his frame in a failed attempt to conceal his scanty loincloth. In a dozen loping strides, he quickly reached Rachel's side.

"Monsieur Michaux," she said, greeting him with restrained civility. "Have you brought me news of my brother?"

Beneath lowered lids, his flint-gray eyes feasted on Rachel. "Alas, mademoiselle, I have labored to find him with little success." He drew out the words as if to prolong his time with Rachel.

His unfettered gaze dragged along the curves of her body. Across her breasts, over her waist, around the swell of her hips. Chabert Michaux's long hair dangled in thick clumps around his face. His chipped front teeth made his words hiss.

Revulsion swelled inside Rachel till she labored to breathe. "Then, monsieur, we have nothing more to discuss," she announced, turning to leave his side.

His large-knuckled fingers clutched at her arm.

"Oh, but Mademoiselle Whitfield, we have much more to discuss. I feel quite certain if you were to give me additional information about your brother's physical appearance—and his capture, of course— my chances of finding him would be that much greater." Chabert Michaux stroked his mustache tips. "Or perhaps . . . if you were to accompany me in my pursuit—"

His lowered voice, the red blotches suffusing his face, the flames rising in Michaux's eyes raised Rachel's guard. She slipped from his grasp.

"My presence at your side, Monsieur Michaux, would be useless at this point, since you've failed to learn any particulars of Zeb's fate. I cannot understand, monsieur," she continued, trying to avert her eyes from his half-nude appearance. "You and your brother are officers from Canada. What possible business can you have this far east of Logstown?"

"You, mademoiselle, need not trouble yourself on my account. Or my travels, since you choose not to join me. There may arise a time in the future, however, when you will be grateful for my personal assistance. And protection. Surely you do not journey over these mountains on your own. Who escorts you?"

"Miss Whitfield? We must depart!" Jonah Butler's call suddenly rang out from Loyalhannon's clustered huts.

Chabert Michaux's eyes hooded into hostile slits as he caught sight of Butler's lanky frame. His mouth crumpled into a snarl. "You, mademoiselle, travel with Butler . . . an English trader without morals?" He spat out the words in a furious torrent.

He seized her again, as if to prevent Rachel from rejoining Butler.

She stomped hard on the instep of Michaux's bare right foot, forcing the Frenchman to release her with a pain-ridden howl.

"Mademoiselle Whitfield, you shall regret your foolish decision to abandon a French gentleman in favor of an English dog!" he shouted as Rachel dashed back toward the Indian village.

"I must leave, Corn Woman," Rachel blurted. "Mr. Butler . . . needs my help with the horses." They scurried along a worn root-studded path toward Butler. "I wish I might stay and visit with you. I should like to learn more about your uncle's use of plants."

Impulsively she hugged Corn Woman as they reached the clearing.

"I will send some parched corn with you to share with the man who . . . is not your man," Corn Woman said slyly. "Ah, and the twining vine with tiny blue-green leaves you pushed aside just now? Remember this, my new friend. The dried stem and leaves make a tea that can render a grown man quite sleepy. You might have need of that knowledge someday."

"Truly!" Rachel stuffed a leafy cluster of the ominous vine through her skirt slit into a concealed hip pocket. For good measure, she hid an additional sample inside her silver locket.

"I have news, Mr. Butler, of which you might be unaware."

Pausing on a trail east of Loyalhannon, Butler dismounted to check the girth on his saddle. "You, Miss Whitfield?" His lip curled in disbelief. "Might this news pertain to another of your bold schemes?"

She sniffed. "Perhaps I should not tell you, impertinent as you are. Perhaps I should simply retain my own secrets, as you keep yours from me."

"I owe you nothing, Miss Whitfield. Not secrets or information."

Her eyes flared. "Quite so. Very well; I shall keep my news to myself and tell you naught."

He smiled. "If you are able. Being a woman makes such containment difficult."

"I hate you, Mr. Butler. For an entire assortment of reasons."

He tipped his felt hat to her. "A comfort, ma'am, to know I have roused your passions." Smiling, he remounted and continued east once more.

Just before sunset they rode into a deserted Shawnee settlement perched on the west slope of Laurel Hill. Thick stands of basswood and speckled alder surrounded three crumbling, abandoned huts.

"This cabin seems the likeliest," Butler commented after surveying all three. "We'll spend the night here."

Tom Blaine kicked at dust with the toe of his

leather boot. "Even left us a stack of firewood. Mighty obliging."

"We shall need more before the night's through, Tom. Fetch us some wood while I start a fire with this brush." Butler set to work by the hut's stone hearth with his bow drill.

"Marvelous to have a roof over our heads tonight," Rachel commented, watching Butler gradually increase arm speed and pressure till his cedar board began smoking. He blew on the new coal, finally birthing a fire in the dust-coated hearth. "How that would have been appreciated during last night's storm!"

Butler swung his gaze in her direction. "Last night, Miss Whitfield? Last night you seemed far more absorbed in vanishing than in appreciating any roof."

"You underestimate me, sir. I can escape anytime I choose. And neither you nor anyone else can stop me."

"I see. So this night shall be a repeat of the last?"

She assumed a solemn pose. "No. No, you see, I have decided to accept my father's wisdom and follow your trail to Lancaster."

Butler propped his fists on his wide leather belt. "Have you, now?"

"Yes." She coughed quietly.

"And what, might I ask, brought about this incredible change of thought?"

" 'Tis clear to me that you need help."

"Do I, now?" His black eyebrows shifted in apparent disbelief. " 'Tis clear to you, eh? I see. In what manner do you propose to help me?" He leveled a sizzling gaze her way.

Rachel fidgeted with her fingers. "In your usual

self-centered manner, sir, you fail to notice how I have already assisted you in countless ways. With the horses. With cooking. With—"

He studied her facial expression more closely. "To be sure. Countless ways, indeed. And so you . . . ?"

"Shall take advantage of your skillful guiding and remain safely at your side until we reach Lancaster. After all, 'tis imperative that you reach Philadelphia as quickly as possible. For England's sake." Her blond eyelashes swept her cheeks as she readjusted her fichu.

"Clever of you to notice."

She ignored his sarcasm. "For me to disrupt you would be . . . well, near traitorous. Besides, my presence at your side can be useful to you."

A dimple deepened in Butler's tanned cheek. "I am indeed grateful for your compassionate change of heart, Miss Whitfield. Might we review just how you suggest being useful to me?" He leaned one arm against a log post behind Rachel's shoulder.

She tensed at his suggestive smirk. "Rest assured, Mr. Butler, I continue to find your coarse, vulgar manner offensive beyond belief. Decency shall prevail at all times, regardless of the urgency of our mission."

"*Our* mission? I do so like the feel of that phrase across my tongue, Miss Whitfield."

Tom Blaine bounced into the hut with a freshly skinned hare. "Parched corn and meat in broth! We shall eat well again tonight, eh, Jonah?"

Butler shook his head. "Lad, your stomach shall lead you to perdition one day."

"Ma said my appetite shan't slow till I finish growing."

At the youth's enthusiasm, Rachel's taut lips softened into a smile. "I lived with two brothers, Tom. I can vouch for your mother's words. Here, hand me the hare and I shall make us a tasty stew."

At dusk, when wolves began their plaintive wails and stray night winds curled around the hut, Jonah Butler reached for his rope.

Rachel eyes widened. "But . . . but we agreed . . . !"

He looped the rope around her waist. "We agreed to nothing, ma'am. You declared that you could escape whenever you wished, but miraculously you no longer care to." He tightened the rope around his own wrist.

She tapped her toe in controlled anger. "I tell you, Mr. Butler, I shall stay with you. I shall cause you no further trouble."

He stroked his whiskers. "I do so want to believe you, Miss Whitfield," he said, mocking her solemnity in a parlor-perfect baritone. "Truly I do. And perhaps I shall one of these dusky September nights." His voice dropped to a low, harsh growl. "But not tonight. Now get some rest. We have an arduous ride tomorrow."

Lying alongside Butler, before the ash-speckled fireplace, Rachel glared at him with pure hatred. Then again, her hatred was not as pure as she might have hoped. Butler lay on his left side, his broad shoulder jutting upward, his thick-muscled arm draped across his chest.

Stars twinkled through gaps in the hut's failed roof. In pursuit of insects, a bat slipped through a ceiling crevice and fluttered at will, then departed.

Rachel watched Butler sleep. Her curiosity stirred.

Men caused women pain in the night, according to Old Eliza. And she would know, having had not one but two abusive husbands. Just what was it men did?

What evil acts did they perpetrate on innocent women?

Jonah Butler was an ogre, of a certainty. Entirely capable of abhorrent acts. Had he done those . . . those vile things to a woman? To more than one woman? Had he thrown up their skirts and viewed their naked bodies with lust?

Rachel shuddered. Her breathing escalated. An odd foreign tingling dashed along her limbs.

What would she do if Butler awoke this very night and decided to inflict his male aggression upon her? Rachel contemplated this dreaded wanton male visitation.

Her lips parted in fear . . . and wonder.

Butler removed the rope for their daytime ride up the slopes of Laurel Hill.

Sunlight struggled to burn through morning mists as songs of exuberant thrushes, warblers, and chickadees punctuated splashes of rain-swollen creeks. Thick emerald skunk cabbage leaves lay in spent heaps along watery seeps and pale pink joe-pye weed blossoms perfumed the air.

When Butler paused to rest his horses, near noon, Rachel tentatively approached the drover. "I feel it wise to inform you, Mr. Butler, that I detected moving shadows as we rode through the forest this morning."

He fanned his perspiring brow with his hat. "Your keen observations please me, Miss Whitfield. A good indication that your primitive survival instincts are wakening."

"Gibe if you like, sir," she tossed over her shoulder

as she helped Blaine water the horses. "Still, you might find my observations useful."

"Ah, yes. You did promise to be useful. To me." He bit into a chunk of roasted groundhog.

Against her better judgment, Rachel watched Butler's teeth and tongue and lips move over the morsel. She felt a coarse sense of . . . of vigorous . . . dear heavens! What was that foreign sensation tingling throughout her body?

Her fingers reached for the silver pendant guarding her vulnerable throat. She traced the curves of that cool protective metal.

"I fear the Michaux brothers might be following us, Mr. Butler."

He paused from eating and met her gaze. "Interesting. However, I've known that all along."

"And you never told me?"

"You never asked, Miss Whitfield. You were too busy with your own plans."

She huffed her annoyance, then continued. "I saw Chabert Michaux at Loyalhannon—with several of his cohorts."

"And you never told me."

"I tried. You failed to listen. Perhaps now you shall respect my confidences."

"So you and Monsieur Michaux . . . conversed?"

"Indeed. In a manner of speaking, that is. He . . . he does not hold you in high regard, Mr. Butler. Then again, neither do I! But I thought you should know of Michaux's hostile attitude. After all, he carries a beltful of hideous weapons. I do not."

Butler's solemn gaze massaged the curve of Rachel's hips. "Do not underrate the ammunition you possess, Miss Whitfield. As for guns, the prospect of you shouldering a weapon is too frightful even for me to contemplate."

"Enjoy your very small joke, Mr. Butler. But Pa taught us all to shoot . . . and shoot rather well. You might be grateful for my assistance someday."

Suppressing a smile, he leered down at her. "Miss Whitfield, even now I cheer the thought of your assistance."

"Philippe, you fool!"

The casual brush of Philippe Michaux's shoulder as he rode sent huge pine boughs swinging in the damp September afternoon.

Chabert Michaux jerked back the reins of his roan gelding and glared at his younger brother. "Dolt! Will you never learn?" he hissed.

"As usual, Chabert, you bark undue criticism." Scowling, Philippe nudged his horse onto a fern-laced side trail.

"You forget, *mon frère,* this time 'tis that scoundrel, Butler, that we follow."

"Hah! Butler causes me no alarm. Did we not get the better of him once before, at Venango?"

Chabert shook his head. *"Oui.* But Butler, I sense, is now a different and far more dangerous man."

"I am his equal in every way."

"Not as you are now, Philippe. Butler has learned the ways of the forest. He passes quietly, like a panther stalking its prey, while you knock branches and make loud noises signaling your presence to every forest creature . . . including concealed men."

"Why do we follow him anyhow, Chabert? Butler is easy prey, leading that cumbersome pack train as he is. Why not kill him right now and be done with it?

That way he will never reach Philadelphia with his news of French army advances."

Chabert smiled, a mirthless twist of his lips.

"We shall kill that bastard Butler, of course. A man who steals French furs and women. But we shall kill him all in good time. He must never even get so far east as Lancaster with his message. His pack train, though, is the very reason we shall allow him to live several more days."

A stiff wind ruffled fringes along Philippe Michaux's wamus. "The pack train, Chabert? Why should that grant him longer life?"

"Ah, those furs, Philippe! Did you see them up close? Possibly the finest I've ever seen. Thick and glossy and richly hued. And worth a great deal of money to the men who sell them in Lancaster. Those men will be you and I, Philippe."

"Us?" A broad smile creased Philippe's leathery face.

"Oui. But why should we do all the strenuous work on the trail, eh, *mon frère?* We shall follow Butler while he and his gangly young assistant labor with those horses and heavy loads."

Patting his sheathed knife, Philippe Michaux chortled. "And we shall kill them just after they cross the Susquehanna River . . . before Lancaster, eh?"

"Unless Butler kills us first, Philippe. To avoid that ugly possibility we must pass through the woods like shadows. We shall make no undue noise, or signal our presence to Butler in any way."

"Or we shall be dead men, eh, Chabert?"

The elder Michaux fingered his ornate scabbard. "Many years have I hunted in these woods, Philippe. I have no intention of allowing an English dog like Butler to end my life." He spat on the dusty earth.

"Soon, my brother, we shall feed Butler's corpse to an Indian stew pot."

"And the yellow-haired woman who rides with him, Chabert? Eli Whitfield's daughter . . . what of her?"

Chabert Michaux tugged on his mustache tips. "A waste to kill her just yet, Philippe. I have other plans for Mademoiselle Whitfield. And when I am finished with her, arrogant Eli Whitfield will finally understand which of us rules these hills."

Managing a brittle smile, he stared east across the Endless Mountains.

Eight

Sweltering summer mists swirled around Rachel's unclothed body as her legs intertwined with Jonah Butler's warm bare thighs. She thrashed and moaned on their shared blanket with increasing urgency. His thick-muscled arms cradled her naked back as his hungry mouth tasted every inch of her.

"No!" she wailed, clawing at Butler's broad shoulders. "I must not! I . . ."

"Must not what, Miss Whitfield?"

Rachel's eyes blinked open from her dream as she awoke nose-to-nose with Jonah Butler. A fully clothed Jonah Butler. She blinked again. "I beg your pardon?"

Lying next to Rachel on the dusty cabin floor, Butler offered her a lazy morning smile.

" 'Tis indeed your most cordial dawn salutation yet, Miss Whitfield. I yearn to hear what it is you must not do."

Her mouth worked. No sound emerged at first. She edged back from him.

"Forgive my impertinence, Mr. Butler. 'Twas only a dream," she said, sitting upright as she brushed cobwebs from her linen skirt and apron.

Still lying on his side, Butler cupped his cheek in his palm. "The intensity of your nighttime emotions concerns me, Miss Whitfield. Indians believe dreams should be carefully discussed and acted on, to avoid illness. Would you care to act out your dream, Miss Whitfield?"

Her eyes flared at his sly expression.

"Certainly not! 'Twas merely a jumble of confused images."

"And that explains why you ardently clutched my shoulders?"

She sniffed. "I have asked for your forgiveness, sir. The dream frightened me, 'twas all."

"I see. And your fright would explain why you wrapped your legs around mine in your sleep?"

Appalled, Rachel gasped. With a slight cough, she groped for the silver pendant dangling from her throat. "'Tis all your fault, sir!" She fingered the rope around her waist. "Binding me so callously to yourself prompted my terrified outburst."

"Then I shall free you."

Butler untied the rope from his wrist. Rising, he extended his hand toward Rachel.

"Free me?" Rachel burst out, gaping at him in anger. "I shall rise from this floor without your foul assistance, Mr. Butler!" Dodging cobwebs suspended from the low cabin ceiling, Rachel unkinked her legs and stood upright.

"'Morning, Miss Whitfield, ma'am." Tom Blaine bounced across the threshold with an armload of kindling. "Thought you might like a cup of hot chocolate to go with your warmed-over pone."

Butler gestured toward the open door. "A fine clear spring trickles from yonder hillside, in case you yearn to freshen up."

Rachel glanced from Tom Blaine's earnest young face to Jonah Butler's seductive slouch.

"Decent of you to allow me fresh water," she said, watching him undo the rope from her waist.

He leaned against the door frame a moment. His gaze followed Rachel to the spring, where a sea of starry blue asters parted to reveal a marauding gray squirrel.

Blaine shuffled his balance from one foot to the other. "Jonah?"

"Yeah?" Kneeling, Butler blew on the ash-covered fireplace coals to revive them.

"You being a man of the world and all, Jonah, I . . . I wondered if I could ask you—"

"Spit it out, boy."

"Well, I was just wondering what it feels like to . . . to, you know, *have* a woman."

"What?" Butler brushed crumbled ash from his fringed linen shirt and swung around to glare at his adolescent assistant.

"You know, Jonah. Do the thing that a man does to a woman. Sleep with her."

"Damn it, boy, did your pa tell you nothing?"

"No. He . . . he never wanted to talk about it. Being around Miss Whitfield reminded me."

Butler's eyes narrowed. "You want to sleep with Miss Whitfield?" he growled.

"No! You see, I have a lovely girl in Lancaster, Jonah. Lily. Her name is Lily Martin, and she has the most beautiful eyes and hair of any girl who ever lived. I met her last time we brought a pack train through town. We kissed. I think Lily might be willing to marry me."

"Then why ask me about sex with a woman?"

Blaine fumbled anxiously with his bone-colored shirt button. "I never had a woman, Jonah. What does a man feel when he loves a woman? In his heart, I mean. And . . . and what does it feel like to touch—"

"I could smell that inviting chocolate all the way outside, Tom," Rachel said, her skirts brushing the threshold as she returned from the spring.

Both gawping red-faced men stared silently back at her.

"Gentlemen? Have I interrupted a private conversation?"

"No! That is—" Butler pawed nervously at his shirt fringes.

"Miss Pone, I mean, Miss Whitfield, the pone is ready." Tom Blaine scurried to ladle out Rachel's serving. His blush intensified.

Rachel squinted at the two. "I sense a conspiracy here, gentlemen. What has happened? You must tell me. I insist! French soldiers, knives at the ready, have us surrounded! Is that it?"

"Calm yourself, Miss Whitfield," Butler began. "Tom merely gave me the news that one of our mares stumbled in the creek."

Blaine nodded all too briskly. "Yes. Yes, indeed! Stumbled in the creek and bruised her leg, she did, poor luv!"

Her hackles rising in disbelief, Rachel studied the pair. " 'Twas not news of the French? You swear? Can the mare walk, then?"

Butler poured steaming hot chocolate into a wooden cup for Rachel. "If the weather holds, and these cursed swamp holes don't swallow us, we should reach the settlement of Bedford by tomorrow. With any luck we can switch a few horses there."

* * *

Riding behind Jonah Butler that morning, Rachel contemplated the broad-backed trader. A born liar if ever she recognized one, was Butler. But why?

Surely the maze of witch hazel thickets and laurel hells surrounding them held the answer. She must have guessed correctly. Wily, perhaps malicious, French renegades likely surrounded them. Sensing Rachel would dash to their sides seeking news of Zeb Whitfield, Butler concealed the truth from her.

The rogue!

Ignoring the rolling motion of her mount's flanks, Rachel studied the surrounding forest. Every branch, tree trunk, and floral wand. No trace of any man— French or otherwise—appeared. How could she dash to them if they refused to show themselves?

Butler led them through hoof-sucking bogs that day. Tortuous labor, Rachel noticed, getting more than a dozen horses through rain-swollen mire. Insects rose in great clouds from soggy, stale-smelling earth.

When they paused to rest the horses, Rachel twitched to avoid insects.

Butler watched her slap at her arms and cheeks. "Rain filled these lowlands deeper than I've ever seen them," he commented.

"This swamp teems with stinging insects, sir." She waved her hands at swarms of gnats. "They feast on every inch of my flesh."

"Come here," he ordered.

She hesitated at his graveled tone. "You seek another opportunity to plaster me with penitential mud?"

"I seek to dump you in Lancaster, ma'am, as I reluctantly promised your father. The day cannot come one minute too soon. Or would you prefer being eaten alive out here in the howling wilderness?"

She glanced over Butler's shoulder at Blaine, busy watering the horses. Tense-mouthed, Rachel slowly advanced toward Butler. Lush emerald sprigs of fresh-picked mint protruded from his large fist.

"Tea? Now?" she asked, staring at the herb.

He shook his head. "Rub this over your exposed skin. And on your clothes. 'Twill repel the bugs."

He demonstrated.

In unhurried, gentle motions, Butler smoothed the leaves of one piquant sprig across Rachel's cheek.

Her breathing slowed.

He leaned closer. His open hand stroked her throat with the scent of mint.

She intended to slap him first, then step back. She did neither.

His hand, large and comfortingly warm, massaged small circles of mint along her nape, across her chin, down toward her shoulder.

Rachel's lips parted. "I . . . I believe you have done quite enough, Mr. Butler."

"On the contrary, Miss Whitfield. I have only just begun."

His mouth whispered dangerously near her ear, though why that should feel so dangerous, Rachel knew not. She pressed one hand against Butler's chest.

"Your useful demonstration is more than adequate, Mr. Butler. If you'll hand me the herb, I shall rub it over the remainder of my body. Uh, my clothing, that is." She scratched at itchy red welts rising along her arms.

"'Twould not do, Miss Whitfield, allowing the varmints to nibble your delicate pink skin." Massaging green leaves along her forearm in a lingering fashion, Butler's hand encircled Rachel's wrist.

Heart pounding, she stared deep into his bark-brown eyes, as if searching for some universal truth.

"All finished, Jonah!" Tom Blaine called out. "You might want to check the girth on that fourth horse. Looks a bit loose to me."

Butler pressed the mint leaves into Rachel's hand and walked away.

Grateful for Blaine's interruption, she sighed long and deep. Fie! Whatever had she been thinking? Allowing that ruffian to . . . to touch her. To *fondle* her! Was that *indecent* fondling? If so, then why did it seem so . . . pleasant?

Men hurt women with their touch, did they not? She would have to be more prudent. More prim and proper, as she had always been at Venango.

As if to ward off the touch of any man, most particularly Jonah Butler, Rachel tightly rewrapped her white muslin scarf around her throat before tucking the loose ends inside her bodice.

On their afternoon ride, Rachel watched closely for Frenchmen who surely crept just on the other side of the wall of trees surrounding them. "They're there," she murmured. "I can feel it in my bones."

Jouncing along atop her shy mare, she glared at Butler's strong back, at the rifle slung across his thick arms as he rode ahead of her. Jonah Butler was an unforgiving man of might. If she bolted once more, he would hunt her down like an animal.

Or would he?

Perhaps Butler had grown more relaxed, more trusting of Rachel.

She smiled.

She would put Butler at ease tonight, when they camped under the trees. Perhaps he would forget the rope. He was especially fatigued today. Maybe sleep would claim his weary body and seduce him into deep slumber.

When they halted for the night on Buffalo Mountain, Rachel helped Blaine feed and water the horses while Butler stomped off in search of fresh meat.

Mitt-shaped sassafras leaves and plump dogwood berries bore the first fragrant traces of early autumn beneath a cloud-strewn September sky.

Rachel watched as Blaine knelt to snatch a cluster of waxy pink pipsissewa flowers and smile at its sweet minty scent.

"A man who appreciates flowers! Touching to behold your tender gaze as you contemplate the pipsissewa, Tom. 'Tis a reminder of someone you care for, is it not?"

Quick ruddiness flushed Blaine's cheeks. "Aye."

"And you miss her?"

"Day and night, Miss Whitfield. Lily Martin is the fairest lass in all of Lancaster. I count the hours till I see her once more."

"'Tis love, then, of a surety. Will you marry?"

"If she'll have me." Extending his hand, Blaine offered a grain mix to the next horse. "Miss Whitfield, 'tis a fact, I am shy around maids. Clumsy as well. Perhaps you could offer me advice on how to properly approach Lily for her hand. I asked Jonah, but he—well, he . . ."

"Jonah Butler? That savage brute? Hah! Tom, Mr. Butler has not the slightest inkling of how to properly approach even a dog, let alone a woman."

"But he is a man, Miss Whitfield. And he . . . he is known to be familiar with women."

She gasped. "Is that a fact?"

"Forgive me if I wounded your sensibilities, ma'am. But 'tis certain Jonah has a way of finding the ladies. Sometimes 'tis the other way around. The ladies seek Jonah."

Rachel's eyes bulged. "Indeed!"

"Which is why I sought his guidance on matters of . . . well, how to kindly approach women. Lily, in particular. Perhaps the moment was wrong. He seemed unable, or unwilling, to offer advice."

Rachel patted Blaine's arm. "You are a kindhearted lad, Tom. A good boy. Allow me to think further on this matter. And I suggest you not seek assistance of this nature from Jonah Butler—surely the most vulgar, crude man I have ever met."

"You hate him then, Miss Whitfield? Truly?"

"Well, of a sort, Tom. Though, I hasten to add, I labor to mitigate that contempt. Hatred is a most unpleasant vessel in which to live."

"Jonah is a good man, Miss Whitfield. Better than he appears to you. Perhaps your harsh opinion of him will soften before we reach Lancaster."

She flinched. Blaine must not suspect her true intentions—that she was about to attempt another escape. Better to let the boy believe her motives were more benign.

"Did I say *contempt?* Oh, Tom, I misrepresented my true feelings for Mr. Butler, indeed a noble individual with merely a few rough edges requiring intervention."

"Entirely true for most men, Miss Whitfield." He leaned closer and lowered his voice. "I have observed that Jonah's . . . rough edges have gentled a bit under your influence on this journey."

Rachel bristled. She clenched her fists to restrain any foolish outbursts on her part. "Surely you are mistaken, Tom."

"Indeed not, ma'am. Jonah's glance gentles, his

tone softens, when he contemplates your presence. Mayhap you are the very woman needed to mold him into a . . . a refined gentleman. 'Tis a high calling for a fine woman such as yourself."

"Mercy! I think n—er, that is, I shall meditate on your opinions, Tom. Further thought may prove that your ideas have merit."

Just then Butler strode boldly back to their camp. "We shall dine on roast groundhog tonight," he announced, scratching his chest.

Blaine nudged Rachel's elbow. "A high calling indeed, Miss Whitfield," he whispered to her. "Mark my words."

After dinner, Rachel stretched her limbs and strolled leisurely through a patch of lemon-scented bergamot beneath a pair of serenading cardinals. "How lovely," she murmured to the two men. Gradually she slipped farther away from the fire.

Rachel had more on her mind than nature's grandeur, however. She intended to map out a midnight avenue of escape. Possibly even seek inquisitive Frenchmen lurking in the area.

Butler joined her. With his rifle. Not at all what Rachel had planned. She fanned her mouth to cover forced repeated yawns.

"An exhausting day, Mr. Butler, would you not say?"

Two steps behind her, he nodded. "Hard work bringing horses through that mire."

Feathering her fingers through the September evening, Rachel yawned again. "I feel certain we shall all lapse into well-deserved slumber the very instant we recline on our pine-bough beds. Would you not agree, Mr. Butler?"

He studied her excessively amiable manner. His eyebrow quirked. "Perhaps."

"Shall we retire, Mr. Butler?"

He extended his arm in a wide sweep. "You first, Miss Whitfield."

"Oh, permit me one quick moment to pick some of those dainty white flowers, sir. I shall be right behind you. Truly."

The flowers she sought were beautiful but quite diminutive. Rachel knelt low on all fours to silently admire the glistening miniature blossoms.

"Do not move."

Frozen in a crouch, Rachel glanced sideways toward the growled warning. Jonah Butler, with his rifle aimed seemingly straight at her, stood twenty feet away.

Had she finally exhausted Butler's patience? Was he about to kill her here in dense woods, where her body would never be found? Rachel had no intention of dying meekly like some pathetic, dim-witted sheep. If this was her moment to expire, she would fling her arms wide and die with panache.

Just as she rose from the ground, a hideous scream reached her from overhead, followed by a shot. A tawny blur whisked past her face and crumpled to the earth with a thud.

A mountain lion!

Smoke wisps curled upward from Butler's rifle, still clenched in his fists.

Gasping at the lion's body and at Butler's gun, Rachel worked to move her lips.

"Close, Miss Whitfield," he barked. "What would you have done had I not been here with a gun? If you had been all alone in the woods . . . in the dark?"

"I am not helpless, Mr. Butler." Strident words,

quickly betrayed by an uncontrollable shivering that seized her.

In a flash he reached her side. "The lion grazed you. Let me help you."

She shrugged off his touch. "'Tis only a modest amount of blood, sir. Nothing I have not experienced before."

She stepped over the mountain lion's body to return to camp. Rachel braced the air with her outstretched hands to offset her trembling legs.

Unconvinced, Butler watched her. Seizing Rachel, he slung her across his left shoulder and bore his rifle across his right. Scowling, he stomped toward camp.

She thumped his back with her weakened fist. "Let me go. Let me go, Mr. Butler!"

"Woman, I can never let you go," she thought she heard him rasp low under his breath.

"What? What did you say, sir?"

He grunted as he deposited her on a fresh bed of pine boughs under faint moon glow. "Have you forgotten my promise to your pa, Miss Whitfield? I shall not let you go till we reach Lancaster. And, God's blood, that day cannot come soon enough. For now, though, 'tis necessary to examine your injuries."

Butler cleaned her slashed arm with cool stream water, then bound it with a muslin strip torn from Rachel's apron. His probing fingers searched for any additional injury.

"Your hands, sir! I shall scrutinize my own body, thank you very much." But Rachel's hands shook too badly for her to examine herself. Much to her complete disgust, she began to cry softly.

Squatting on his haunches by Rachel's side, Butler opened his arms to her. "I shan't hurt you, ma'am. You know that. I only want to help you."

"Help?" she wailed. "A curious concept of help you harbor, sir. Knotting a thick rope around my midsection each night as if I were some sort of heinous prisoner. If I had a gun, I would shoot you!"

Tears dampened Rachel's flushed and angry cheeks.

In a tentative gesture, he touched her tangled golden hair, no longer covered by a mobcap. "Do you not understand? I want only to protect you from harm. And from yourself."

Brushing tears from her cheeks with her knuckles, Rachel shrank from his touch. "Where, sir, is your demon device of rope tonight?" Through her tears, she glanced at their fire, flickering in the starry night.

After setting a wooden cup of water at her side, he edged back toward his own crude pine bed. "Not tonight, Miss Whitfield," he muttered. "Not . . . not tonight."

Nine

The sting of a laceration along her left arm woke Rachel at dawn. Her fingertips probed the ragged edges of a linen bandage Butler had wrapped round her upper arm. Absentmindedly, she felt for the rope knotted at her waist.

Missing.

"Stand!" Addressing his restless horse, Tom Blaine checked the mare's fetlock. "Feeling better?" he called to Rachel minutes later, while swinging a heavy pack up onto a bay gelding's back.

Rachel winced. She patted her arm once more. "I believe so, Tom. Yes, I . . . I feel certain." She glanced searchingly around their camp.

"Looking for Jonah?"

"Of course not." More guarded this time, she moved only her eyes as she pretended to casually survey the horses.

"Third mare down the line chipped a shoe. Jonah's looking her over."

"You need help, Tom. Shame on me. I slept late and shirked my duties." She struggled to rewind the plait of autumn-gold hair at her nape.

"Jonah said no, ma'am. Said you needed to rest that arm. Good thing he went with you last night. You were lucky, Miss Whitfield."

She clucked her tongue. "A curious form of luck, I should say."

"Crouched low like you were, all quiet and alone, that big cat thought you resembled his next meal. Jonah saved your life."

Rachel blinked back her unspoken gratitude. 'Twas not possible for her to verbalize thanks to the uncivilly coarse Butler. She reached again for the absent rope knot at her waist. And scanned the tree line for her captor. Somehow Rachel felt a mysterious, almost disagreeable lightness at being untethered from Butler.

"Perhaps," she reluctantly acknowledged. "But I should not be here at all on these mountains were it not for heathenish Jonah Butler."

Blaine furrowed his brow while tightening a leather girth. "'Tis odd," he muttered.

"What is?"

"Oh, nothing, ma'am." Blaine seemed embarrassed.

"You must tell me, Tom. I insist."

"Well, 'tis only that you scald him with your words. And . . . and he barks at you as if you were a perpetual annoyance. And yet—"

Blaine's face pinked.

Rachel caught at his billowing sleeve. "Finish, Tom, I beg of you."

"Well, 'tis just that, despite your words, when you look at Jonah, a curious glow shines in your eyes and lights up your whole face."

"Nonsense!"

"And, despite his scolds, when Jonah looks at you, the weathered lines in his face soften."

"All of it false, Tom. You imagine these things because you miss your sweetheart so. 'Tis all. No one has a more energetic imagination than a young love-struck swain." She brushed pine needles from her apron and began silencing horse bells with soft moss for the day's ride.

"That arm must rest, Miss Whitfield."

She tensed at the sound of that familiar deep voice. "I shall determine when and if I rest, Mr. Butler."

In two strides he was upon her. "Woman, your vexing attitude tests my . . ."

"Your *what,* sir?"

She glared up at him. Foolishly she paused a moment to search his tanned face for signs of that supposed tenderness toward her that Tom had proclaimed.

At her delayed proximity, Butler moistened his mouth. His large fists gripped his leather belt. "The cat fair gashed your arm last night. I shall have a look at it. Eli will enact bloody hell upon me if you end up losing an arm to inflammation."

He reached for her.

Rachel stepped back. " 'Tis fine, sir. No need to touch me."

Butler knit his bushy black brows together in scorn. "Woman, though you think otherwise, I am not the devil. I have never harmed you with my touch. Though I must say the thought was indeed oft tempting. Perhaps that is precisely what you need—the strong hand of a man."

"Beast!"

"Now I shall unwrap your bandage for a look—with or without your approval." He clutched her wrist with one hand while unwrapping her bandage with the other.

She winced as he gently exposed her wound.

"Just as I thought: an angry wound, ready to fester.

I fetched some plantain leaves to draw out the soreness." He applied leaves to her wound, then rewrapped it with the linen strip.

Halting his chores, Tom Blaine tipped his head sideways as he peered at the antagonistic pair leaning near one another.

"Well?" Butler bellowed. "You stand gawping, Tom, when there's work to be done. What do you find so interesting, lad, eh?"

"Hm? Oh, uh, well, Jonah, I was just looking for, that is—"

With a wink at Rachel, Blaine resumed adjusting girths.

"Now, Chabert! Should we not kill Butler now? Surely the time is right!"

Twitching with impatience, Philippe Michaux rested a forearm against his horse's wither as he watched Butler's pack train snake down a laurel-tangled valley.

"Resist the temptation, Philippe. Now is not the time." Chabert Michaux stroked the food-soiled tips of his mustache.

Philippe repeatedly fingered his powder horn. "From here I have an excellent shot at the English troublemaker. And at his lovely companion, who he binds to his side each night with a thick rope. I ask you, Chabert, what sort of man chains a beautiful woman to his side?"

The elder Michaux scowled. "An inadequate man who cannot keep her near with sweet words and love-making."

"Mademoiselle Whitfield is restless, Chabert. Perhaps she needs to be rescued from Butler's surly clutches." Philippe grinned wide, exposing his darting fleshy tongue. "Perhaps she needs the enticing lovemaking of a Frenchman. Several Frenchmen, even!"

"Restrain your overzealous urges, Philippe," Chabert snarled. "Allow me to do the thinking."

Cocking his head sideways, Philippe utilized his one remaining eye to glare at his elder brother. "You always have, Chabert, though I oft resent your arrogance. Despite grand notions you nurture about your brilliance, your ideas are no more clever than mine."

"But this time, *mon frère,* you shall see my plans are perfect. Butler must not be killed yet. Harassed, perhaps. Annoyed and even ever so slightly wounded on occasion. But he must remain healthy long enough to drive that pack train up to the Susquehanna River. We shall benefit from the fool Englishman's labors."

"And the woman, Chabert?" Philippe licked his lips. "What of that saucy blond woman, eh?"

"Ah, Mademoiselle Whitfield is a little witch, Philippe. All in good time we shall make her pay for her sullen rebuff of my attentions."

Philippe smirked. "How that will pain her poor father!"

"Eli Whitfield spat in the face of France. We shall teach that cocky trader a valuable lesson. 'Tis not wise for Englishmen to ignore orders from a French army on the move."

Philippe Michaux focused his one good eye through a rifle sight at Jonah Butler.

Chabert caught at his brother's sleeve. "The knife, Philippe, not the rifle. Your accuracy is far greater with the knife. Besides, I want no marks on Mademoiselle Whitfield . . . yet."

* * *

"Can they last, Jonah? Till we reach the Bedford settlement, that is?" Tom Blaine wiped his brow during a brief pause to rest their horses.

Scrutinizing the pack animals, Butler's face darkened. "Pray God they have enough strength left to climb at least one more incline. Bedford, I think, lies on the other side of this hill."

Riding through a mountain pass that afternoon, as her gaze trailed along steep tree-tufted hills, Rachel suddenly spotted smoke curls rising from a cluster of chimneys.

"Thank God! A settlement!" she cried, pressing the bandage against her aching arm.

Dismounting at Bedford, a small outpost nestled in a long valley between Sideling Hill and the Alleghenies, she walked back the line of horses to begin feeding them.

Butler blocked her. "Heed my advice, Miss Whitfield. Go indoors and rest that arm. Tom and I will manage, with the help of the blacksmith over there."

More grateful than she cared to admit, Rachel trudged toward a log tavern. Braced at the doorway, an attractive woman dressed in crisp homespun greeted her.

"What bliss! Another woman to converse with!" the jolly woman exclaimed, opening her arms in salutation. "Welcome to the Red Rooster Inn, my dear. Do come inside for a cup of tea. My name's Molly Stonewell. Simon will help your husband with the horses."

Rachel's skirt whispered across the stone threshold. "Mr. Butler is not my husband," she replied, entering the humble log tavern.

"Eh?" Molly crooked a beseeching eyebrow.

"We simply travel together, 'tis all."

"Indeed! A widow such as myself hears of these arrangements, though only occasionally. Have some tea, my dear, and tell me of these matters." Swinging a wrought-iron crane outward from her cavernous fireplace, Molly retrieved her teakettle from a metal hook.

"'Tis not what it seems, Mrs. Stonewell. Mr. Butler is my . . . captor."

Molly nearly dropped her wooden noggin. "Then you . . . you are his slave?"

"I should rather die first."

Molly eyed Rachel cautiously over her mug. "A fine-looking man, is your Mr. Butler, ma'am. Why should you resent him so?"

"My father, Eli Whitfield, runs a trading post on Turtle Creek, near the Ohio River. Even as we speak, the French army descends the Allegheny River. They captured my poor brother, Zeb, and spirited him off to some godforsaken Montreal prison."

"Dreadful, indeed! But what has this to do with your Mr. Butler?"

Rachel paced warped plank floorboards in front of the tavern's fireplace. "My father insisted that Jonah Butler escort me out of harm's way to Lancaster. Mr. Butler has a reputation for knowing the best route across the Endless Mountains. Among other things."

"Then you do not value his reputation?"

"Not in the least, I daresay."

Molly solemnly studied the facial expression of her guest. "Tut. Here come the men for victuals and some liquid for their parched throats. Perhaps we ladies shall speak more of this later, eh?"

After a meal of roasted venison, potatoes, and cabbage, Molly watched Butler inspect and redress Rachel's injured arm.

"Splendid medical attention, Mr. Butler," she observed. "Miss Whitfield is clearly in excellent hands."

"I have no choice, madam. Miss Whitfield's father entrusted her to my care." He finished rewrapping the linen dressing. "I intend to see her safely to Lancaster." He signaled to Blaine. "One last check of the horses before bedtime, Tom."

Molly Stonewell peeked out her smoke-stained window to be certain the men were out of earshot. "Ah, your handsome Mr. Butler reminds me of my own dear departed husband, Rachel. He, too, had fine large hands and strong shoulders like your . . . like Mr. Butler."

"Doubtless your departed husband was far more personable and kind, Molly." Toying with the frayed edges of her apron, Rachel watched embers play and spit in the wide fireplace.

A warm peach glow softened Molly's cheeks. "Men are much like clay, my dear. They can be manipulated and molded to almost any shape you desire."

"Hmph! I have no interest in reshaping Mr. Butler. He ties me to his side at night to prevent my escape."

At that bit of information, Molly's eyes sparkled. "Does he, now?" Her lips curled into an impish grin.

"Can you imagine such cruelty?" Rachel asked, carefully tightening the neckerchief that crossed her bosom.

"Possibly. Tell me, my dear, have you ever been married?"

"No. And I have no intention of doing so, Molly. Men in their rough, selfish haste only cause a woman pain and suffering. I shall have none of that nonsense."

"No?"

"Certainly not. What would be the purpose?"

"Rachel, my dear, I believe for your sake that we need to converse further about . . ."

"About what? Men?"

"Yes. I fear you labor under some serious misinformation."

"Old Eliza taught me all I need to know, Molly. She gave me this pendant to . . . Dear God!"

"What is it?"

"My pendant! 'Tis gone! Somehow I lost it back in the woods."

"A precious stone perhaps?"

"More than that. 'Twas a silver pendant known to save the life of its wearer at least once. Old Eliza gave it to me, along with her advice."

Molly patted her hand. "With handsome Mr. Butler to watch over you, my dear, you shall have no need of the pendant."

Rachel rubbed anxiously at her naked throat. "Oh, Molly! Do you not see? With Mr. Butler strapped to my side, I shall need the pendant's protection more than ever."

Molly's advice ended abruptly when Butler and Blaine, along with five other overnight guests, shuffled back inside her tavern.

"I suspect 'twill be quite cool tonight," Molly warned with an odd sideways glance, as Jonah Butler unrolled his and Rachel's blankets on the plank floor. Molly lowered her voice to a guarded whisper. "I would advise you to sleep close by Mr. Butler's side tonight, Rachel. To avoid an undue chill, that is." Her sly smile sparkled in the dusk as she bid them good night and traipsed up a narrow flight of stairs toward her own room.

Butler glanced at his rope, then at Rachel.

"Your arm shall require a fresh application of plantain in the morning, Miss Whitfield," he said, by way of subtle warning. "To offset inflammation. I shall oblige you at dawn."

She glared at him. "Your rope is quite unnecessary tonight, Mr. Butler. Lightning flashes signal an approaching storm. And those flea-ridden dogs by the tavern door will sound the alarm if anyone tries to enter, or depart, in the night."

"I derive comfort from that thought, ma'am." He stretched out his muscular frame next to Rachel on the bare wood floor, with an assortment of travelers and dogs packed close around them.

"Beast!" she hissed to him. "Remove your hand from my arm at once or I shall . . ."

"Shall what, Miss Whitfield?" he whispered. "I fear 'tis the rope, or my judiciously placed hand."

"Nothing, sir, is judicious about the placement of your hands!" Her bosom heaved in anger.

The weathered crease on his left cheek deepened. "Shall I utilize the rope instead?"

Her breathing slowed. "No," she whispered back, "you heathen!"

Lying quite still in the hopes Jonah Butler would quickly succumb to sleep, Rachel watched the crackling fire toss shadows along chinked logs of the tavern wall. Distant thunder echoed over mountain walls surrounding Bedford. Stray lightning flashes flickered past narrow tavern windows, made sooty from constant cooking fires.

Wedged as she was in the shadowy darkness against Butler's lanky frame, with his arm draped over hers, Rachel recalled Old Eliza's words: "In their rough haste . . . men plunge in and cause pain. Do not expect to enjoy it, child."

Rachel listened to Butler's soft buzzing snore. Lying so close to the predatory fiend, she could breathe in his masculine scent. She inhaled again, more slowly this time. The musk of a vigorous man. Of Jonah Butler. Not unpleasant, actually. Leaning a bit closer, Rachel explored Butler's proximity. A curious urge, unfamiliar in its demands, made Rachel stir in restless need.

She longed to touch the drover's sleeping form. Had to, in fact. And didn't know why.

Howling winds bent trees low and thrashed cabin walls with escalating rain. Inside, smoke from the fireplace tinged the air with a pungent tang mixed with the odor of leftover venison stew.

A threatening night. A night when all the senses were taunted by the elements and aroused with a hint of fear.

A night when Rachel wished for comfort.

Men . . . cause pain, she heard again in her mind.

Even so, a birth of unfamiliar urging forced Rachel to study Butler's sleeping form as he faced her. His hair, darker than ever in deepening shadows, lay sprawled against the plank floor. Bushy jet brows framed his closed eyes, fringed with coal-black lashes. His husky frame bulged with strong muscles earned laboriously on rugged Pennsylvania trails.

Harsh rain pounded the cabin till Rachel suspected chinks would loosen and walls might collapse. She stared up at the roof. Could this humble shelter protect them all from the storm's frenzy?

"Mr. . . . Mr. Butler?" she whispered.

No reply.

Somewhere outside, wolves howled their displeasure at this raging night.

Choosing the lesser of two evils, Rachel snuggled close against Butler's side and cautiously draped her fingers on his broad chest. Almost as if she were touching a serpent. She breathed in his familiar masculine aroma. Comforting, this time, knowing he was near.

Zeb?

Her brother would have to wait one more night for salvation from a frightful Montreal prison. Rachel closed her eyes. Shielded by Butler's brawny body, she felt strangely secure.

Dawn pinked the windows with first light, next morning, as Jonah Butler rolled onto his side and rubbed his eyes. He smiled. Like a trusting soul mate, Rachel Whitfield lay pressed tight against his body. Her relaxed fists burrowed along his chest.

He studied the sweet innocence in her sleeping form. Downy flaxen lashes curved over her cheeks. Loose strawberry-blond tendrils spilled across her narrow shoulders. His eyes traced the curves of Rachel's shoulders. Her breasts. Her hips.

The wench.

A spitfire who delayed his progress and fought him every step of the journey. One day soon he would be free of Rachel Whitfield's meddlesome distractions. *Forever,* thank God.

The smile vanished from Butler's craggy face.

His fist, twice the size of Rachel's slender one, lingered for a moment over her sleeping form. In an awkward gesture, his fingers spread toward her splayed-out curls. Gently he touched those silken strands. The rosy fire of first sunlight ignited pale reds and golds and earth browns in Rachel's shining hair.

He stroked her cheek . . . till, stirring slightly in her sleep, she whimpered.

Butler extricated himself from Rachel's unknowing embrace and stood up. Like some guardian angel hovering above her, he stole one last look at her curled and feminine contortions.

A small muscle flinched in his stubbled jaw.

He took the slobbering, panting dogs with him to the stable, where Bedford's blacksmith already worked at stoking the fire.

" 'Tis none of it good, the news we hear from the Allegheny," Isaac, the blacksmith, grumbled. He rolled up his linen sleeves as heat billowed from the red-hot fire.

Patting his horses, Butler checked them over for briars and sores. "From Indians? Or from the French?"

"Both," the aging German replied, as two Lenape men clustered near him for conversation.

"The earth trembles from the multitude of French on the march from Presque Isle," a smooth-faced Lenape buck insisted. "They walk with hatchets uplifted."

Butler scowled. "How far south have they progressed?"

"The Rivière au Boeuf, when last we heard."

Butler nodded. "The upper reaches of the Allegheny River. And likely picking up speed." He hoisted a mare's hoof to examine one shoe.

"A summer drought slows the Allegheny to a trickle," one Lenape commented. He smiled wickedly. "And slows the bateaux of the French army as well."

"They build new forts as they go," his companion asserted. "All the while, Frenchmen tell Indians living along the Ohio that they come only in peace, to help Indians . . ."

"Bah!" Butler exclaimed.

"—and to watch over the English."

"The first true statement!"

Isaac hesitated over his anvil. "You have valuable business contacts in Philadelphia, Jonah. You must tell them, that they might understand the danger threatening us all. Tell the politicians, the Quakers, the militias."

"Make them understand," both Indians agreed.

"War between the French and English for control of the Ohio Valley? 'Tis certain it shall erupt shortly," Isaac fretted, watching his carefully built fire.

Jonah ran his hands over the last horse's rump and nodded. "Indians who live and hunt out there will be trapped between two powerful nations."

"All of them forced to choose an ally, my brothers," the eldest and most blunt of the Lenape visitors advised. "Much blood will spill across those mountains, Jonah. Tell the English in Philadelphia so they will believe."

Head shaking in agreement, Jonah Butler gestured toward his pack animals. "Half my horses are lame and exhausted from the journey. And I have much more distance to cover."

The blacksmith scratched his forehead with a grimy thumb. "Give me some time, Jonah. A few more hours. Bedford is a small settlement, but . . . perhaps I can supply you with the horses you need."

Ten

Hard by the Red Rooster Inn's fireplace, Molly Stonewell eased her spinning wheel next to the tape loom where Rachel labored.

"Kind of you indeed to assist me, Rachel. 'Tis a grand opportunity for us to chat together . . . alone." She glanced nervously over her shoulder, as if expecting intruders. "I feel it imperative to resume our conversation of yesterday."

"Of the most expeditious way to roast venison?"

"Ah, no, dear. I had other meat in mind, actually."

"You . . . do not mean men, surely."

Molly's treadle worked furiously under her fast footwork. "Indeed I do, Rachel. I want to impart information with you that might . . . might bring true joy to your suitably upright but rather, er, restricted existence."

Rachel straightened her spine. She fiddled with her fichu. "I have all the information I need, Molly."

"But clearly you do not, my dear, for you have denied yourself the touch of a man. A loving man, that is."

Rachel coughed quietly. "This does not interest me, Molly. I seek to avoid the pain men inflict on women." Her fingers worked furiously at the small loom.

"But not all men bring pain to a woman, Rachel. In fact, most do not. With their big gentle hands and tender kisses over a woman's body—"

"Stop!"

"You need to hear this, Rachel. Truly. A woman undressed by a gentle man warms under his touch till her body cries out for more."

Rachel gasped. Her eyes bulged. "Not true, surely! None of it!"

"His loving, persistent kisses rouse a woman to kiss him back with knowing passion." Molly's smile brought a rosy glow to her cheeks.

"I shall not listen to more."

Molly glanced out the window. "Dear Rachel, we have little time left together. Isaac and the other men will soon gather the horses Mr. Butler needs. But hear me out. When a good man, a man like your Mr. Butler, makes love to you, you will reach a pinnacle of ecstasy so thrilling that you will cry out for the sheer joy of it."

Rachel's jaw sagged. "Molly, this sounds frightfully improper."

"Ah, but 'tis highly proper, my dear. With the right man, of course."

"And . . . and you remember all this jubilation from your late husband?"

Smiling, Molly pinked from throat to ears. "Let us just say, my dear, that I . . . that men— Let us just say that this conversation was one I felt you needed to hear. And leave it at that."

"You have allowed more than one man to undress you?" Rachel marveled at the very concept.

"One more thing, quickly, Rachel, before the men return. Remember I advised you yesterday that men were much like clay in the hands of a clever woman?

You possess far greater control over a man than you realize."

"Control? A diminutive woman over a towering man? Surely you err, Molly."

"Listen carefully to my words, Rachel. Men approach the tavern even as we speak." Molly stepped back from surveying the window. "Little time remains for our private woman talk. And clearly there's much you need to know. How you dress, or move, can vastly affect a man. For instance, the manner in which your hips sway as you walk, or how you flutter your fan or blink your eyes."

"Blink my eyes? How absurd!"

"Or smile at him. Appropriate smiling is quite effective, actually."

Jonah Butler, accompanied by four Bedford men, strode toward the tavern doorway.

"Impossible, Molly," Rachel whispered. "I simply cannot imagine smiling and blinking at a thorny man such as Mr. Butler. 'Twould be an exercise in futility."

"Try it, my dear. Merely as a learning exercise, you understand, for you need to practice these skills. Every woman needs expertise in these matters. Our safety, our very survival depends upon proper use of our feminine powers."

"You . . . you make it sound so dire, Molly."

"One last thing, my dear. Simply placing your hands upon a man's chest, as you smile, oft renders him sufficiently helpless in your grasp."

"Hush, Molly!" Rachel held a finger to her lips. "No more on these matters. I should not wish the men to overhear your . . . your feminine counsel."

Butler stomped across the tavern threshold. "We leave at once, Miss Whitfield."

"The horses?"

"Isaac arranged trades for our weariest animals. With French soldiers on the move, 'tis more vital than ever that I reach Philadelphia posthaste. How fares your arm this morning?"

" 'Tis improving by the day, sir."

He studied her facial expression. "You have been known to lie, Miss Whitfield. I shall have a look at that arm and make my own determination."

Rachel tensed in anger. Jonah Butler's arrogance infuriated her. She opened her mouth to hurl a sharp retort. From the corner of her eye she caught Molly Stonewell's knowing wink.

Rachel sucked in a deep breath and blinked at Butler. Twice.

"Something wrong with your eye as well, Miss Whitfield?" he asked.

She took a half-step back from his imposing frame. And smiled. "Why, no, Mr. Butler. I simply am marveling at the day's brilliant sunshine after last night's drenching downpour."

Butler cocked his head sideways. "You seem . . . different somehow today, Miss Whitfield. More amiable, perhaps. A brief rest here seems to have benefited you."

Was it possible? Or did she only imagine a softening in Butler's brutish manner? Was Molly Stonewell's cunning advice actually true?

She caught Molly's nod.

"I fetched some sassafras bark for your sore arm, ma'am."

"How very thoughtful of you, Mr. Butler!" Molly exclaimed, nudging Rachel. "Was that not thoughtful, dear Rachel?" Molly soaked the bark chunk in a kettle of water.

Thoughtful? Rachel clenched her teeth to avoid undoing the scene. A man who tied her up with rope each night—or threatened to—could scarcely be deemed thoughtful.

"Oh, indeed," she responded in flattened tones. She quickly undid the bandage on her arm, herself, to avoid Butler's touch.

He scrutinized her wound. "The redness diminishes. Are you quite certain it does not pain you? Or throb?"

"Quite," Rachel affirmed.

He dabbed the sassafras infusion against her jagged wound, then rewrapped the bandage. "Finished, Miss Whitfield. We shall bid the gracious settlers of Bedford farewell and depart at once."

Brooding, Rachel trudged toward the string of packhorses.

"Your dejected manner, Miss Whitfield," Butler called out, as he neared to help her mount, "due, perhaps, to the additional mountains we must cross? Or from leaving your new friend?"

Face downcast, Rachel fingered her bare throat. When she finally looked up at Butler, tears rimmed her eyes. "My pendant, Mr. Butler. My silver pendant is gone."

At the sight of her tears, he cleared his throat. "In the tavern, perhaps, Miss Whitfield. I shall take time to—"

To stop him, she caught at his fringed sleeve. "No. 'Tis no use, Mr. Butler. The pendant must have been lost as we crossed that last mountain."

He shifted awkwardly from one foot to the other. "We haven't time to go back and look for it." His voice, gentle and low, rasped over the difficult words.

"I know."

"Perhaps I can find another one for you in Philadelphia."

"No. This necklace was special."

"A gift from a treasured friend?"

"Oh, yes, Mr. Butler. Old Eliza's gentle ways comforted me so when my mother died, years ago. She gave me the necklace with the assurance that it would one day save my life."

"A superstition. And you believed it?"

"Yes," Rachel answered simply. "She said the pendant saves the life of its wearer one time; then it must be passed on to someone else." She dabbed at her welling eyes with her palm.

"Farewell, Mr. Butler!" Isaac called out, waving both arms at the trader. "And Godspeed."

Distracted for a moment, Jonah Butler waved back, then turned his gaze toward Rachel. "I regret you no longer have your favored pendant to protect you, Miss Whitfield. But I promised your pa I would watch over you. And so I shall. Now . . . we must ride, ma'am."

Bypassing the Warrior's Path, they plodded up Tussey Mountain along narrow ledges. Thick leathery rhododendron leaves obstructed trails. Watery seeps trickled down along pale green-crusted rock faces.

Rachel mourned the loss of her protective amulet, Old Eliza's special gift to Rachel. The talisman she'd hoped would keep her safe on her journey to rescue Zeb in Montreal.

She gripped the reins with fierce determination.

"Nothing shall deter my mission to locate Zeb," she whispered, riding past dangling vines thick as a man's wrist. "Not the loss of my necklace. And contrary to what he believes, not even swaggering Jonah Butler."

They followed a high ridge for several miles. Tiny chipmunks, tails upraised, skittered among leaf litter as scarlet tanagers trilled into breezes scented with the damp moldering air of early autumn.

East of Warrior Ridge, Butler halted at a branch of the Juniata River to rest his horses.

Leaving his gun and bullet pouch propped against a fallen log, Tom Blaine ambled up from his end-horse position. "Back in Bedford, I saw Isaac give you some venison jerky, Jonah. Sure would taste good after that ride. Me being a growing boy and all, you understand."

Butler handed Blaine a chunk and laughed. "Never saw a stomach quite so prodigious as yours, boy. Impossible to fill."

"I shall rejoin you gentlemen in a moment," Rachel announced. She followed her declaration with a slight smile to allay Butler's suspicions before slipping behind tight-woven branches of maple-leaf viburnums.

A short while later, shimmering witch hazels rustled alongside a narrow swale.

Butler spun around. "That you, Miss Whitfield?"

"No, fella," a strange male response growled back. "'Tis me."

An unshaven backwoodsman advanced on horseback. A long Pennsylvania rifle lay propped across his arms. "An' I come to ask you a favor, my friends. The dust is thick, you see. And my thirst torments me somethin' fierce."

The stranger's eyes rolled in an uneven stare.

Tom Blaine gestured toward creek water sparkling in the afternoon sun. "The water here is finer than most, sir. Join us and refresh yourself."

The stranger spat contemptuously. "Don't want no damned creek water." He stroked the carved butt of his rifle. "You men are traders. I intend to have me some of that nice throat-clearin' Monongahela whiskey your critters are hauling."

Butler swept his arm in a half-circle. "We head east, my friend. Nothing here but furs and skins from the frontier."

"Liars!" the stranger barked. In one blinding motion he raised his rifle and aimed it straight at Butler's chest. "A keg is strapped to that middle horse. 'Tis whiskey, and I want a big drink of it. *Now!*"

"Easy there, friend." Butler's rifle lay ten feet away. His hand edged closer to his knife scabbard.

Hands shaking, the stranger squinted through his rifle sight. "I can shoot the hairs off a coon's muzzle, you bastard. Make one more move and you're a dead man."

"And I can split the hairs on a coon's muzzle with my rifle," came a feminine response from the bushes behind him. "Drop your gun at once, sir, or you shall be dead before you strike the ground."

In disbelief, the stranger maintained his stance. "No woman shoots that good!" he shouted.

"Then I shall prove it to you, sir. Say your prayers," Rachel replied.

"Bitch!" the scraggly stranger snarled.

A shot rang out that creased his hat brim.

"The next shot, sir, will divide your backbone. Drop your gun at once."

Letting his rifle slip to the ground, the stranger twisted in his saddle in search of his assailant as Jonah Butler and Tom Blaine lunged for their own weapons.

The stranger gaped at Rachel and groaned. "Bested by a mere slip of a wench!"

Butler guffawed. "Albeit one who shoots like a mountain man."

"I warned you, sir. Now relinquish all your weapons to my friends. Even the knife that bulges beneath your shirt. Remember, I still have my gun trained on you."

Reluctantly, the stranger yielded his assortment of knives, bullets, and powder to Butler and Blaine.

"My thirst—" he moaned.

Butler handed him a gourd of fresh water. "Now be off. And stay out of trouble. This is rough country, friend, and your next encounter may be your last."

They watched him ride north across a rock-strewn stream.

Jonah Butler turned back toward Rachel and, with a laugh, reached for the rifle she clutched. "You never cease to surprise me, Miss Whitfield. Did Eli teach you to shoot like that?"

"No." Rachel cleared her throat. "Not exactly."

"Your brothers, then?"

"N-no."

"Then . . . ?"

Rachel's hands trembled as her shoulders sagged. "Pa said guns were for men. This . . . is only the third time I ever shot one."

Butler's brows hoisted. "You mean . . . ?"

" 'Twas a lucky shot, I fear. I was in the bushes and heard the villain's threats. I crept through the brush toward the last horse and snatched Tom's spare rifle."

"You once threatened to kill me if you ever got your hands on a gun."

She coughed quietly. "Yes. I believe I said that. And I meant it, too."

He cupped her chin. "Still?"

She sniffed. "At times. Yes."

"Yet you saved my life."

"I had to, to save Tom's. His life is more valuable than yours, you see."

"Witch," he muttered. "I shall have to make very damn certain you never get your hands on another gun while I'm around."

He sliced off a piece of jerky for Rachel before apparently rethinking his words.

"Then again, Miss Whitfield, perhaps 'tis time to see if you *are* a murderess. You shall have to be, you know, if you still plot to hunt for Zeb." He handed the rifle back to Rachel.

She gaped at the gun, then at him. "Why are you doing this, Mr. Butler?"

"You need to know, Miss Whitfield, even more than do I . . . can you kill a man?"

She gulped.

"Now is your opportunity." He spread his arms wide before her. "I present to you a broad target, ma'am."

He certainly did. She could readily see that.

Jonah Butler, with his hard-earned muscles, offered Rachel his burly shoulders and husky chest.

She swallowed hard.

"I shall not kill you . . . *this* time, Mr. Butler. But do not aggravate my temper in the future, lest you suffer the unpleasant consequences. I shall stay with you as long as I choose. Or depart whenever I choose."

He leaned toward her. His long shadow cooled her flaming cheeks. His huge might made Rachel choke on her own harsh words.

"When you threaten me, Miss Whitfield, golden sparks warm the blue-green of your eyes."

Rachel felt suddenly weak in Butler's close proximity. Golden sparks inflamed not just her eyes but her entire pulsing body. A frightening urge made her want to reach out and glide her palms up over Butler's unyielding chest.

She took a step back from him and stared at the earth.

"I . . . I shall help Tom with the horses now," she whispered.

"Plagued with scurvy and fevers, you say, monsieur?"

Frowning, Chabert Michaux picked at his mud-caked fingernails with the point of a knife.

A mixed-blood Shawnee he'd encountered on the trail nodded. "And dysentery. Sickness forced your leaders to send more than two hundred Frenchmen back to Montreal."

"But still our army progresses south from Presque Isle, eh?" Seated on half-rotted logs surrounding a small fire, Chabert Michaux watched a pair of Shawnee gnaw appreciatively on venison chunks.

The mixed blood spoke, using both French and Shawnee words. "Dry weather there makes streams shallow. Frenchmen grow weary from the long portages."

"When rains come men carrying canoes stumble and sicken in the thick mud," a second Shawnee commented, biting off another chunk of meat.

"But still they progress south, eh, messieurs? With their supplies, they manage across the Presque Isle-Le Boeuf portage?"

The Indian pair nodded.

Fierce gusts blew Philippe Michaux's shaggy hair against his empty eye socket as he nudged his older brother. "'Tis not good, Chabert. Men living out in the open, breaking their backs with labor, with not enough to eat, wracked with fevers. What if the English discover our problems and capitalize on them?"

Chabert's eyes glittered. "Have I not oft told you, Philippe? A determined handful of Frenchmen can best an entire army of Englishmen any day. How those redcoats love to deliberate! They move slower than a drunk at dawn. In the end they accomplish nothing."

"But what if Jonah Butler reaches Philadelphia in time to rouse them?"

A slow smile worked its way across Chabert Michaux's mouth.

"Philippe, my dim-witted brother, must I remind you once more that Monsieur Butler will never reach Philadelphia? Or Lancaster, for that matter."

"Should we not kill him right now, Chabert? You know, to be certain he . . ."

Chabert gripped his younger brother's arm. *"Non.* You may play with him, Philippe, as a cat toys with his captured mouse. But you may not kill him yet. He must drive that pack train all the way to the Susquehanna River for us."

"Then we shall kill him and seize those valuable furs, eh, Chabert?"

"Oui. I glimpsed those pelts before Butler left Turtle Creek. Some of the finest quality furs ever to be traded."

Philippe giggled foolishly. "You and I, we shall become wealthy men, Chabert, eh?"

"And meanwhile the French army, despite their

sickness and hardships, will conquer the Ohio Valley. The fleur-de-lis shall flutter over new French forts all the way to the Mississippi."

Philippe fingered the sharp edges of his hunting knife. "Then I may finally gut that arrogant Jonah Butler, eh, Chabert?"

"Oui, Philippe. But my knife will be on the bastard first. Butler stole my woman . . . and furs that should have been mine. I shall repay his treachery with some mountain justice of my own."

Eleven

"Vultures, Mr. Butler! Circling up ahead."

Rachel contemplated the graceful soar of predators drifting on rising currents of warm air.

Descending a long dry ridge, Butler led his pack train through a gap in Sideling Hill. When he paused at a rippling creek to rest the horses, he saw the scavenging birds much closer.

"Something big, to attract that many birds," Butler commented.

Rachel sipped cool water from her cupped palms. A small scarlet blotch peeking through shrubby witch hazel caught her eye. "Strange. An unnatural color out here in the wilderness. Mr. Butler," she called, bringing it to his attention.

She tiptoed behind Blaine and Butler as they investigated. Her hand suddenly flew to cover her nose. "'Tis . . . 'tis the body of that man who accosted us!"

"Poor sod," Blaine commented solemnly. "Been ripped to shreds by some varmint. Maybe a bear."

"And still wreaks of whiskey," Butler added. "Somewhere in these hills he found another trader who gave him the liquor he craved."

Rachel shuddered. "A hideous death. Worse, even, than if I had shot the poor devil." She watched silently as the two men buried what remained of the vagabond.

Passing through broken foothills of Shade Mountain, they paused for the night in a high meadow between the Cove and Tuscarora Mountains.

Rachel peered at charred remains of log dwellings. "They caught on fire?" she asked the trader as he groomed horses.

He shook his head. "Place is called Burnt Cabins. They were torched."

"Torched?" Busy hobbling horses, Rachel's hands suddenly froze in midair. "But why, Mr. Butler?"

"Burned by Pennsylvania officials. To keep white men from taking over Indian land. All this land west of the Susquehanna belongs to Indians."

"Will it work, Mr. Butler? Burning cabins to drive off overzealous Englishmen?" She threaded another grapevine hobble around a gelding's pasterns.

He shrugged. "I doubt it. 'Twill be no more effective than when a Seneca chief like Tanacharison, on the Ohio, warned French soldiers not to descend the Allegheny River."

"War, Jonah! Mark my words!" Blaine exclaimed. "I can see it coming, sure as apples in autumn. France and England will soon battle one another to the death for control of the Ohio River."

"Sadly," Rachel added, "Indian nations will be trapped in the middle."

Butler's features darkened under his slouched hat. "All the more reason for me to reach Philadelphia quick as possible."

She watched Butler relax with his pipe that evening by their fire. A sprinkle of stars glittered in the clear September sky. Maple trees showed early hints of burgundy and gold. Meadowlarks trilled in scorched-over fields and a faint perfume of fading summer flowers filled the twilight air.

"You truly draw comfort from these hills, Mr. Butler," she said simply. "I see it in your posture. Your shoulders ease as you contemplate nature."

Wolves howled on a high ridge somewhere in the settling darkness. A panther split the night with its bloodcurdling scream. Listening to them, Rachel edged closer to Butler's side at the fire.

"I never heard you mention, Mr. Butler, where you are from."

" 'Tis so."

" 'Tis so . . . what?"

"I never mentioned it to you."

"Then tell me, sir, unless it be a dark and dangerous secret, where you are from."

He dumped out the contents of his clay pipe bowl. "I, Miss Whitfield? I am from the sky. The trees. The earth."

"You love being out of doors," she observed.

" 'Tis my home."

"But where are your parents?" she asked, as Tom Blaine returned from mediating a horse squabble.

"Hah!" Blaine exploded. "Jonah's parents live in Philadelphia, in a fine large house with many glass windows."

Butler scowled at the youth.

"Truly?" Rachel asked, stunned. "Why have you not mentioned that, sir? Surely not something of which you are ashamed?"

"They have their lives. I have mine."

Fluttering bats, pursuing insects, swooped low in the darkness as wolves resumed their chilling cries. Rachel slid another inch closer to Butler. "A curious paradox. You choose this life—a rugged one where death stalks you on every mountain, in every valley. Meanwhile, your parents live a sedate city existence in Philadelphia. Are you estranged from your family?"

He glared at her. "Do you perpetually pester men with unwarranted questions?"

She'd struck a sore point. Lovely. She decided to press on.

"Let us just say, sir, that I have an exquisite sense of curiosity."

"Let us just say you are nosy, Miss Whitfield."

Irritating Jonah Butler? Rachel rather enjoyed it. "Have you a wife in Philadelphia, Mr. Butler, whom you are avoiding?"

His frown deepened. "I have no wife in Philadelphia."

"Or Lancaster, perhaps?"

"I have no wife cached anywhere, Miss Whitfield, because I am not married."

"Do you disdain the wholesome, morally upright state of marriage, Mr. Butler?"

"Yes. As do you."

She flared. "Nonsense, sir!"

"Then why have you not married? Would no right-thinking man have you?"

Her lips worked. No sound emerged. She let out a deep breath. She was not about to tell Butler how much she feared marriage. Or the touch of a man.

Blaine lit his own pipe with a reed ignited by their fire. "Why, any man would be proud to have Miss Whitfield for a wife, Jonah," he said slyly. "Truly, a woman more beautiful than a September sunset."

"But more tart and troublesome than any evening sky." Easing up from the ground, Butler stretched his lanky frame, then tramped off to investigate a pair of quarrelsome mares.

Blaine shook his head. "Jonah seems more peevish as we get farther east."

"Perhaps, Tom, there truly is someone in Philadelphia he wishes to avoid."

Tart and troublesome was she? Rachel intended to make Jonah Butler pay for that stinging critique. *Zeb,* she reminded herself. Rescuing Zeb Whitfield was more important than anything in her life.

Except, for reasons she failed to understand, tormenting Jonah Butler.

Studying the plum and coral tones of the vanishing sunset from a craggy fern-swept ledge, Butler snapped a stem into small pieces.

Rachel Whitfield managed to strike directly at the source of his irritation. Matilda Hattersley awaited him in Philadelphia. No way to avoid her. Not this time. His parents would see to that. In their zeal to cage him forever in some Philadelphia brick-and-glass counting house, far from the seduction of backwoods mountains and comely wild maidens, they continually thrust wealthy Matilda at Butler.

"Jonah?"

Butler whirled around.

"'Tis only me, Jonah," Blaine muttered, approaching shyly. "I . . . just wondered if we could talk a bit. You know, man to man."

"Sounds serious, Tom." Butler twisted a glistening jewelweed seedpod in his callused fingers.

"I need your advice on a sensitive issue. Jonah, I shall likely marry soon," the gawky youth announced. "Remember that talk we never quite finished?"

The seedpod snapped open in Butler's hands.

"You know what I mean, Jonah. About how to . . . what to do that first time when a man—You being a man used to having your way with women, I hoped you'd consider sharing your . . . your knowledge about—"

"Damn it, boy! You think I crawl in bed with every woman I meet?"

"No. That is, well, maybe."

Butler made a fierce noise low in his throat. "Tom, when the time comes, you, being a man and all, will know what to do. And how to do it."

"But I oft turn clumsy, Jonah. And my body is big. What if I . . . *hurt* her, Jonah? Lordy, I would never want to hurt sweet, delicate little Lily Martin!"

Butler shook his head. And smiled. "Tom, just remember to take your time. If you love a woman gently, she won't break. Take your time. Remember that more than anything."

"With what? What should I do first?"

"God's blood, boy! You and Lily love one another. 'Twill be a time of joy as you reach for one another. Kiss her. Women love to be kissed. And held. Warm her in your arms till she hugs you back."

"Have you ever been in love, Jonah? Even with Collette?"

"Love?" Butler's expression darkened. "That crazed way young bucks get when they lose their minds for a doe in heat? When they throw all caution to the winds and risk their lives for just one brief fling with their ladies?"

Butler laughed harshly. He fingered a tiny, fine-worked leather pouch dangling from his belt.

"No. You have not, Jonah. I can tell," Tom offered quietly. "But you'll know. When that day comes, your feet shall leave the ground and you will soar through the clouds at the very thought of your love. I hope you find her soon, Jonah. Maybe you already have and fail to realize it."

Butler clapped Blaine on the shoulder. "You, Tom, are an old-fashioned romantic. No place on this rough trail for romance."

"Love is too exuberant to be missed in this life, Jonah. Maybe—?"

"You harbor more advice, Tom?"

"Maybe if you approached Miss Whitfield differently—"

"Romance . . . with that pestilential . . ."

"Sneer if you like, Jonah, but your eyes betray you. Your face gentles when she nears. Especially when you think she does not notice."

"The look you see on my face is nothing more than solemn responsibility. I promised her pa I'd fetch her safely to Lancaster—despite all her shenanigans."

Tom grinned. "Solemn responsibility, eh? 'Tis not the look I saw in your eyes."

"Tom, boy, methinks too many days and nights out on these mountains have corrupted your perceptions. I shall have to get you back to civilization."

"When love strikes, Jonah, you will know. There can be no going back. And never . . . never again will you be the same."

"You hear that?" Attuned to the sounds of all his animals, Butler suddenly cocked his ears to the left. "Miss Whitfield's mare. Likely that leg of hers still bothers her. I shall have a look."

Seated by the open fire, Rachel glanced up from her mending at Tom Blaine's return. She laughed as he reached for an extra chunk of roasted ground-hog.

"Mr. Butler still seem peevish?"

Blaine finished his mouthful. "He keeps a lot inside, Miss Whitfield. And cloaks his thoughts with a tough exterior."

"I could not agree more!"

"Still, I think one day soon he might show you a tender side to his personality."

She sniffed. "I could not be less interested. The sooner we part, the happier I shall be."

Blaine washed down the meat with a swallow of water. "Though Jonah does not confide it, ma'am, I can tell he thinks kindly of you."

"Hah! That immoral rascal? Not likely."

The chilling wail of wolves unsettled Rachel. Fallen leaves rasped across dry grass. Bats crisscrossed low over burned-out huts.

"Tom?" Glancing around the darkness that gradually swallowed their campsite, Rachel noticed the vacant rope. The same one Butler used to bind her to him. "He's been gone quite awhile. Where . . . where is Mr. Butler?"

"Checking on one of the mares. I'll see if he needs help."

Alone by the fire, Rachel spied the crescent moon through tree branches that somehow assumed a menacing new angle. She tugged her trade blanket up over her shoulders.

Blaine returned, blank-faced, through the darkness. "He's gone. No sign of him."

Rachel's eyes widened. "Vanished? But Mr. Butler would never abandon his pack train."

Blaine fashioned a torch from a split pine knot. "Something is wrong. I must look for him."

Rachel leaped up from her log seat. "I shall come with you."

"Stay by the fire, ma'am. I may need your services here, though I hope I am wrong."

Rachel watched the torch slice through darkness up a steep wooded ridge. "A perfect time to escape," she murmured on a sigh. Yet, oddly, she felt bound here by some invisible tie.

The torch returned toward the fire. Much slower, this time, than when Blaine had departed. Rachel heard footsteps. Nervously she worked her fists open and closed. She seized a small knife Blaine had used to cut roasted meat.

"Tom? Tom, is that you?"

She heard feet shuffle through underbrush. Owls and wolves and fluttering bats conspired to alarm Rachel. *Now!* Now she could dash off to rescue Zeb. Yet some imperceptible force held her close to this infernal fire.

"I care not a whit what becomes of the scoundrel!" she whispered into the night. "Truly." She was indifferent to Jonah Butler's fate. Without her fierce captor, her life would become infinitely easier. Yet . . .

Her breathing escalated.

What if Butler lay wounded somewhere in the darkness? What if she were never to see that towering rogue again? Those piercing dark eyes that seemed ever in search of her, that thick, shining black hair, his sparkling white teeth framed by a rare smile, Butler's husky hard-muscled frame. And . . . and the touch of his large, strong hands.

A cold emptiness suddenly swept over Rachel.

Tom Blaine emerged through the darkness with a bloodied Jonah Butler slung over his shoulder.

Rachel snatched the torch from Blaine's hands

while he spread Butler out before the fire. "My God! What has happened?" she cried, above Butler's moans. "A mountain lion?"

Blaine swept Butler's dark hair back from his forehead. "Looks more like a knife mark to me, ma'am."

"I'll fetch water!" She snatched up a spare kettle and filled it at the stream.

Rachel tore a strip from her white apron, dipped it in water, and daubed Butler's grazed skull as he slowly opened his eyes. "I shall have no apron left if this nonsense continues," she muttered.

Butler's face worked at making a smile. His eyes fluttered closed again.

"His arm is sliced as well, Tom. Try to fashion a sling for him while I clean and bind his wounds. We *must* halt this bleeding."

Butler groaned. "Wha—what happened?"

"Suppose you tell us, Mr. Butler," she asked.

"In the dark . . . something struck . . ."

"Easy, Jonah," Blaine cautioned. "Hold still till we get the bleeding stopped. I think someone hurled a knife or ax at you."

"The horses . . . a man . . ."

"You mean, when you checked the horses, you encountered a man in the dark?"

"Hush, Tom," Rachel insisted. "He grows more agitated when you question him. Let me finish wrapping his wounds before further interrogation."

Holding his head on her aproned lap, Rachel dabbed cool stream water on his scalp wound, then wound a linen strip salvaged from her apron around his head. "Now for his arm," she said, rolling up Butler's bloodied sleeve.

Rachel winced at the sight of Butler's mangled arm.

"Not . . . not part of Eli's deal," Butler murmured, his eyes half closed. "You, nursing my injuries."

She blotted his upper arm laceration with clear water. "Your brutal rope, sir, might have kept you safe tonight if you remained bound fast to me in camp."

Butler's hand groped for her wrist and held fast. "No. They might have struck you instead."

She studied his pained expression. For a long moment she stared at that large hand clasping her own wrist. Did Jonah Butler suffer agonies from his physical wounds? Or . . . was it possible that the scoundrel actually fretted for Rachel's safety?

Her cool fingers stroked his forehead. Strange, that she would caress the blackguard she had feared for so long. Stranger still that she found great calmness in comforting him.

She reached for a wooden mug of water and offered it to Butler.

He drank gratefully. "Thank you, ma'am."

" 'Tis Tom who saved your life tonight, Mr. Butler. All that food he eats built a body strong enough to fetch you back here."

"But what of the man, Jonah?" Blaine begged. "What do you remember?"

"Bastard . . . in the dark. French, I suspect, from his garb. After our horses. Or maybe trying to steal one of the loads."

"And you accidentally stumbled on him?"

"Aye. Afterward, in my confusion . . . thought I heard him call another *Renard.*"

"Renard?" Rachel gasped.

Her astonishment startled Blaine. "You know of him?" he asked.

"Renard—the Fox—is the Devil himself, Tom! The same man who attacked and captured my brother,

Zeb. But . . . why is he here now? What would make him come this far east?"

"After something, likely."

"Or someone," Butler volunteered weakly.

Rachel frowned. "One of us?" Her fingers explored a small scar on Butler's cheek. "They tried to kill you once before, Mr. Butler. At Logstown."

He managed a rueful smile. "Who shall succeed at that onerous task first, Miss Whitfield? You, or the French demons?"

Rachel eyed his strained expression. Butler struggled to joke, but he was in pain. Perhaps a lot of pain.

"Get well first, Mr. Butler. I require a worthy adversary. One who's fit and healed. Then we shall discuss who receives the honor of annihilating you."

Blaine piled split logs on the fire. "A cool evening tonight. I put extra kindling beside the fire, Miss Whitfield. Whichever of us wakes during the night can easily add more fuel."

"Thank you, Tom."

Blaine patted Butler's sleeve. "Miss Whitfield and I shall lie on either side of you tonight, Jonah. Should you need help, just call out."

Rachel found sleep an elusive concept that night. She watched Butler's still form. Occasionally his closed eyes flickered, accompanied by a restless twist and moan.

He suffers, she thought, yet refuses to cry for help.

She once intended to poison him with herbs. Or shoot the villain. Indeed. That, she thought earlier, would have been divine retribution. Anything to be rid of Jonah Butler's smothering captivity.

Now she studied his ragged breathing.

If Butler died from his wounds, or developed morbid fevers from them, she would immediately be free to seek Zeb in his wretched French prison. Exactly what she wanted, was it not?

Butler moaned again in his fragmented sleep.

On the next ridge, wolves howled chilling litanies. Mammoth branches swayed overhead in September gusts rich with the scent of moldering wild ginger.

Reclined at Butler's side, Rachel glanced out into the darkness and picked nervously at her fingernails. Who circled the camp this fearsome night? If Butler was correct, it was the demon Frenchman Renard. What if she bolted into the black night and screamed out his name? Would he seize her and guide her to Zeb?

She could dash into the woods this very instant. The incapacitated Jonah Butler was in no shape to stop her.

Pack-train horses whinnied softly out in the darkness. Their bells made faint music as the horses shifted positions. At Rachel's side, Butler thrashed in his sleep. A muffled cry slipped past his lips.

"Mr. Butler?"

She eased up his head to receive a sip of water. His forehead felt warm to her touch, yet he shivered.

"Ma'am?"

"Have you anything in your saddlebags for pain, sir? Anything I might offer you?"

"Dogwood bark."

She offered him sips of tea made from the bark.

"To heal, Mr. Butler, you must sleep." She rechecked his bandages for fresh blood. "None," she murmured with a sigh of relief.

Old Eliza had cautioned Rachel of men's urges to hurt women with their painful touch. She glanced down at a wounded Jonah Butler. Uncertain, now, whether she feared him or yearned to sleep close to him, she cautiously lay down at his side.

"You must live, Mr. Butler," she whispered into his ear as he thrashed in his sleep. "You must live to carry your vital warning of French invasion to the Philadelphia authorities."

She covered Butler with a blanket. She reached for his hand as if about to caress a venomous serpent. Slowly, gently, she stroked his tense fist and murmured comforting words into his ear.

"All will be well, Mr. Butler. You shall live to deliver your message. The frontier settlers depend on you to do so. I . . . I shall take care of you."

Gradually, Rachel's whispered consolation and gentle caress took effect. She watched Butler's fist relax into an open hand. His thrashing ceased. His breathing slowed.

Tight-strung and wary, Rachel kept close watch on forest shadows as well as the slumbering Jonah Butler. Noises. Did they never cease? Did the forest creatures not sleep? Or were those rustling noises the sounds of human footsteps?

Twelve

Horses. Horses nickering for food and water. Restless horses invading dreams.

Groaning, Rachel rolled over in her sleep.

Men's voices. Sounds of leather being stretched and tied to tramping horses. Men's voices?

Rachel rubbed her eyes and struggled to sit upright by a near-extinguished fire at dawn.

"That one over there, Jonah?" Tom Blaine queried Butler.

Unwilling to believe her ears, Rachel patted the ground beside her. Butler's lanky frame was . . . gone! She rubbed her eyes again. This time she saw two men labor over the bulky loads of packhorses. Her eyes widened.

"Mr. Butler!" she cried. Rising from the damp ground, she worked at a scold but scarcely knew what to say.

With his good arm, Butler tipped his felt hat toward Rachel. "Ma'am?"

"Sir, only last night you were more dead than alive. You cannot possibly labor as you are. You shall be dead before noon."

"Only if you shoot me, Miss Whitfield. I have no time to die. At least, not right now. Too much other work to get done."

She rubbed remnants of sleep from her eyes and stomped over to scrutinize him.

"Your bandages, sir! At least allow me to inspect them for fresh bleeding." On tiptoe, she reached up to examine his head wound.

Watching in silence, he permitted her close scrutiny. When her balance teetered as she examined his dressings, he steadied Rachel.

She felt his large hand, warm and surprisingly firm, on her shoulder.

"You've never been this close to me before, Miss Whitfield," Butler commented, his voice husky.

His proximity inhibited Rachel's breathing, much to her annoyance. " 'Tis purely for medicinal reasons, I assure you, Mr. Butler. But you're too tall. Best if you sit down for a moment while I rewrap your dressings."

He obliged by easing down onto a lichen-covered boulder.

Standing over Butler, Rachel finished knotting the linen strip at his temple. Only then did she notice his pallor. With the fingers of her left hand, she lifted his chin for further scrutiny.

Butler winked up at her. "We must do this more often, Miss Whitfield. Far more interesting than lashing one another with ropes, though of course that had its alluring aspects as well."

"Can you not cease being a morally deficient scoundrel even when ill?"

"No."

"Be serious. You, sir, are white as a ghost. I beg of you, take a day—a morning, even—and tarry awhile."

He grew somber. "No time for that self-indulgence, Miss Whitfield."

"But you must! What good will it do if you faint dead off your horse three miles down the trail?"

Butler clenched his jaw. "I shall not faint, Miss Whitfield."

She blew out a sigh. "Stubborn, pigheaded man. Here, let us slip your arm from the sling so I can have a better look. Hmm. Very sore indeed."

She applied a poultice of crushed mullein leaves to his wound, then rewrapped the dressing.

"I am doubtless stronger for your ministrations, Miss Whitfield. Thank you, ma'am." Butler worked his frame up to a standing position.

She caught at his good arm. "I urge you again to rest, Mr. Butler. Else I fear Tom and I shall have to bury you yonder. With my disdain for you, I fear the grave would be a shallow one at best." She stared unflinchingly at him.

He leaned close to her. His long shadow shielded her slender frame. "Then you would finally be free of my domination, Miss Whitfield, as you've so ardently wished. Without the trouble of having to shoot me."

"Doubtless I shall always view you as a despicable cad, Mr. Butler. But you have a job to do. A mission to complete. Many British lives—including possibly my own father's—hinge on your safely completing that mission. I wish to be free of you, Mr. Butler. I . . . I do not wish you dead. Please take proper care of yourself."

In the saddle, Rachel maintained a guarded watch over Butler's figure, one horse ahead of her. Though she suspected he wobbled in his saddle at times, Butler never paused.

A fierce man was Jonah Butler, she noted. A man unwilling to yield, even to affliction.

It was late in the morning before he pulled to a halt

on the approach to Kittatinny Mountain. Dogwood berries showed an early autumn blush as hawks soared in a vibrant blue sky and September gusts hinted of rain-washed hemlocks.

"He pauses for the horses, Tom," Rachel commented as she added tinder to the fire, "but not for himself. Perhaps a nice stew will put some color in his wan cheeks and strengthen him."

Traipsing over a deeply worn trail, she collected leaves of lamb's-quarter, mustard, cress, and blackberry to flavor a stew thickened with ripe nuts. She smiled wryly, recalling that not long ago she intended to poison Jonah Butler, or sedate him at the very least, with plants.

Now, temporarily, she sought plants to heal him.

"The man, or men, who struck Jonah still shadow us," Blaine reminded her. He swung his gaze warily over surrounding inclines.

"Their motives seem unclear, Tom. Surely if they wanted to kill Mr. Butler, or any of us, they could have done so by now." She tasted a sample of her stew.

"Unless they're waiting to steal the furs."

"The furs? But then why wait, if that be their purpose?"

Blaine smiled. "Perhaps they intend waiting till closer to Lancaster, to spare themselves the labor of tending the pack train."

"But I sense more involved here, Tom. Might these men possibly have a grudge against Mr. Butler? One of them might have been the Fox, a cunning French killer."

Tom's face lengthened with concern. "Miss Whitfield, I have a favor to ask you. I know you longed with all your heart to bolt north toward Montreal and find your brother."

"Zeb? Oh, yes, Tom! I *must* help free him. I owe Zeb that much."

"I . . . I ask you to wait on that, ma'am. For the sake of Jonah's mission. For his health. I ask you to stay with us till Lancaster, ma'am. You know Jonah. No tougher man lives. And he feels indebted to your pa. If you vanish, Jonah will . . . will go after you. Even if it kills him."

Rachel picked at her fingers. She could not tell Tom—not even Tom—that she fully intended to escape when they reached the Susquehanna. Well before Lancaster.

Butler shuffled toward them. "Pray, what might you two conspirators have to discuss?"

"Why, indeed, Mr. Butler, Tom was raving about the tasty therapeutic stew which I just made to strengthen you."

She watched him struggle to feed himself with his left hand. When the food spilled, she seized a spoon and fed him herself.

"You have not spoken of your family, Mr. Butler," she said, ladling rich broth into his mouth. "Will you stay with them when you reach Philadelphia?"

"Aye."

"You seem reluctant, sir. Will they not be thrilled to see you once again?"

"Likely." He savored her cooking. "Delicious stew, ma'am."

"You avoid my gaze, Mr. Butler. As if something in Philadelphia displeases you. Or you are reluctant to return there."

His eyes danced with mischief. "Or I am wanted for criminal charges there."

She sniffed. "Altogether possible, Mr. Butler. You are, after all, completely devoid of morals."

"Shall I confess to you my prior sins?" He massaged his stubbled jaw.

A rosy glow flamed Rachel's cheeks. "That would be indecent, sir, for a scoundrel such as yourself."

He pondered a moment. "I should like to think of myself as a *mercantile representative,* Miss Whitfield. Sounds ever so much more polite than scoundrel."

"With that stubbled beard of yours, today, Mr. Butler, you look more like a pirate."

"A pirate, eh? Do you fancy pirates better than scoundrels, Miss Whitfield?"

Rachel clicked her tongue. "Your color pales again, Mr. Butler. I sense you overexert yourself with demented mocking humor. Rest a bit. Lean back against that maple trunk. I shall fetch your razor and shave you. 'Twill make you feel better."

"Feel better? My God, woman! The thought of you with a razor at my throat fills me with complete dread."

She smiled with wry indifference. "Rest easy, Mr. Butler. If my hand slips, I shall bandage you at once. Have I not already proven my skill at dressing wounds?"

He eyed the razor she grasped. "Your humor eludes me, Miss Whitfield. Particularly when I am weak and you bear a lethal weapon in your hand."

"Lean back against this maple, Mr. Butler," she insisted, pressing against his strapping chest with her opposite hand. "Even weak, you are far more forceful than I, a mere woman."

Seated on damp ground, Butler braced his head

against the tree trunk. "I have decided to retain my beard after all. It suits me."

"I saw you scratching at your ticklish whiskers, sir. You will likely feel much better after I am finished with you."

"After you *finish* with me? God's blood, woman!"

"Hush, you vile man." On her knees before Butler's seated figure, Rachel leaned close and carefully scraped bristled whiskers off his cheeks. "Now lift your chin," she ordered.

He grunted. "This is the part I truly fear."

"I pride myself on being gentle, Mr. Butler. Higher, sir. Lift your chin . . . yes, just so."

Shaving the bull-necked, strong-jawed Jonah Butler proved more unsettling to Rachel than she anticipated. Perching herself close to his broad shoulders to reach his throat, she felt her hand weaken. What was there about this odious man that invariably made her feel this way?

Only inches from her face, Butler's bold stare reduced Rachel to trembling apprehension. Did she fear the pain he might visit upon her? Was that the sensation she experienced? Hadn't Old Eliza warned her of men's cruelty to women?

Surely it was fear. What else could make goose bumps skate over her limbs in this alarming manner?

"There!" With a quick splash of cool spring water over Butler's clean-shaven face, Rachel leaned back to admire her handiwork.

"Could not have done better meself, Miss Whitfield," Blaine commented. "A fair barber we have in our midst, Jonah."

Butler explored his shaven jaw and throat with the fingers of his good hand. "Eh? Most importantly, my neck remains unbloodied and intact." His gaze wandered leisurely from Rachel's waist up over the laces of her bodice to her face. "Still, I shall feel safer next time shaving myself," he grumbled.

From a kneeling position at Butler's side, Rachel rose to her full height. "Altogether fine with me, sir. Next time I shall be happy to let you perish from whisker itch."

She flounced off to cleanse his razor in a cress-overgrown rivulet.

Tom Blaine glanced at Rachel's disappearing back, then at Butler's terse expression. "Life is quite full of trials as it is, Jonah," he began. "Ordinarily you are a most amiable man. When not crossed, that is."

Still seated on the mossy earth, Butler closed his eyes and leaned back against the furrowed tree trunk. "I sense this is a lecture of sorts, Tom."

"Oh, no, Jonah! 'Twould be improper, a hired hand upbraiding his superior."

"And yet . . . ?"

"'Tis the way you treat Miss Whitfield, Jonah. It puzzles me the way you go out of your way to vex her. As if you make a special, calculated effort to ruffle her feathers."

"You err, Tom. I treat her the same roughshod way I treat you. Or anyone else."

"Not so, Jonah." Tom polished off a second bowl of stew. "You treat her . . . differently."

"Pure imaginings."

"You look at her differently, too."

"Balderdash!" Butler wedged himself upright and studied his ever-hungry assistant. "See what comes of letting you dally for a rest? The Devil starts playing tricks on your mind. We best get going before you contemplate the remainder of my sins."

Returning from the stream, Rachel saw Butler preparing to ride. "Mr. Butler, you look—"

He scowled at her. "Hale and hearty, Miss Whitfield. Ready to ride."

She shook her head. " 'Twas not my observation, sir. Your face is pale as cream and beaded with perspiration. You are weak, yet unwilling to admit it."

"Weak?" Butler snorted as he tested a leather cinch. "Nonsense, Miss Whitfield. You and Tom share obscured vision this morning."

"Stubborn man! Shortly you shall become food for the wolves, just like that pathetic whiskey-soaked man you recently stumbled upon."

Pausing, he aimed a crooked smile at her. "I should think that would please you immensely, Miss Whitfield. To be free of me at last."

"It *will* please me immensely, sir. I shall celebrate your demise. But only if you feed the wolves after you have completed your Philadelphia mission to save Pa and all the other frontiersmen. Not one minute before."

"Ah, that's what I so love about you, Miss Whitfield. A woman possessed of a tender heart fair brimming with compassion for your fellow man."

Her expression softened. "Tarry here awhile, Mr. Butler. The rest would surely strengthen your body and spirit."

Butler met her pleading gaze. He hesitated. Moistening his mouth, he took a step toward her, then apparently thought better of it.

He gestured toward a foreboding western sky crowning the top of a shaggy claret-and-gold-tipped mountain. "A delay will leave us trapped below North Mountain in that festering storm. 'Tis vital we push on at once."

Riding her sweet-tempered mare tethered behind Butler's gray gelding, Rachel had ample time to observe the trader's broad shoulders and tapered waist. Far too much time, in fact. She managed to avert her eyes from his figure initially.

But not for long.

Jonah Butler was a ferocious man. Unyielding. Determined. Bull-strong, even when wounded. She knew he suffered now with pain that he disclosed to no one. A man that fierce, when healed, would let no man—or woman—halt him from his resolves.

Rachel shuddered.

Coarse, shameless Jonah Butler, if he cared to, would rip off Rachel's clothes in his madness and fling them away with abandon. Crazed by primitive male urges, he would furiously mount her, as Old Eliza had warned, without a single thought to her comfort or pain. No doubt the brazen Butler would impale her with his manhood.

Oh, fie! Indecent to his core!

Mouth agape at the envisioned trauma to her person, Rachel clutched with one hand at her fichu.

But what if Old Eliza was mistaken about men? What if a rare few chose not to brutalize women with their ardor? If that were the case, then which sort might Jonah Butler be?

Gentle? Or swinish?

"Hah!" she murmured. "The answer seems entirely obvious." A bully dedicated to flagrant use of rope, curt tongue, and stolen kisses, doubtless Jonah Butler thrust his untamed vicious bulk atop helpless women and ignored their pitiful squeals for mercy.

Oh, fie on him! Fie!

Watching Butler's thighs balance against his mount's barrels, she studied the trader's husky body.

The angle of his neck and wide-set shoulders. The rolling might of his back muscles. The implied strength in his arms and large hands.

Glaring at the trader, she moistened her lips and swallowed hard. Her gaze softened. Once more she contemplated Butler's brawn . . . then moistened her lips again.

"Disease and exhaustion, you say? You saw it first-hand?"

Scowling, Chabert Michaux ladled up gruel and handed it to an Indian seated before him on the ground.

The hungry Ottawa nodded. "Frenchmen weary carrying supplies and ammunition over the portage from Presque Isle to Fort Le Boeuf. The path turned to marsh from all their traffic. They sank in the mud up to their knees."

"Mon Dieu! And they had to build a new road?" Chabert's expression darkened.

"They carry heavy loads. And sicken by the day with fevers and other ailments." The Indian sucked in mouthfuls of corn gruel.

"But our men are resolute, *mon ami,* are they not?" He handed a gourd of gruel to the Indian's squat companion.

"They vow daily to drive all Englishmen east of the Ohio."

Chabert Michaux smiled wide enough to expose his chipped front teeth. *"Merveilleux!"*

Philippe dashed up to the seated men huddled by a low fire. "They slowed their pace, Chabert. Just as you said."

"You took a chance, Philippe. 'Twas a miracle Butler did not see you."

"I am too fast for that English fool."

"Never underestimate that particular trader, Philippe. Butler is dangerous. He would gut you on sight."

"Instead, we shall tear Butler apart, eh, Chabert?"

"Patience, *mon frère.* All in good time. For the moment, we shall play amusing little games with Monsieur Butler."

"To slow him?"

"Yes, while our army has a chance to reach the forks of the Ohio."

"I brought you a present, Chabert. Look!" Philippe held up a shining silver pendant.

"Where did you find this?"

"Near Butler's last camp. You seem especially pleased by the trinket, Chabert."

Holding up the gleaming necklace before his own eyes, the elder Michaux beamed. "Oh, Philippe, this time you have truly outdone yourself. Do you know to whom this necklace belongs?"

Philippe Michaux shrugged. "A beautiful woman?"

Chabert nodded. "But not just any beautiful woman, *mon frère.* This necklace belongs to Mademoiselle Rachel Whitfield."

Puzzled, Philippe scratched under his worn cap. "Does . . . does this arouse you, Chabert? To possess jewelry from a woman you desire?"

"Perhaps. But not in the manner you suspect, fool. This precious necklace will offer me the perfect opportunity to approach Mademoiselle Whitfield with my most tender felicitations."

"You . . . do not intend to court the woman?"

Chabert tipped back his head and laughed harshly. *"Non, mon frère.* Ultimately, I intend to seize her as a hostage."

"A hostage?"

"Oui. Though, of course, I will first amuse myself with her for a tempting little interlude."

Philippe wiped his grimy hand across his stubbled jaw. "I have not had a woman for a long time, Chabert. Not since we struck out in this open wilderness. I must have a turn with the Whitfield woman as well."

"And so you shall, Philippe. Have we not always enjoyed games together?"

"But you said *hostage,* Chabert. Who will pay money for Mademoiselle Whitfield?"

The elder Michaux's eyes narrowed. "That, *mon frère,* is what we shall find out."

Thirteen

"Gentlemen, your shirts need immediate attention," Rachel declared.

Tom Blaine grasped torn edges of elbow shirt holes. "The briars fair ripped my sleeves apart."

"I brought my darning needle and thread. It seemed likely the wilderness would pose threats to our garments. Tom? Your shirt, please, and I shall mend it for you."

Blaine peeled off his linen hunting shirt and lingered at Rachel's side while she worked. He studied Jonah Butler's figure bent scrutinizing horseshoes.

"Miss Whitfield, ma'am?" Blaine shuffled from foot to foot.

Rachel labored over her stitches. "Yes, Tom?"

"I respect your . . . your feminine opinions, ma'am."

"Thank you, Tom. Most kind of you."

"So . . . so I wondered if I might ask a question of you." Blaine glanced warily in Butler's direction. "While Jonah is not around."

She eyed Blaine cautiously. "Yes?"

"'Tis about Miss Lily Martin of Lancaster. My sweetheart. A finer girl never walked the earth, Miss Whitfield. Well, except you, of course, ma'am."

"Thank you, Tom. You love Miss Martin very much, do you not?"

"Oh, yes, Miss Whitfield. I count the hours till I next see her. I wish never to be separated from her again. That is, if she'll have me for her husband."

"But what is it you want from me, Tom?"

"Advice, ma'am. In particular, how to woo a fine young woman. And ask her to marry me in such a majestic way that she cannot possibly refuse."

"But how would I know of such things?"

Blaine peeked once more in Butler's direction, then back at Rachel. "Just suppose a man wanted to marry you, ma'am."

Rachel flinched.

"Just . . . just supposing, ma'am, is all. How would you want a man to properly approach you so that you'd be highly inclined to consent? Nay, unable to resist the proposal?"

She hesitated. What could any man possibly say to convince her of matrimony? Nothing, likely. But red-faced Tom, all stammering and embarrassed, seemed so eager to seek Lily Martin's hand in marriage. Rachel pondered a moment.

"Your advice would be most appreciated, ma'am."

With a sigh, Rachel handed Tom's mended shirt back to him. "I . . . I suppose great tenderness, Tom. Kind words to your sweetheart. Yes, gracious, flattering words, most likely. You might want to consider a gift of some sort."

"Gift?"

"Yes. Likely Miss Martin would appreciate a gift of say, wildflowers. Or perhaps something you made, like one of those wonderful wooden bowls you craft so beautifully."

"Might I touch her? A hug, perhaps?"

"At a decent interval, I suppose. A proper suitor should maintain acceptable decorum at all times, Tom."

"And a kiss, ma'am?"

"A kiss?"

Wide-eyed, Rachel recalled the fervor of Jonah Butler's stolen kiss back at Turtle Creek. Without seeking permission, Butler had swept her into his arms and kissed Rachel passionately. She would never forget the warm thrill—unsettling in all its untempered lust—of that searching kiss.

"A kiss?" she repeated, fumbling for words. "Well, perhaps a demure, chaste kiss, Tom. A brief peck on the lips. But only, of course, with Miss Martin's permission."

"I shall try all these things, ma'am, and hope they work. Let's see, flattering words, flowers and gifts, a hug, and . . ." Blaine broke into a wide grin. "A kiss!"

She cautioned him with a tug at his arm. "Do be slow and tender, Tom. You must not rush Miss Martin, hear? If your heart is in the right place, I feel certain your proposal will succeed."

When Butler rejoined them, she turned on him. "While we tarry here to rest the horses, Mr. Butler, I shall darn your shirt as well. And we shall see how your arm progresses." She reached to untie the knot securing his sling.

Butler's brown-eyed gaze drifted lazily across Rachel's shoulders. "You offer me no choice, then, Miss Whitfield? I must strip off my clothes and stand naked before you?"

Astonished, Rachel blinked at him.

"You jest, Mr. Butler. I doubt you are troubled by any sense of decency whatsoever."

"Is that what plagues you so, Miss Whitfield? Your sense of decency? Is that why you bind your scarf so tightly around your throat and twist your shining hair into a prim little bun?" One corner of Butler's mouth curled slightly. "Or is it because you fear the touch of a man?"

She bristled. "You speak nonsense, sir. Indeed, I fear no man. Now, I shall avert my eyes if the idea of removing your shirt offends you. Your wounds must be tended, even if you prefer that I not mend your shirt."

Dropping the sling, he eased his fringed linen shirt up over his head.

She tried not to look. Oh, truly, she tried not to marvel at those casual curls of black hair adorning that great hard-packed sweep of a chest.

Rachel swallowed. A futile exercise. Her mouth remained dry.

'Twas dangerous, standing so near Jonah Butler. The smell of his warm maleness intoxicated Rachel with unfamiliar urges. Indecent urges. Butler stood mere inches from her. She ached to reach forward and glide her palms up over his bronzed, bulging hardness.

Ignoring Butler's sullen-lipped taunt, Rachel busied herself examining his lacerated bicep. She dabbed it with water to cleanse off dried blood, then retied the dressing over a poultice of crushed mullein leaves. Her fingers dallied, drifting over his arm a bit longer than Rachel intended.

Almost . . . almost a caress.

"Am I making progress, Miss Whitfield?"

His low voice seemed unduly close to her ear as he observed her meanderings.

"Progress?"

"You seemed . . . perplexed by my arm."

With a hasty series of throat clearings, Rachel abruptly released his biceps. "Indeed. Progress. Yes, Mr. Butler, I feel both your head *and* arm wounds are healing, though you must still take care, sir."

She grasped his torn linen shirt and sat down with her sewing reticule.

The September sun brought a glow to Butler's exposed golden skin. Basking in the warm rays, he flexed his body in a half dozen ways to ease out minor aches.

Rachel vowed not to look. Just as she had that first day at Venango when she beheld Jonah Butler stripped to his loincloth. 'Twas not proper for a woman to . . . to contemplate a vigorous man's well-formed dimensions.

"Hmph! Badly torn, difficult to mend," she muttered, tugging her needle and thread through the frayed fabric.

Framed by a background of delicately frost-singed autumn leaves, Butler held up a mug of water and allowed the cool liquid to trickle down his throat. His lips, shining from the water, gratefully received its wetness.

Over her sewing, Rachel stole a peek. The sight of Butler's mouth and strong jaw brought back forbidden memories of his kiss. Oh, that sultry kiss stolen at Turtle Creek! Memories of the trader's coarse, rousing embrace even now made Rachel tingle in that forbidden zone above her thighs.

Despite her pledge to avoid the touch of men, despite Old Eliza's warning . . . that unholy tingling in Butler's presence grew stronger by the day.

Bronzed and gloriously masculine in his near nakedness, he sensed her gaze. Defiantly, he stared back. Penetrating, fierce, indiscreet, that look spoke to Rachel of some mysterious, hungering need.

"You approve, Miss Whitfield?"

"I beg your pardon?"

"Of what you see?"

Warmth crept up her throat. "I have no idea what you mean, sir! I . . . I was simply observing that you seem, that you still—Your pallor remains a matter of concern, sir, 'tis all."

Tom Blaine returned from grazing on wild nuts. "The horses seem restless, Jonah. A tad irritable. I caught the third horse nipping at Miss Whitfield's mare again."

"These hills weary them," Rachel commented, finishing the last stitch on Butler's shirtsleeve.

Butler peered east. "They sense an approaching storm. Far on that next ridge is a smoking chimney. A settler of some sort."

"Amiable, I hope," Rachel commented.

Butler yanked his shirt back on. "We shall aspire to reach that farmer before this storm strikes."

A raw wind drove fine mists into their faces as they rode east. Mists that turned into bold drops. Then a furious downpour.

Clutching her hooded cloak around her head, Rachel sighed with relief when at last they approached a cabin with beckoning smoke curling up from the chimney.

A stern, square-bodied farmer emerged from the cabin.

"Where you headed with those packs?" the dour man inquired.

"Lancaster," Butler responded. "Mind if we rest here till the storm passes? We'll tend the horses ourselves."

The ruddy farmer scanned Butler's pack train. "How many of ye are there?"

"Three."

"Two men and a woman?"

Butler nodded. "Tom Blaine is my assistant."

The farmer's lower lip jutted forward. "The woman . . . she your wife?"

"Nay."

"Blaine's wife?"

Butler shook his head. "Nay."

Blocking passage to his doorway, the burly farmer crossed his hair-matted arms over his chest. "Ye're not married? Not bonded in holy matrimony? None of ye?"

" 'Tis so." Butler answered. "We travel together out of necessity, not legal bonds."

The florid-faced farmer suddenly broke into a huge grin. "Welcome, sirs, to my humble home. Muh name is Benjamin Buckman. Folks call me Ben." He gestured broadly toward the front door of his primitive log abode.

Following Rachel and Tom inside, Butler glanced round the shadowy interior. "Thank you, sir, for sheltering us from the storm. Tom and I shall tend the horses now."

"Oh, wait, sirs!" Buckman insisted. "We shall help you. That is . . . my *daughters* will." Beaming, he pointed toward two dough-faced, determined-looking women bolting from the cabin's shadows. "Gentlemen, this here is Maisie." One homely, eager girl dipped slightly. "And over there is Delilah." At Buckman's second introduction, a gap-toothed, buxom maid bounced forward.

"Welcome!" the girls trilled in unison, lunging toward Blaine and Butler.

"Yuh see, my friends, we do not oft get company in these parts," Ben Buckman commented with a wide grin. "Ye are most welcome, indeed."

All six of them trudged toward Buckman's barn to feed and water the horses. Maisie and Delilah clung tenaciously to Butler and Blaine's arms.

Dishing out grain in the stable, Ben Buckman turned to Rachel. "My daughters are single maidens, Miss Whitfield, though not for lack of suitors, mind you." He grinned and nudged Butler's ribs. "Ye gentlemen behave yourselves out here in the barn. I insist! My tender young girls frighten easily. Do you not, my little gems?"

"Oh, Pa!" Maisie snickered, tugging wide open the scarf that covered her cleavage.

"How you do embarrass us!" Delilah added, before stroking Butler's arm suggestively.

"Miss Whitfield," the farmer began, "a fair maiden such as yourself must beware of suffering chills on such a forbidding afternoon. Come inside, where my, uh, fire might safeguard your health."

A bit wary, despite her rain-sogged state, Rachel nevertheless gratefully followed Buckman toward the cabin. "The others . . . ?"

"Oh, them? Doubtless they shall join us shortly. That is, when they . . . finish their work."

Inside the cabin, Buckman seated himself beside Rachel on a wooden bench before the fireplace and vigorously rubbed his hands. "My . . . my *fire,* you will observe, Miss Whitfield, is quite warm. Entirely suitable to comfort a troubled maiden such as yourself."

Hands folded neatly on her lap, Rachel sat primly. She sensed uneasily that the square-shaped farmer intended greater meaning to his words. "Yes. An altogether suitable fire, sir. We appreciate your kind hospitality."

He edged closer to Rachel on the bench. "We rarely get visitors here, ma'am. Your company is most welcome. Pray tell me, ma'am, how is it such a . . . a comely maiden as yourself remains unmarried?"

The sight of Buckman's thick, hair-matted hand ardently massaging his thigh made tiny hairs prickle along Rachel's neck.

"I . . . I was to be married out on Turtle Creek last winter, with my father's blessing," she lied. "Alas, poor, dear Sylvester died of the ague one week before our wedding."

"A pity. Rest his soul." Buckman slid another inch closer to Rachel. Thunder crashed over the mountains outside.

Rachel moved nearer to the bench's end. "However . . ." Deepening her falsehood, Rachel cleared her throat. "However, Mr. Buckman, I am pleased to announce that I am on my way to Lancaster to marry another respectable gentleman. Uh, Mr. Aloysius T. Threadwell. Dear, honorable Aloysius! Mr. Butler was kind enough to assure my poor, concerned father that he would escort me to my betrothed."

"Fortuitous, then, Miss Whitfield, that you paused to retreat here from the storm." Buckman leaned against Rachel's shoulder.

"Sir?"

Buckman's hand crawled toward Rachel's waist just as the cabin door blew open on a gust. "Damnable weather!" he grumbled, turning toward the rain-splashed doorway. "Oh! Mr. Butler! 'Tis you, sir."

Lightning flashes silhouetted Jonah Butler's lanky frame braced in the doorway.

Grateful for the interruption, Rachel rose from the bench and darted to the trader's side. "How did you and Tom fare with the horses, Mr. Butler?"

"Well enough, ma'am, that we can journey out of here as soon as the storm abates."

Ben Buckman jerked upright. "Oh, but Mr. Butler! My beloved daughters and I would not hear of it. You must avail yourself of our hospitality overnight. The rest will do you and your horses good." Buckman stole a sidewise glance at Rachel. "Very good indeed, sir."

A lazy smile smoothed Butler's lips. "Miss Whitfield's betrothed, the very honorable and upstanding Mr. Threadwell, would never forgive me if I tarried unnecessarily with his intended."

Rachel caught his wink. "Quite right, Mr. Butler. Dear Aloysius, though a man of compassion, has a fearful temper when angered."

"Mr. Butler? Mr. Butler!" Breathless, Delilah Buckman darted inside her father's cabin. "Oh, there you are, sir! I wondered where you disappeared to."

Butler presented Ben Buckman a token of his gratitude—ginseng and a fine fisher skin—when the storm ended later that afternoon. The farmer and his two petulant daughters watched sullenly as Butler organized their departure.

"Nothing but trouble here," Butler whispered to Rachel as he helped her mount. "Though a rest would do us all good, we must ride. Did Buckman—?"

"No, though I feared I might have to fetch a musket and rescue you and Tom. Unless, of course, you relished Maisie and Delilah's charms." She offered the drover a sly glance.

He snorted. "Not to my liking, Miss Whitfield."

"But I thought you . . . that men like you did not discriminate where women were concerned."

His fingers grazed her chin. "There's much you do not know about me, Miss Whitfield."

At his touch, urgent heat warmed Rachel's sensitive flesh. Heat that frightened her. A pounding, primitive, unrecognizable urgency that threatened to cancel out Old Eliza's warnings.

"Nor do I care to, Mr. Butler," she replied, mounting her horse in breathless haste.

They rode for several hours. Past a flock of crimson-wattled turkeys scratching through oak leaf litter for acorns. Beyond cinnamon-colored cattails bent low in a stagnant marsh. Beneath bobolinks bubbling their euphoric songs in an autumn breeze spiced with minty bee balm.

Descending North Mountain, Jonah Butler fought to ignore the ache in his arm and the throb in his head. No time to indulge in personal sympathies. He was only halfway to his ultimate goal—Philadelphia.

The Pennsylvania Assembly would abhor his message and shun his advice. If the governor took one side, the assembly would likely take another. All would politicize about "saving the people's money." Paying to send guns into the backwoods for farmers' protection? "Bloody hell!" he muttered. They'd fight it with every ounce of their political clout.

Matilda Hattersley most likely awaited him in that bustling city on the Delaware River. His parents would see to that, damn it, with their infernal zeal for urban social climbing. Wealthy Matilda, all icy reserve and crisp bloodless manner.

Butler moved his sore arm in an effort to ease the ache. Rachel Whitfield, as well, played at being prudishly virginal.

Butler knew different.

He knew it from that absurd moment at Turtle Creek when he impulsively gathered her in his arms and kissed her. Beneath her frigid exterior lay a sensuous woman unlike any he'd ever met. A woman terrified by her own deep passions. And damn it all, Butler longed to repeat that stolen kiss. Something he must never do.

He roamed free as the autumn wind across these mountains. He loved the wild, unfettered life of a frontier trader. And it was making him wealthy. No woman belonged in that harsh life with him. Not poor Collette, not ice-cold Matilda, and certainly not . . . not vexatious Rachel Whitfield.

The throb in Butler's head spread to his chest. And his groin.

Only a patient, tender man could free Rachel Whitfield from her terror of intimacy. A man who could control his own passion long enough to move slow. To hold back.

Butler didn't know if he had that much patience.

Riding down a slope dense with witch hazel and berry bushes, Butler brought them to the sweeping Cumberland Valley for evening camp. A meadowlark's slurred whistle mingled with the sound of stream water tumbling across smooth, round stones.

Rachel delighted in the abundance of low plants thriving in the more open sunlight.

"While you men tend the horses," she announced, "I shall prowl in search of plants for our soup pot." Onions, cress, lamb's-quarter, purslane, these she added to Tom's contribution of a fat brook trout for soup. As the meal simmered, she busied herself pinching and sniffing the plethora of plants.

"Find something?"

Rachel jerked upright. "Uh . . . no, Tom. I was just, uh . . . 'twas nothing, really." She shook off her inner guilt.

"More food for the stew pot?"

"No. That is—"

Blaine glanced over her shoulder. "Dunno the name of that one there, but my aunt once warned me of its noxious properties."

"Did she now?" Rachel cleared her throat nervously. "Indeed, a blue-green-leaved vine of similar description can cause sleepiness, Tom. But not this one." She coughed again. "Likely this plant is something else entirely."

"No? Then perhaps you found something more palatable, Miss Whitfield. I see you clutch bluish leaves in your other hand."

"Just . . . just a few fragrant mint leaves is all, Tom, to form a pleasing sachet. You know how I do so love sweet-smelling herbs. Now, shall we offer our assistance to Mr. Butler?"

Catching Tom by the arm, she steered him away from the vine-sprawled rise where she stood.

"Your brother, Miss Whitfield," Blaine asked over their evening meal. "You never told us why you dared risk your life to find him."

She fidgeted with the worn threads of her coarse white apron. "Zeb is my brother. One never needs an excuse to save one's brother."

She avoided his level gaze.

Butler studied her manner. "More to the story there, I wager."

A chill pine-scented wind whipped across the wide valley as a full moon mounted the night sky. Butler retrieved a spare blanket from one of his pack bundles.

"'Tis the coldest night yet, Miss Whitfield. Here's extra warmth for you."

In handing her the blanket, his rough hands brushed her own slender fingers. Like a bow drill against resistant wood was Jonah Butler's touch against hers. Hot and thrilling, sending incendiary sparks clear to her thighs. And to the forbidden region just above.

Rachel craved more.

Leaning close—so close she could breathe in his warm maleness—Jonah Butler seemed to be offering what she sought. His penetrating gaze unsettled her as chilly winds billowed her skirts and caught at her wide-brimmed straw hat.

"Best sleep close to me tonight, Miss Whitfield," Butler urged from somewhere low in his chest. "You'll need my body heat to keep you warm."

"Good night, Mr. Butler. I . . . My own body heat will be quite sufficient tonight, thank you all the same."

Rachel wrapped his blanket offering tightly around her shoulders to ward off perceived intrusions of the leering pack drover. But most of all, however, to lock in her own rising urges. Turning from Butler to hunker down by the fire, she heard his voice rasp one final torment.

"I am available, Miss Whitfield, should you need me."

Reclining on her unrolled blanket by the crackling fire, Rachel willed her pounding heart to slow.

A fine madness seemed to plague her waking moments and afflict her nightly dreams. All of it having to do with the rogue trader, Jonah Butler.

Men caused women pain. Old Eliza, beaten and abused by two drunken husbands, had stressed that fact. Thoughtless creatures absorbed only in their own pleasures, their own well-being, men brought sorrow to the women who loved them.

Rachel knew all this by heart.

Yet despite her armor plate of knowledge, she yearned to reach out and explore every inch of Jonah Butler's warm masculine body with her hands. With her mouth. *Needed* to, in fact. She craved the feel of his mouth on hers. Should the instance arise again, she feared she would not slip from his grasp. Rachel knew she would kiss Butler back and clutch at him and mewl for something too explosive even for her to comprehend.

That moment must never be allowed to happen.

Zeb Whitfield might still be alive. And if he was, he would be counting on Rachel's childhood promise.

She had no choice. Not really. Rechecking the fresh cache of tiny blue-green leaves she'd hidden in the pocket belt beneath her petticoat, Rachel glanced over at Butler's form in the dark.

Fourteen

"I tell you, we must do something, Chabert." With his lone remaining eye, Philippe Michaux peered anxiously at his brother. "Despite foul weather, those wretches progress over these infernal mountain ranges."

"See how you tremble, *mon frère!*" Chabert patted his brother condescendingly. "You forget that, in the end, my plans always work."

Philippe scraped mud from his quivering fingers with a bone-handled knife. "But you always use *me* to accomplish your deeds, Chabert. Always! And if my neck shall be on the line, I insist you heed my words." Philippe pointed his knife at his brother for emphasis.

"Careful where you point that, Philippe. I should not want you to grow careless in your . . . agitated state."

"My aim is true, I tell you. Even with one eye," he shouted, ignoring the winds that tore at dried secretions across his empty eye socket.

"Then save your aim and venom for the guts of Jonah Butler."

"With pleasure shall I disembowel that arrogant English trader!"

Chabert's gray eyes glittered. "Not in haste,

Philippe. We shall not dispatch Monsieur Butler too quickly. He does not merit such a compassionate death."

"What have you in mind?"

"Death by inches, *mon frère.*" He tilted back his head and guffawed. "When the time is right, we shall tie Butler to a tree and slice him to death slowly."

"The same for his assistant?"

"Quite likely."

"And the woman?"

Chabert Michaux massaged his jaw in slow arcs. "Mademoiselle Whitfield is far more useful to us alive than dead, Philippe." He grinned. "I feel certain she will relish the pleasure of watching her captor tortured. We shall enjoy her lovely body as often as we feel the need."

He fingered Rachel's silver pendant, dangling from his own throat.

"Hah! That would be suitable punishment to her father for disregarding French orders to move east."

"Eli Whitfield will not learn of our little pleasures with his daughter, *mon frère.* At the proper time, we shall deliver her silver pendant to Eli and demand ransom for Mademoiselle Whitfield."

"When, Chabert? Surely we must act soon. Another two days at most and those scoundrels will reach the Susquehanna. Butler must not be allowed to rouse the English while fever and exhaustion force our own soldiers to retreat back to Canada."

"Patience, Philippe. Patience. We will not allow Butler an opportunity to reach Philadelphia. Or Lancaster, for that matter. Your day of entertainment draws nigh."

"And meanwhile . . . ?"

"Meanwhile, *mon frère,* you and I shall find interesting ways to slow Butler's progress."

Rachel's moccasins sank into rain-sogged earth by Muddy Run as she gently stroked her mare. "She seems peckish, Mr. Butler. Sara is normally quite sweet-natured. I worry for her welfare."

Sunset rays, orange as a monarch's wings, slanted across Rachel's upraised arms. Mitt-shaped sassafras leaves tickled her ankles, and sticktights clung to her skirts as a pair of thrushes warbled their evening songs.

Butler smoothed his hands over the mare's shoulder and chest. "That forearm troubles her, Miss Whitfield. Likely that's why her personality worsens."

"A kinked muscle?"

"I expect so."

"Pa always said the best remedy for that in a horse was a short walk to ease the ache."

"Try walking her after you finish eating. With some luck, we can sustain her till we reach Shippensburg tomorrow."

Wolfing down an extra portion of gruel, Tom whooped. "Then Carlisle, then the river, then Miss Lily Martin!"

"How many days till we reach the Susquehanna, Mr. Butler?" Rachel asked, dodging windblown fly ash from their fire.

The grizzled drover took his time answering her query. He chewed on a blade of grass. "A day. Or ten. Depends on the weather, the horses—"

"And whoever is out there visiting mischief on us, right, Jonah?" Blaine added.

Butler cautiously studied Rachel's demeanor. "Why do you ask, Miss Whitfield?"

"Idle curiosity, 'twas all, sir." She retucked hair at her nape that had already been re-pinned twice since morning. Her mobcap had long ago vanished in that first deluge. "One cannot traverse these Endless Mountains without wondering when we shall see something different. Such as . . . such as the wide Susquehanna, for instance."

"And Lancaster!" Blaine exclaimed, exploding into a sunny grin. "Ah!" he sighed. "Lily awaits me there." He gulped another portion of corn mush.

Rachel laughed. "At least, Tom, you shall be well-fed and healthy when you finally meet your Lily."

Butler frowned. "Rash talk, Miss Whitfield. Health is never a given, especially out on the frontier. Even for a sturdy young buck like Tom."

Her smile faded. "Quite right, Mr. Butler. My mother died giving birth at Venango."

Still scrutinizing Rachel, Butler drew on his pipe. "'Twill do you good to visit with your elder sister again, Miss Whitfield. Safe in Lancaster. Away from frontier perils."

She avoided his pointed gaze. "Yes. Quite right, indeed, Mr. Butler."

Blaine's eagerness shone from his eyes. "Well, I say to you all we shall have a *glorious* celebration when we reach Lancaster. Before we send Jonah on his way to Philadelphia, that is."

"I leave the celebrating to you, Tom. A quick change of horses for me and I shall be off. After I sell the furs, that is."

Hearing her troubled horse nicker, Rachel rose from the log where she sat and smoothed her skirt.

"You ride with a heavy heart, Mr. Butler. As if dreading what awaits you in Philadelphia."

Butler eased his lanky frame to its full height and snorted. "What awaits me? You mean a handful of politicians who want backwoods furs without the expensive trouble of protecting frontiersmen? Why, Miss Whitfield, whatever made you think I was not eager to greet those same men?"

She studied his brooding demeanor. "Your family, Mr. Butler. Perhaps they will soften your anger."

She saw his face darken at her words.

Blaine patted Rachel's shoulder. "A visit with your sister will cheer your spirits as well, Miss Whitfield. Thank goodness you abandoned your plan to hunt for your brother."

"Yes," she whispered softly, pinching at the folds of her linen apron. "Yes. Well, I shall offer dear Sara a brief walk to ease her soreness before it grows dark."

Butler watched her shuffle away toward her speckled bay mare.

"A mistake, boy, to ever mention Zeb Whitfield to that headstrong sister of his." Butler rearranged a pack loosened by the day's ride.

Evening winds whistled through waving hemlocks and rustled burnt-orange maple leaves.

"But she's changed, Jonah. You never use the rope anymore. The two of you seem, well, a tad more cordial to one another. And—"

Butler exhaled deep and long. "Tom, just when I begin to think you understand women—even a trifle—I realize . . . you do not." He knocked soggy earth from his pack with a closed fist.

"Oh, and I suppose you do, Jonah. A man who ties

up a sensitive, pretty woman like Miss Whitfield and snarls at her at every possible opportunity. Eh?"

"Sensitive?" Butler spat. "That woman, Tom, is conniving from the moment she wakes till the moment she sleeps. She never abandoned the urge to reach her brother in Montreal."

"Then if you know so much about women, and Miss Whitfield in particular, Jonah, why did you just now let her disappear along with one of your horses?"

Butler worked his mouth. No sound emerged at first. "Because— Oh, hell, Tom, because—"

"I watch the two of you, Jonah. A stubborn mountain man like yourself, you don't even realize how the lines in your face ease whenever you look on Miss Whitfield."

"You speak gibberish, Tom." Butler knelt to retuck another fur bundle.

"Scoff if you like, Jonah, but if you spoke kind words to her, flattered her even, she might never leave your side."

"Never leave my side? God's blood! An abomination like that would render me sleepless for a year!" Butler exploded. Still, he grew uneasy over Rachel's absence.

He was about to wedge tobacco in his pipe bowl when they both heard the scream.

"Bloody hell, Tom! 'Tis herself! Something's got her!"

They dashed in the direction of the cry.

Through deep viburnum tangles snarled with bittersweet and grapevine. Past heaped ferns concealing rabbit holes from the unwary. Thrusting aside giant fuzzy-leaved mullein stands. At the men's bounding approach, squirrels and bluejays scattered with noisy scolds.

"Damn, Jonah! I don't see her!"

"No excuse, boy. We've got to find her."

They crept down a rubble-lined trail littered with pebbles scattered by recent downpours.

"I never should have let her . . ." Butler blurted out, heading for a ravine. He found her there, lying in a twisted heap. Her horse stood nearby, nickering softly.

"Walk Sara back to camp, Tom. I'll fetch Miss Whitfield."

Kneeling against the earth, Butler scooped Rachel into his arms. He kissed her deathly still form—her cheek, her forehead. When he pressed a kiss on her hand, she moaned softly.

His hand explored the curving recesses of her neck and back. "Thank God, your neck's not broken!" he whispered.

Rachel's eyes fluttered open. " 'Twould have . . . have saved you the trouble," she murmured.

"What happened?" Still kneeling on the ground, Butler cradled her in his arms. He swept aside tall fern fronds that tickled her face in the encroaching dusk. Eyes closed again, Rachel lay limp in his arms.

"So sudden," she murmured. "Trying to recollect. Mud and stones gave way. Sara slipped. I reached for her and . . ."

"Looks like she rolled downhill."

"Oh, Mr. Butler! How is she?" Rachel groped outward in search of her mount. "My poor sweet Sara."

Butler cradled Rachel securely in his arms. "Hush, woman. Sara is on her way back to camp with Tom. I would guess she's better off than you right now." His wind-chapped hand swept stray strawberry-blond tendrils back from Rachel's forehead.

On the next ridge a pair of wolves howled in the enveloping dusk.

"We must get you back to camp."

"I shall walk," she insisted, struggling to stand upright. But a loud roar filled her ears, and the world suddenly tilted at crazy angles.

Standing, she sagged against Butler's hard-walled chest.

His arm encircled her waist. "Your face is ghostly white, Miss Whitfield. You shall not walk. Not tonight."

She barely managed a smile. "Then shall you drag me behind you with your blasted rope, Mr. Butler?"

He swept her into his arms and walked toward their camp. "No. No rope tonight."

His words brushed past Rachel's ear in a warm, pleasurable rush as she reluctantly permitted Butler to carry her. In her weakened state, would this be the night Butler inflicted his wicked way on her?

She worked at mustering physical strength. Locked in Jonah Butler's arms, none seemed to appear.

"But your own injuries, Mr. Butler. Your head, your arm?"

"'Twould appear, Miss Whitfield, that we shall nurse one another throughout this journey." His mouth lingered near her cheek as he spoke. "Tonight 'tis my turn to tend you."

She clutched at the fringes of his hunting shirt—purely to keep from falling out of his grasp, Rachel assured herself.

"Were you running away, Miss Whitfield?"

His abrupt question stunned her. "Why, no, Mr. Butler. I was merely exercising poor Sara's leg. Have you not observed my keenness to join my dear sister in Lancaster?"

He eyed her distrustfully. "Then you have abandoned all cockeyed notions of slipping alone through the woods to Montreal?"

On a sigh, she snuggled against his chest. "Can you not see, Mr. Butler, that thought is furthest from my mind? I am compliant in all regards, sir."

He grunted his disbelief. "I should like to believe your words. Even in your weakened condition, your tone fails to convince me."

At the fire, Tom Blaine rushed forward. "Miss Whitfield! Is she . . . ?"

"More safe than not, Tom. But argumentative, as always."

Biting back a grin, Blaine reached for Sara's reins. "I see you have matters well in hand, Jonah, so I shall tend to the mare's needs."

"Put me down at once, Mr. Butler, or I shall box your infernal ears. Up here, like this, I can reach them quite readily, you know."

Still bearing Rachel, Butler met her gaze for a moment. His dark eyes flashed an intense message Rachel felt deep within her body. Curiously, 'twas not pain, or evil, or the arrogance of a tormentor she read in those penetrating eyes.

Instead, it was the look of the tormented.

Rachel feathered her fingertips over Butler's tanned face. Horrified at her own intimate gesture, she recoiled. "I . . . was, uh, examining your head wound, Mr. Butler, which, by the way, seems to have—" Rachel's faint words drifted into the twilight as Butler's face pressed close to her forehead.

She relished his strength, his warmth, his masculine aroma that aroused her concealed urges.

"Perhaps, Miss Whitfield, we need to spend time this evening carefully investigating one another's injuries." Butler's voice rasped deeper on each word.

Rachel stirred in his arms.

"I think, Mr. Butler, that we have most likely completed our mutual examinations for the evening."

A subtle grin caught at Butler's mouth. "Tomorrow evening, then?"

His playfulness alarmed her. "Put me down, Mr. Butler. At once. I should not wish to keep you from your day's-end chores."

He deposited her gently on his own worn blanket.

Rachel's eyes flared wide. "Mr. Butler?" Did the hulking drover assume she would spend the night huddled with him on the same bedding?

She pointed to the blanket.

"Its softness will comfort your newly acquired aches, Miss Whitfield." He covered her with her own blanket.

"But . . . then you shall have nothing on which to sleep, sir."

"The earth is my blanket. Rest easy, ma'am."

Rachel watched the trader finish grooming his horses. *Men caused pain.* Old Eliza, who'd born eleven children and knew of these things, had said so. Yet somehow when Rachel saw the wind whip Jonah Butler's dark hair around his handsome face, when she felt his strong arms hold her close, when his husky voice caressed her ears, oh, how she struggled against Old Eliza's words!

A screech owl's quavering call echoed from giant hemlocks to the north.

Rachel trembled in shame. Somewhere in that sinister direction, poor Zeb lay shackled in a French prison. He counted on Rachel's resolve to free him, of that she was certain. Her long-ago promise ensured that. Yet for a brief while, after her perilous tumble from Sara, she felt only a vibrant urge to cling to Jonah Butler.

Doubtless all because her head had been jostled in the fall. Doubtless.

She contemplated the reticule that lay heaped near her place at the fire. Inside were the leaves and stem of that vital blue-green plant. Rachel plucked nervously at Butler's frayed blanket edges. She would use that dried herb to sedate Jonah Butler just before they reached the Susquehanna River.

She smiled at the thought of her domination over Butler. Was he convinced he controlled her? Thanks to the herb, and her plan, she knew the reverse to be true.

At first light next morning, Rachel crept from her place of repose. Butler and Blaine already labored over the horses. Reaching for her reticule, she retrieved a handful of the blue-green leaves. Sudden foot scrapes alarmed her.

"Tom!" Rachel busied herself rearranging her skirt folds. "I did not hear you approach."

"Growing up in the forest teaches a man to move light of foot, Miss Whitfield. Thankfully, you seem much improved this morning."

She clutched the herb behind her back. "My head aches a bit. But I can still help with the horses. Oh, Tom, how is poor Sara this morning after her dreadful tumble?"

He stuffed roasted rabbit meat in his mouth. "Able to walk. Still favors her leg, though. Jonah is looking her over now. What have you there, ma'am?"

"These?" Rachel cleared her throat. "'Tis only some herbs that, uh, my pa always insisted would dis-

pel pain and provoke vigor. I found them over by that
boulder this morning."

"And you . . . ?"

"I was about to make a tea of the leaves. Mr. Butler and I, with our assorted aches and wounds, would
greatly benefit from the herb's salubrious effects."

"Hmm. Dispel pain and provoke vigor? I should
like to drink that tea as well, Miss Whitfield."

"As well?" Rachel blanched. "If . . . if you feel the
need for its therapeutic benefits, Tom. Though I wonder if that be entirely wise."

"A man out on these mountains can never be too
vigorous, eh, ma'am?"

Too vigorous?

The thought of Jonah Butler's raw strength, and
precisely what he might do to her with that unharnessed might, made Rachel shudder.

"As you say, Tom."

She made a tisane of the herb. In sufficiently large
doses, the blue-green leaves would render a grown
man sleepy, according to the Lenape women at Loyalhannon. How large was that dose? She needed to
know. No point in knocking out Jonah yet, before
they reached the Susquehanna. Today would be
merely . . . *a test*.

Rachel smiled at the thought of her own petite
might. And duplicity. Two leaves? Three? She settled on two for a start.

"I say, Miss Whitfield, you seem perkier than I expected this morning," Butler commented, striding
toward her after checking the straps on his packs.

"See here, Jonah, the answer lies in Miss Whitfield's herbal tea." Blaine arranged the scabbards of
his weapons carefully on each hip.

Butler's eyebrow peaked. "Is that a fact?"

She nodded. "Yes. The Indians taught me that these leaves soothe away body aches and pains, leaving a person feeling refreshed."

"And vigorous, Jonah. Miss Whitfield says it makes a man more vigorous."

The corner of Butler's mouth quirked. "Does it now? Most interesting. Just which herb are we discussing, Miss Whitfield?"

"The name?" She feathered tendrils of her pinned-back hair. "The precise name eludes me at the moment, Mr. Butler. But I'm certain of the leaf."

"She made enough for us all, Jonah."

Butler bent down to sniff the kettle's pale green contents. "Why, I feel better already."

Rachel set out a mug of the tea on a rock ledge. "Oh, but you must drink it, Mr. Butler. To obtain full measure of the herb's therapeutic effects, that is."

Accepting the mug cautiously, Butler dangled one hand on his leather belt. "Do join me, Miss Whitfield. Together we shall banish all our cares."

She reached for a mug of plain mint tea she'd poured for herself. And smiled. "Indeed, sir."

Butler halted. "Merciful heavens, was that an angry sow bear I just saw yonder by that laurel clump?"

With a gasp, Rachel set her mug down on the rock shelf and peered at the shrubs. "I see nothing moving, Mr. Butler."

"Keep looking, Miss Whitfield. One can never be too careful."

Tom shook his head. "My eyes are keen, Jonah. There's no critter out there that I can see."

"Hmm." Butler scratched his jaw. "Could have sworn I saw a bear. Well, always the possibility I was mistaken. By the way, delicious tea, Miss Whitfield.

I feel mercifully invigorated already. Drink up, ma'am. On the trail we shall need you to be hearty as well."

Rachel stared hard at the lone mug remaining on the rock ledge. A pattern of wet traces marked the stone. The cups seemed to have been switched accidentally.

Or on purpose.

She raised the remaining mug to her lips. Mint masked the presence of her devious tisane. Was this liquid plain mint tea? Or the sleeping potion?

Rachel took one cautious sip. Then another.

Glancing over at Jonah Butler to determine his physical state, she caught him staring back at her.

Fifteen

"With you?" Rachel's sputtered attempt at indignation failed. Her tongue, seemingly loosed at both ends, refused to cooperate.

Jonah Butler adjusted the cinch on his spunky gelding. "We have no choice, Miss Whitfield. Sara is too lame for you to ride this morning."

"But—"

Staving off a grin, Tom Blaine worked at nonchalance. "Jonah is right, as usual, Miss Whitfield. Besides, with your fresh injuries from that fall last evening, far better you should ride with Jonah on his horse than walk alone."

Rachel sulked. "We shall crowd one another on that animal." She gestured toward Butler's mount.

"We shall manage, I wager. With any luck, when we reach Shippensburg shortly, we can trade Sara for a gamer mare."

Climbing up onto his saddle, Butler pulled Rachel behind him as Blaine gave her an assist. "Do hold tight, Miss Whitfield," Butler drawled. "I should not wish to lose you."

Unwilling, yet oddly relaxed, Rachel threaded her arms around Butler's hard-muscled midsection. Her head and bruised legs no longer ached.

And Butler's warmth felt . . . inviting.

Tilting forward, she leaned her head on his back as they rode across a small creek and proceeded deeper into the Great Valley.

His palm covered her two hands clasped over his abdomen. "Sleepy so early in the morning, Miss Whitfield?"

She yawned. "Only a little. Must be from that lovely scent of mint on cool, dry September breezes. You never told me, Mr. Butler, why did you become a frontier trader?"

"Same reason as your pa, ma'am. Filthy lucre."

"But Pa stays put at his post out west. You continually rove these mountains. You have other reasons, I wager."

His chest muscles tightened beneath her grasp.

"Smell the fresh pine scent of that air, Miss Whitfield."

She breathed in. "Yes?"

"See those scarlet dogwood berries decorate rich green spaces betwixt the earth and those giant flame-colored maples?"

Her eyelids half closed, Rachel nodded. "Lovely, indeed."

"Hear the music of water tumbling across stones, thrushes warbling, and wind whistling through a thousand leaves?"

"Those are your reasons?" Rachel yawned again.

"All of them."

Her head nestled into the small of his back. "I do not quite believe you, sir. Are you . . . are you not just a *trifle* drowsy, Mr. Butler?"

"Not a bit, Miss Whitfield. Your tea banished my aches and restored my vigor, as promised. Have you more of that beneficial herb somewhere in your possession?"

"A few leaves," she murmured, savoring Butler's hard brawn.

"I suggest you brew more this evening, ma'am. That, uh, seems to be when my soreness plagues me the most."

"I shall attempt to oblige, Mr. Butler."

"'Twill only be a few more days till we reach Lancaster, ma'am. A cup of your tea each night and you shall be in fine shape, with all your injuries healed when you arrive at your sister's house. In fine shape indeed."

"Are you smiling, Mr. Butler? Somehow I sense that you are smiling."

"Only at the glorious freedom of being alive out on these hills, ma'am."

"Are you holding my hands, Mr. Butler?"

"In what sense, ma'am?"

"Well, you know, holding my hands."

"Oh, no, Miss Whitfield. That would be improper. And you know I always strive to maintain proper decorum. No, I merely brace your arms so that you do not tumble off my horse."

"Proper?" Rachel hooted. "Mr. Butler, you are a carousing, indecent rascal who steals kisses from unwilling women."

"Carousing? Wherever did you hear such unkind sentiments about me?"

Her cheek rested comfortably against his broad back. "From Tom. He implied that you . . . well, that is—"

"Miss Whitfield, have I harmed you in any way—indecent or otherwise—since we started this journey?"

"Other than the odd rope burn? I suppose not. But you did steal a kiss back at Turtle Creek. Altogether naughty of you, Mr. Butler. Are you certain you're not just a tiny bit sleepy?"

"No, ma'am. I am not at all sleepy. Would you like another kiss, Miss Whitfield?"

"Certainly not!" Her tongue, uncooperative at best, labored with those *t*s.

"I just wanted to be certain you were properly cared for, ma'am. Rest easy, now. We have a long ride ahead of us."

She never slept. Not actually. But somehow the rolling gait of Butler's horse lulled Rachel into gentle dreams of hammocks in summer breezes that lifted and stirred myriad pine boughs.

Low knobby hills blended into a string of miles.

Butler signaled a halt to Blaine. "Time to rest the horses, Miss Whitfield."

Blinking her eyes open, Rachel felt a rush of embarrassment at her intimate proximity to Jonah Butler. Her arms were locked tight around his midsection, of all things! Her bosom pressed forward into the well of his back. Her thighs lay sprawled tight against Butler's long legs.

She eased down off his horse.

Butler dismounted. "Quite an entertaining ride, Miss Whitfield," he commented, flicking a pebble from his mount's front hoof.

Rachel's hands fluttered to her hot cheeks. For some reason her memory evaded her. Had she said or done something improper? "The scenery? Is that what you mean, Mr. Butler?"

He grinned wickedly. "That would have been sufficient, in and of itself, Miss Whitfield. But your sparkling and witty conversation made it far more interesting."

"My . . . conversation?"

"Quite."

"But I slept all the way. I . . . I'm sure I did."

"Not *all* the way, ma'am." Butler's mouth twitched into a sidewise grin.

Her lips parted. "Dear me! Perhaps my head injury affected my speech. If I have offended you in any way, sir—"

"Not at all, ma'am. No, I was not offended in the least."

Rachel shifted uncomfortably at the sight of his brazen stance. Even worse, the feel of Butler's warm, hard body and the memory of his disturbing stolen kiss made it more difficult by the minute for Rachel to control foreign urges rising within her.

She caught at his sleeve.

"Perhaps this head injury has altered my personality, Mr. Butler. Help me by telling me what I said. Or did."

"Or what you begged for?"

"B-begged . . . for?"

He bent down and kissed Rachel's lips.

Unable to resist, she savored the warm, insistent press of his kiss. Her cool fingers edged up against Butler's chest. Instead of pushing away, she clutched at his fringed shirt.

"That," he whispered into Rachel's ear, "was merely the first thing you asked for."

She gasped. "But, sir, you must tell me—"

Tom Blaine dashed up just then, interrupting them with his enthusiasm. "The trout here are of prodigious size, Jonah. This big, at least!" Blaine flung his arms wide to indicate.

"Food, Tom," Butler said with a nod. "'Tis the first and last thing you think about."

"Nay, Jonah. Miss Lily Martin—'tis she who's first and last in my thoughts, always."

Later, as the men finished feeding and watering the horses, Rachel sat alone on a boulder that sprouted delicate maidenhair ferns from its clefts. Clutching a petite bouquet of white boneset flowers and starry purple asters, she watched a cardinal pluck ripe berries from a gnarled dogwood branch.

"You love flowers, do you not?" Butler asked.

His sudden presence startled Rachel. He stood with one forearm resting on a bent knee propped against the boulder.

She sniffed a bergamot sprig tucked in the center of her bouquet. "Flowers, Mr. Butler? They feed my soul with their ambrosial grace and beauty." She lowered the bouquet to her apron folds. "But, sir, you simply must tell me what scandalous things I committed or said, that I might be certain it never happens again."

"You need not worry, ma'am. I shall not divulge your playful bent to a soul. Not even Tom. Your secret is safe with me."

She cringed. "My . . . my *playful* bent?"

"Hidden urges, ma'am. Some folks struggle hard to conceal them. Sooner or later, though, such inner devilment wriggles to the surface and demands to be—"

"Mr. Butler! Surely 'tis only my head injury. Or the morning tea, perhaps. I have no inner devilment, I . . . I feel certain." Rachel's hand flitted to the thin cotton scarf snugly encircling her throat.

"None?"

"Not a speck, sir."

A September breeze, sweeping across the gentle rise, released a wheat-colored tendril from Rachel's tightly pinned bun. When she reached to tuck it back,

Butler caught her hand. Lazily, he wound the silken strand around his own callused finger.

Leaning down, he cupped her face in his two hands and kissed her firmly on the lips.

She enjoyed that kiss. Far too much. "Mr. Butler, really, sir, you must stop doing that," she whispered, hesitating to back away.

"I was only complying with your earlier demands, ma'am."

"I know. But 'tis wrong. Improper, you understand? Surely my lascivious requests were born of yesterday's fall that resulted in my head injury."

Butler scratched his chin as if somberly pondering her remarks. "You think that's the likely explanation?"

"It has to be."

"I see. Then you do not harbor closeted cravings that threaten to destroy you if unfulfilled?"

"Certainly not!"

"Because, sadly, they will, you know. 'Tis the quickest way to ill health and an early grave—ignoring deep-seated longings that torment a person and eat out the soul."

She clasped her hands together in her lap. "I harbor no inner lust, sir. Toward you or any man. 'Twas only my poor battered head. Or . . . or the tea."

"Ah, yes. The tea, Miss Whitfield. Have you more of those leaves?"

"Only a few." Rachel shifted uneasily, evading Butler's stare. She intended to conceal the truth from this hulking trader. Those leaves, steeped in a tea, would stupefy him when she decided to escape. Though obviously she would need a much stronger dose to drug such a large man.

And be absolutely certain she consumed none herself!

He crossed his arms over his chest and solemnly contemplated Rachel. "Yes. Perhaps you're right, Miss Whitfield." He let out a long sigh. "I suppose a woman like you would never possess raw passion."

Turning his back on Rachel, Butler returned to douse their afternoon fire.

She clutched her diminutive bouquet and willed her breathing to slow. Pain. Pain and cruelty and anguish. Was that not man's sole legacy to women?

"I want no such vicious torture. None of it!" she murmured, sniffing the bergamot-scented flowers.

Why, then, did it hurt so much to watch Jonah Butler's towering figure stride away from her?

Oh, he was correct, of course. She could confess to no one how desperately she ached to glide her fingers over his bronzed, roping chest and arms. How she needed to taste his searching mouth and smell the musk of his aroused male ardor and feel his strong arms envelop her in his muscular warmth.

Dear God! She ached to toss off her clothes and make love with coarse, indecent, amoral Jonah Butler!

What sort of madness had swept over her? Could she contain it long enough to rescue Zeb?

She rode on Butler's horse with him again that afternoon. The brooding trader remained strangely quiet.

Approaching the southern fringes of Conodoguinet Creek, Butler halted to rest the horses that sunny afternoon.

"I swear, Tom," he insisted, "you grew another three inches just since we left Ohio."

"Taunt if you like, Jonah, but I saw the finest red

raspberries back there ever grown. Somehow the birds missed 'em. You two will thank me when I fetch a hatful back for you."

He headed off on foot.

Rachel sipped a handful of stream water, then splashed more over her sun-kissed cheeks. "Have you ever been married, Mr. Butler?"

He scowled. "We had this conversation before, Miss Whitfield."

"You seem anxious to reach Philadelphia, while dreading it all at the same time."

He joined her at the stream. "Your fertile imagination keeps you busy, does it not, Miss Whitfield?"

She dabbed at withered grasses with the toe of her moccasin. " 'Tis a woman. Your wife, perhaps?"

"I have no wife," he growled.

"A sweetheart, then? A sweetheart who pleads with you to remain in Philadelphia." Masking her anxiety, she studied Butler for signs of flushed embarrassment.

He betrayed none.

Stoic and rock-jawed, Butler sat on a moss-covered log and twisted blades of grass. "No raging wife could equal the fury of Philadelphia politicians when they hear what I have to say. They want their furs *and* money served up on a silver platter."

"Perhaps a skirmish at the Ohio forks will convince the French that—" Recognizing the folly of her own words, Rachel glanced away at trickling stream water.

"You know better, Miss Whitfield. Nothing short of all-out war between France and England will resolve which nation controls the Ohio River."

"And your parents? How will they feel about all this potential carnage?"

"My parents are Quaker pacifists."

"Pacifists?" She digested this revelation. "Then they will reject your urging the Pennsylvania Assembly to arm backwoodsmen with British guns and soldiers."

"Precisely."

"And . . . the woman who waits for you? She is a pacifist also?"

Butler's jaw clenched in silence. That was when they both heard the dreadful scream. Tom Blaine's scream. Hard on Butler's heels, Rachel dashed toward the shrubby mound where Tom had last been seen.

Blaine, stunned, stood with his hands propped against a shagbark hickory.

Butler reached him first. "What is it, boy?"

Blaine worked to move his mouth. "Snake . . . a rattler, Jonah. Got my ankle!"

"Dear God!" Rachel cried.

Poking grasses with a long stick, Butler searched for the snake. "Be vigilant, you two!" he warned. "The serpent might still be around." Careful to avoid touching the bite mark, he pulled Blaine's loose-edged legging up to examine the youth's ankle.

Blaine trembled. " 'Tis a dry bite, Jonah, right?" he begged. "Jonah?"

"Bloody hell, Tom. Wish I could say that. Careful, Miss Whitfield!" he warned, blocking Rachel's eager advance with his arm. "The poison could affect anyone who comes in contact with it."

" 'Tis venom, then. Lord have mercy, Jonah. Is that what you see?"

"Two bites, Tom. A truly provoked rattler. Sit down. I'll try milking the bite." Butler squeezed down hard against Blaine's leg. Blood oozed from the puncture wounds.

Rachel clutched at her apron. "I know plants well.

I shall search for snakeroot. Surely some grows nearby!"

"Be careful, Miss Whitfield," Butler warned again. "If the rattler's still around, you could be its next victim."

Rachel's search for the snakebite remedy proved futile. Dejected, she returned with only a handful of plantain leaves.

"None?" Butler asked.

"No. But snakeroot grows plentiful. Surely as we ride we shall spot some." Rachel labored to sound optimistic while making a poultice of crushed plantain. "How . . . how do you feel, Tom?"

Blanched and tense-lipped, Blaine stared at his leg. "The skin feels tight there," he answered, pointing to the red puncture marks on his calf.

A death sentence? No, Rachel prayed, as she tied the poultice to Tom's leg with a cloth strip from her apron. Tom must not die! A good-hearted boy with a beloved sweetheart awaiting his arrival, his life could not be over yet.

'Twas not possible!

Butler slung Blaine's arm over his own shoulder and walked the youth toward their horses.

Silently, Butler examined Rachel's mare. His knowing hands prowled every inch of her glistening black-splotched legs. He turned to Rachel. "Miss Whitfield, we need a change of plans."

"Only tell me, Mr. Butler, I beg of you."

"With luck we can make the settlement of Shippensburg well before nightfall." He took a deep breath. "Your mare's leg, I think, seems strong enough for that distance."

"So I shall resume riding behind you?"

"No. Tom will. If he needs help, I shall be close at hand."

"Then, I shall ride—?"

"Tom's horse. Tail end of the pack train. I must ride up front to guide us. You willing?"

"Of course."

"Several things to watch for, Miss Whitfield."

"Name them, sir," she responded with far more assurance than she felt.

"Packs that loosen and sag off any horse. Horses that nip at the critter ahead of them. Limp animals that might have cast a shoe or picked up a stone."

Butler hesitated.

"Yes? What is it, Mr. Butler? For Tom's sake, you need only ask."

"Watch out for the Frenchmen who, for their own devious reasons, shadow our every move. At some point they'll try to kill us. You understand that."

She gulped. "I understand."

"Watch for my hand signals to halt, or pick up the pace."

"But how will I communicate with you when you ride more than a dozen horses ahead?"

"Can you whistle?"

She nodded, but her attempt produced only a meager lisp.

"Here, like this." He demonstrated.

On her second attempt, the shrill sound pricked the ears of all the horses.

"Perfect," Butler announced. "Now, Tom, boy, we've got a pack train to move. Ready?"

From his resting place on a moss patch, Blaine nodded.

Butler walked the pack train's length with Rachel, then helped her mount the last horse.

Brow furrowed, she locked eyes with the swarthy drover. "Can we save him, Mr. Butler? We must, you know. No better boy walks the earth."

Taciturn, the trader swallowed hard. He patted Rachel's horse, then walked away.

Every muscle tightened within Rachel's body. Her eyes swung in steady, vigilant arcs as she recalled Butler's terse admonitions. Earlier, when they descended into the wide Cumberland Valley, she had watched anxiously for signs of the sinister Frenchmen who trailed them. Was one of them the Fox?

And who was the woman who awaited Butler in Philadelphia? Did he love her? If so, then why did Butler seem uneasy about seeing her again?

And why did Rachel care so?

Snakeroot. She scrutinized every ledge, every mound of brush for the vital plant that might save Tom Blaine's life. And found none.

When the fiery sun slanted low against the autumn horizon, Butler signaled a halt.

Rachel slid from her mount and dashed forward as Butler eased Blaine off the second-in-line animal. "Mr. Butler? Tom? What is it?" she begged.

One glance at Blaine gave her the answer she dreaded.

Sixteen

"Ahead lies a treat for our senses, Philippe," Chabert Michaux announced, easing his horse across Burd's Run, deep in the Cumberland Valley.

"An English settlement? Chabert! You think that wise? Even in this rain?" The younger Michaux yanked his garish trade blanket tighter around his face.

"Certainly, *mon frère*. We are civilized men." His chipped front teeth glistened as Chabert Michaux laughed enormously at his own statement. "Are we not merely weary travelers in search of a warm meal and a roof over our heads?"

"And a woman, *mon frère*. Mmm!" Grunting, he rubbed at his groin. "I have not had a woman since we left Ohio."

A cool, steady drizzle dampened Chabert's leather wamus and breeches as his horse exited Burd's Run. "Patience, Philippe. Indeed, you shall have the most arousing woman of them all shortly. If, that is, I choose to yield her to you."

"Mademoiselle Whitfield? Chabert, you speak as if we have already captured her."

The elder Michaux fingered the silver pendant he wore concealed beneath his fringed shirt. "In essence, *mon frère*, we have, though Mademoiselle Whitfield does not yet know it." Fleshy lids hooded his watery gray eyes. "Nothing, I sense, shall interfere with our plans."

"A rich load of furs in our possession. That haughty Englishman, Butler, dead with his heart cut out. And—"

"And shapely Mademoiselle Whitfield in our arms."

Philippe Michaux avidly licked his lips. "Eli Whitfield will yield all in his storehouse to free his luscious daughter. When will you send him her silver pendant?"

"Not quite yet, Philippe. Mademoiselle Whitfield's necklace shall serve us one or two additional ways."

Smoke curled from the chimney of a stone dwelling just ahead. Trees obscured what appeared to be two or three additional cabins.

Philippe Michaux clutched his blanket tighter against the angled rain. "Mmm. I can almost smell the roasted meat, Chabert. And bread! Oh, surely, for a price, the madame will sell us bread."

"We can afford to make time for it all, *mon frère.* A superb place to tarry in comfort while Butler's pack train crawls across the mountains in this rain."

"Butler's young assistant seems ill."

"Excellent! Then Butler shall require even more time to reach Philadelphia." Suddenly Chabert scowled. "He must pay, Philippe. Excessively. For stealing my woman, for seizing furs I should have had, for ignoring our warning to halt trading on the Ohio—oh, Monsieur Jonah Butler shall pay handsomely for all his sins."

"And I, Chabert, shall caress him with my knife first. I'm quite skilled with my knife, you know. The natives taught me clever ways to keep a man alive for hours while making him wish he were dead." Managing a crooked grin despite the rain, Philippe massaged the scabbard of his knife.

They hitched their horses in front of the two-story stone building.

A stout woman greeted them at the doorway of her inn. "Welcome to Shippensburg, sirs."

Crumpled in Jonah Butler's arms, Tom Blaine moaned on a series of rapid breaths.

Rachel patted his arm. "Poor Tom!" she murmured, reaching to stroke his forehead. "His blood pounds furiously, Mr. Butler. I can feel it. He sweats, yet shivers from chills. If only it were not raining!"

White mist punctuated by cool showers obscured Rachel's vision of all but the nearest trees.

Butler nodded. "His leg grows more swollen, even while it bleeds."

Abruptly, Blaine rolled on his side and spattered vomit across a patch of square-stemmed cleavers. A drizzle washed his face as he collapsed back on the ground. "You can ill afford to lose more time, Jonah. Move on. Leave me here. 'Twas meant to be."

"Unthinkable, Tom!" Butler exploded. "No more such twaddle. Shippensburg lies just ahead. We shall see how you fare by then. But under no circumstances shall we abandon you in the woods."

"Feel dizzy, Jonah. And thirsty. So thirsty." Saliva dribbled from Blaine's lips.

Rachel fetched him a mug of cool springwater. Propping his head with her arm, she pressed the mug to his mouth. "Sip, Tom. The water will make you feel better."

Above his head, she frowned at Butler. A silent stare that bespoke her concern for Blaine.

Butler scanned the sky. "This rain is here to stay till evening. We must move on."

Lying on the ground, Blaine trembled. "I cannot walk, Jonah. Or ride. Leave me."

Butler winked at Rachel.

"Have you not learned yet, Tom, never to argue with me when I've made up my mind?" he chided, slinging Blaine's arm over his shoulder and pulling the youth to his feet.

Rachel slipped to Blaine's other side and supported his arm. Staggering under his limp weight, she helped Butler walk the youth to the second horse. She watched as Butler tied Tom Blaine to his saddle with the same rope he once used to bind Rachel.

"There, Tom, you see?" she said, exuding far more enthusiasm than she felt. "Mr. Butler and I shall impart our vigor to you. You shall fare well."

Grasping Rachel by the elbow, Butler pivoted her toward the end horse. "I shall help you mount."

Blaine retched again.

"Stay with Tom," she insisted. "I will mount on my own."

"Then give me a signal when you are ready to ride." Butler's dark eyes fixed on Rachel.

Back in her saddle, she glanced forward at Butler's tall, commanding form. He waited for her wave, then launched the pack train.

A curious journey, Rachel thought, pondering their dilemma through the sharp sting of an autumn downpour. All three travelers had changed on this journey of the heart. Gentle Tom Blaine, so full of vigorous young manhood, so in love with his Lancaster sweetheart, might never live to see her. Jonah Butler, an indecent, amoral, scandalous backwoodsman, turned out to be . . .

Rachel still had not deciphered the bold trader.

A mercantile representative, he oft labeled himself with a wink of those devilish dark eyes and a thrust of his lean pelvis. Despite appearing the perfect scalawag, Jonah Butler watched over Tom and Rachel with an almost paternal concern. Tall and strong and protective of his charges, the crude drover could at times be almost tender.

Had he changed on this journey?

More frightening, had she?

Rachel's hand fluttered to the naked spot on her throat where Old Eliza's silver pendant had once rested. The pendant that was to save Rachel's life on this journey was gone. And with it, her security.

She had to find Zeb, she had to safeguard herself from the wretched excesses of cruel-handed men, and most of all . . . most of all she had to smother the growing impulses arising from within her own savage breast. Frightening impulses. Cravings that urged Rachel to reach for Jonah Butler's hard-muscled body in the night and taste his arousing kisses till dawn.

She pulled a blanket tighter around her shoulders. "I shall not yield," she whispered, staring ahead at Butler's strong, fierce physique. "I shall not!"

Arms crossed over her ample chest, a stout woman peered through the evening rain at three approaching figures.

"Kicked by a horse?" she asked, sizing up Tom Blaine's trembling frame as Jonah Butler and Rachel struggled to walk him inside the tavern.

Butler shook his head. "Bitten by a rattler."

"Poor lad!" the tavern owner's wife exclaimed, dabbing at her nose with a handkerchief.

"Have you room for him, then, madam? Till he recovers, that is. I shall pay you well in ginseng and furs."

She purred at the sound of Butler's offer. "Name's Anna Snyder, sir. Always room for one more. You can stretch him out on the floor near the fireplace. Have you a spare blanket to soften his bum?"

"I shall fetch it, Mr. Butler," Rachel insisted, "while you reckon with Mrs. Snyder."

"What about you and your wife, sir?"

"Oh, we are not married, madam," Rachel replied, releasing Tom's limp arm as she strode across the threshold.

"Not married, eh?" Mrs. Snyder's eyebrow peaked. "Then will you two be staying here as well?"

Butler eased Tom's gangly frame onto the bare planked floor. "This night only, madam, with your kind permission. If this rain lets up by first light, Miss Whitfield and I shall head east with the pack train."

"A woman?" Anna's husband scoffed. "Never heard no such thing! Manning a pack train? 'Specially with a slight woman like that 'un?"

Dashing back inside with her own blanket—thickest of all they had—Rachel was startled by every face staring at her. Her hand flew to her face. "Have I—?"

Butler retrieved the trade blanket from Rachel's arms. "They question your ability to muscle the pack train across Pennsylvania, Miss Whitfield. They do not perceive your skills as I do."

Kneeling on the dusty wood floor, Butler rolled Blaine toward him as Rachel smoothed the blanket into a bed.

Overhead, loud boots clumped against a second floor.

"You have children, Mrs. Snyder?" Rachel asked.

"I do indeed, miss. Fourteen, to be exact. But

that?" She pointed upstairs toward the commotion. "Them's other guests. Two Frenchies and two Injuns."

Reluctantly, Butler rose. "I must tend the horses. I leave Tom to your tender care, ladies."

From her commodious fireplace, Anna Snyder ladled out a bowl of venison broth and brought it to Rachel. "A handsome man, your Mr. Butler."

"I assure you, madam, he is not *my* Mr. Butler. I do not own him any more than he owns me." She crouched at Blaine's side and eased his head up on her arm. "Some broth, Tom. Please try, I beg you."

"Cannot," the youth whispered through sagging lips. "So . . . nauseous."

Rachel gently massaged Blaine's forehead. Tears welled in her eyes as she pleaded once more. "Please try to drink, Tom. For me, please. And for Lily Martin, who awaits your arrival in Lancaster."

"My mouth . . . numb. Leg pains me so. Will I live, Miss Whitfield?"

With a dash of her knuckle, Rachel dabbed away her tears. "Of course you shall, Tom, dear boy. We shall entertain no further talk of you dying. A sip of broth, now, I insist."

But when Tom slurped the meat juice, he retched soon after.

Butler returned in the dark. He motioned Rachel outside for a discussion. "The rain abates, Miss Whitfield. We shall leave here at dawn."

"Tom cannot leave, sir. Surely I should stay here to nurse him."

He studied her earnest, upturned face. "None would do it finer. But I cannot leave you here. I promised Eli—"

"Pa would understand, I feel certain."

He stared at her long and hard. "I cannot go back

on my word to your pa. As well, your services will be useful on the drive east."

"But could you not hire some stouthearted male to ride with you?"

"None are available."

Noisy voices presaged men descending the tavern's stairway. French accents. Heavy boots clomped into the tavern's main room.

Butler looked up. A frown briefly flickered across his tanned countenance.

"Monsieur Michaux," he said, by way of greeting.

Chabert Michaux's eyes brightened. "Monsieur Butler! A pleasant surprise," he gushed, though his expression remained level. "And . . . and Mademoiselle Whitfield!" He lunged for her hand. "Always a delight!"

"You know one another?" the tavernkeeper asked. "'Tis unusual. Especially since you shall be spending the night together."

Chabert Michaux stroked the food-speckled tips of his mustache. "All of us under the same roof for a night. Only imagine!"

"'Course, the Frenchies, having arrived here first, got the upstairs bedroom," Mr. Snyder announced. "But I expect before bedtime you old friends will have much to discuss in front of the fire, eh?"

Rachel's glance bounced from Jonah Butler's fierce glower to Chabert Michaux's cold scowl. Locked in a mutual glare, the two men seemed poised to seize each other's throat. She stepped between them.

"Monsieur Michaux," Rachel began, "what brings you this far east?"

"The same as your . . . escort, mademoiselle. Trade, of course. I might ask the same of you, *ma chérie.*" His greedy eyes ravaged the shape of her throat and bosom.

She experienced a slight sigh of relief as Butler knelt to attend the groaning Blaine. At least the two adversaries might mute their antagonism for a while till she could divert them.

"Monsieur, at Turtle Creek I once spoke to you of my heartbreak over my brother's disappearance."

Butler flinched at hearing her words.

"Indeed, mademoiselle. To be sure, your anguish distresses me greatly."

Michaux's feigned distress fooled Rachel not one jot. She bit her cheek to keep from screaming at the liar. Perhaps she might still outwit him.

"'Tis likely, from what my family learned of other captured English traders, monsieur, that if Zeb lives, he is held in some Montreal prison."

"I wish to assure you, Mademoiselle Whitfield, that my brother and I continue to seek news of Zeb's whereabouts."

Control. What was it Molly Stonewell had tried to teach Rachel about controlling men? An occasional eye flutter, a tilt of the hip, a wave of one's handkerchief? Certainly worth a try where Zeb's fate was concerned.

She blinked twice at Chabert Michaux. "But, monsieur, your steadfast assurances produce no news to comfort my poor heart as of yet."

Firelight illuminated Chabert Michaux's blotchy red face and twisted nose, obviously broken in some long ago fight. As he stirred under her scrutiny, a slight silver gleam peeped from inside the rolling collar at his hair-matted throat.

"Ah, monsieur, your necklace reminds me of my own missing pendant," she lamented.

Michaux abruptly readjusted rawhide strings lacing the front of his wamus. "Come sit beside me here on this bench, mademoiselle, and together we shall discuss your plight."

Rachel turned aside. "I no longer wish to merely discuss it, Monsieur Michaux. I insist on firm answers. Since you have none, please excuse me. I must attend Mr. Blaine."

With Rachel's back to him, and Jonah Butler's harsh stare facing him, Chabert Michaux seized his brother and retreated upstairs.

Tom Blaine's fitful tossing and turning that long night disrupted Rachel's slumber. She placed a cloth soaked in cool springwater over his forehead and held his hand as he moaned.

At first light, when Butler slipped outside to harness the horses, Blaine tugged at Rachel's arm.

"Promise me . . ." he begged, trailing off his faint words.

She leaned closer to better hear him. "What is it, Tom?"

"The two of you will leave now?"

Her gut tightened at his implied abandonment. "Yes, Tom. Though I yearn to stay here and tend you, Mr. Butler insists I go with him. Mrs. Snyder assures us she has experience in these matters, that she will nurse you back to health."

Nodding assent, Blaine wrenched in pain. "Promise me," he begged again.

Tears spilled from her eyes. "Please do not distress yourself so, Tom. It only worsens your agony."

He clenched her hand in his. "Stay with him, Miss Whitfield. I know you still ache to seek Zeb, but that can only lead to your destruction. Stay with Jonah.

He would lay down his own life for your safety. No man on earth would protect you as well."

She hung her head. "Tom, you do not know what you ask of me."

"And Lily. When you reach Lancaster, find her, please, and tell her I loved her with all my heart. Please!" Blaine twitched in a series of spasms that left him limp.

Butler walked back into the tavern.

"We will have to leave Sara here, Miss Whitfield. Mr. Snyder has agreed to tend Tom and the horse for us."

"Oh, how I shall miss my shy little mare!"

Butler shuffled awkwardly from foot to foot. "'Tis the only way, ma'am. When Tom recovers, he can ride Sara into Lancaster for you, eh, boy?" He knelt and gently patted his assistant farewell.

"Aye, Jonah," Blaine whispered.

Cheeks moist with tears, Rachel kissed Blaine good-bye and followed Jonah Butler out of the tavern.

The September day blazed with a glorious sunrise of radiant, clear peach and gold. A pair of plump gray mourning doves cooed salutations on breezes rich with sassafras and goldenrod.

Mounting the pack train's end horse, Rachel felt torn in a half-dozen directions. How she hated leaving poor Tom! And Sara, too. Would Tom survive? His plea for her to remain with Butler—how must she regard that near deathbed plea? And what of Zeb, her own dear, trapped brother?

Rachel raked her fingers through her hastily pinned hair and struggled with her priorities.

At their first stop, farther up the Cumberland Valley, Rachel labored to help water and feed the horses. Even so, when she glimpsed husky Jonah Butler close up, that foreign, powerful urge stirring within her threatened to boil over.

Alone with Rachel, Butler appeared quiet. Almost indifferent to her presence.

His nonchalance annoyed her. And inflamed that mutinous urge deep inside her.

Love? No, surely it could not be. Impossible that Rachel might have fallen in love with the scoundrel captor, Jonah Butler.

She fought back intoxicating memories of the drover. Butler, nearly naked at Venango. The feel of his hot kisses. Each memory hurled her into a fine madness that required—

Oh, dear God! What was it she felt driven to do?

Rachel coughed nervously.

She was merely about to flex her will, 'twas all. To test her powers. To practice lessons learned from Molly Stonewell, who spoke of the necessity for controlling men's behavior. Nothing improper in that, surely. If she could control brawny Jonah Butler, perhaps she could also throttle her own reckless yearnings.

An exercise in control?

Certainly. Nothing more.

Rachel stared hard at Butler's commanding figure, about to light his pipe. Her tongue traced an eager path over her teeth and moistened her lips. Slowly, she loosened the scarf wrapped tightly around her throat. Ever so slightly. Following Maisie Buckman's example, with one finger she tugged her bodice lower across her full breasts.

Seventeen

Quieter than ever, sullen Butler ended their rest stop abruptly. Almost avoiding Rachel. She found his aloof manner disconcerting.

Strong gusts soaring in off the Alleghenies teased the brim of Rachel's straw *bergère* hat as she rode east, late that morning. Surely Carlisle lay not far ahead. There, Butler would secure a worthy male assistant. A sturdy man well able to help him ferry across the widespread Susquehanna and continue the pack train to Lancaster without her.

"I shall slip away from you as you ferry over the river, my reticent Mr. Butler," she murmured into the wind. "And thankfully I shall never see you again!"

Her abdomen tensed.

Mere apprehension at the thought of her solitary trek north to Montreal? Surely not regret that she would never see Butler again. That event would gladden her. Surely.

When Butler halted to rest the horses early that afternoon, she helped him water each animal.

"Your pipe, Mr. Butler?" she asked, handing him the clay item as he settled onto a fallen log. Carelessly, oh, so carelessly, she allowed her hands to brush against his larger coarse ones.

Butler drew back, seemingly indifferent to her presence.

"A warm afternoon," she murmured, gently loosening her fichu. She breathed deeply, permitting her bodice to slip lower. And bent down to hand Butler his tobacco pouch.

His neck muscles worked at swallowing. "Springwater, yonder, would refresh you, ma'am." He fastened his gaze on a distant heron in flight and made no move toward Rachel.

Control. Why, despite her efforts, could she not dominate Jonah Butler as she'd hoped? As Molly Stonewell advised was so vital for a woman to do? They neared Carlisle, then the Susquehanna River, yet Butler remained indifferent to her presence.

"You seem unduly quiet of late, Mr. Butler. Is it your concern over Tom?" Carefully tucking her skirts beneath her, Rachel settled down beside him on the mushroom-dotted log.

"I've done all I can for the boy."

"Then . . . have I angered you in some way?"

He surveyed the idle blond curl dangling from beneath Rachel's straw hat. A blue vein coursed a path to his firm jaw. "You labor hard, Miss Whitfield. I have no complaints." He tore his gaze from her and stared at the ground.

Alone with the scandalous trader in this rugged wilderness, where twittering songbirds and drifting butterflies mixed with heady autumn-scented sunshine, Rachel savored Butler's nearness with all her senses. His natural male scent, his warmth, the bulge of his thick upper arm brushing her own shoulder. Oh, Lord! What *was* this demon urge that made her so restless?

Rachel flexed her shoulders. "Horseback riding for days strains the back," she murmured.

Seated next to her on the log, Butler watched Rachel work her shoulders in small arcs. He reached over. His big hand spread to exert gentle pressure along her back. Across both her shoulders. At her nape.

Rachel closed her eyes. "Mmm. That helps, Mr. Butler. Truly."

He studied the curve of those blond lashes over her cheeks. The fullness of her lips. The angle of her throat. "I should like to do much more."

He watched those pale lids fling open to expose Rachel's unusually colored eyes. Blue-green eyes that bore reflections of sky and grass and earth.

"M-more?" she asked.

"To relieve the ache of your travels."

Rachel's hand fluttered to her corset strings, as if to affirm that they were still closed. "My ache?"

"If you wish." Butler's whisper tickled her earlobe.

Abruptly he rose and strode back three paces. He plowed one hand through his coarse dark hair before leaning against a rough-barked hickory trunk.

Her gaze wandered to his matted chest hair, scarcely covered by his half-laced hunting shirt. "Thank you, Mr. Butler. Shall I rub your back now? To ease your ache, that is?"

Locking eyes with her, he tilted his head. "No, Miss Whitfield. That would not be wise just now."

She marveled at the dazzling whiteness of his teeth, the jovial lines rimming his unsmiling eyes, the undeclared might of his arms. "You feel the horses have rested long enough?" Her voice echoed with hollow disappointment. Hands balled into fists, Butler moved toward Rachel, then apparently changed his mind. He dumped out his pipe's contents and crushed the embers with his booted heel.

"Time to ride, Miss Whitfield."

Zeb! Zeb must be rescued, she reminded herself during that tortuous next hour. Nothing on earth mattered so much as saving her battered brother. Nothing. Not the value of the packs they transported. Not French aggression down the Allegheny River. Not these savage urges building inside her toward her captor, Jonah Butler.

Especially not Jonah Butler.

Her gaze fixed on Butler's burly frame, far ahead where he rode. Her captor. An amoral scoundrel who perpetually lived on the fringes of decency. And yet, curiously, a man who fiercely guarded Rachel and Tom Blaine.

Born to ride was Jonah Butler. She could tell by the way he sat his horse. A man who crossed these mountains like some fearless free spirit. He found women where he chose, then left them on a moment's notice. Not the marrying sort.

She feared him, she resented him, she . . . she *needed* him, for reasons she could not comprehend. A mounting, consuming hunger every minute of the day threatened to overtake Rachel's reason.

Love? Dear God, no! Was this what love felt like? She would not allow it. Men *hurt* women with their self-centered ferocity. She would have none of it! She—

Rachel's gaze returned to feast on Jonah Butler's commanding figure.

A thrown horseshoe prevented them from reaching Carlisle that night. They camped outdoors, beneath a rising slivered moon. After a cold meal of Mrs. Snyder's biscuits and ham, Rachel huddled alone by the crotch of a sycamore. She would ignore Butler, just as perversely as he ignored her.

He watched her pick at a thorn wedged in her index finger.

"Splinter?" he asked.

"'Tis nothing," she sulkily replied, still rubbing at her finger.

Dousing his pipe, Butler crossed the distance to her. He took her hand in both of his and pressed out the offending thistle. Then he kissed her sore fingertip. And her nine other fingers. One by one. Slowly.

Gently, he stroked her bare throat, then released her.

She met his gaze. Her breathing grew ragged.

"Why do you fear a man's touch so, Miss Whitfield?"

She looked away. "You err, Mr. Butler. I fear noth—"

"You fear men. You fear me. Like some tense, untamed filly. Curious, but afraid all the same."

Let him think that. Let him believe she never wanted him to touch her. That would save her the humiliation of groveling for whatever it was her rebellious body seemed to crave from Jonah Butler.

"Do you plan to marry someday?"

"Marriage? I plan to be useful to my family, Mr. Butler. Marriage need not be part of the arrangement. I gather it certainly is not part of yours!"

A haunted look flickered across his solemn face. "Aye. I'm not the marrying sort, Miss Whitfield."

As if toying with the Devil, she went after him. Facing him squarely, she shouted, "I know what sort you are, Mr. Butler. The sort who steals kisses from innocent women and binds them with ropes."

Eyes blazing, she stood mere inches from him.

Butler seized her by the nape. He lowered his head and kissed her mouth.

She wanted to slap him!

To that end, Rachel drew back her hand. Instead, she trailed her fingers up his sleeve.

His kiss dropped to her throat. "Rachel," he whispered, voice husky.

In a moment of blood-pounding madness, she stood on tiptoe and returned his kiss.

His arms slid around her waist. He drew her snug against his chest and deepened the kiss. She felt those glorious muscular planes and angles of Butler's male body. A body that did not frighten her so much as comfort her with its enveloping warmth.

She leaned back in his arms a moment. Her fingertips explored the weathered lines of his craggy face. Was this it, then? Was this what her entire body had demanded throughout their journey?

A kiss?

"Mr. Butler," she murmured, "I have never been kissed like this. Should we—?"

His mouth trailed across her cheek and found her earlobe. His lips teased her senses. His tongue demanded entrance. His teeth gently claimed her lobe.

"I smell wildflowers on your skin," he whispered, nuzzling her throat, "and taste honey on your lips." He drew her into a tighter embrace before offering Rachel a lingering kiss.

Suddenly he released her.

"'Tis not fair."

Stunned and gasping for breath, she gaped at him. "What do you mean, Mr. Butler?"

"You were entrusted to my care."

"But . . . you have not abused that trust."

He crossed his arms over his chest. "Believe me, Rachel, this is the hardest thing I've ever done. I look on you with a lust that I can scarcely contain."

Lust? Was that the emotion she, too, felt? Was that the demon that tormented her poor body with urges too strong for her to comprehend? Lust?

Or *love?*

How would she ever know? She crossed the short distance to Butler and, on tiptoe, planted a kiss on his lips.

He kept his arms crossed. " 'Twill not do, Rachel Whitfield," he growled. "Hugging and kissing you out on these hills."

She glanced around at the fading sunset. "Out on these hills, Mr. Butler, we are all alone." She tickled his mouth with her lips.

"Wench! I must be strong for us both." He backed off in a pretense of examining a loosened pack.

Sighing evening breezes caressed Rachel's cheeks, where only a few moments earlier Jonah Butler had kissed her. She watched him check the final bundle. Untying the ribbons of her straw hat, she pulled pins from her long golden-red tresses and shook her hair loose.

"What are you doing?" he asked, looking up from his saddlebag.

"Letting the evening breeze float through my hair, Mr. Butler." She fluffed long curls free.

Over his shoulder, he watched.

She slipped off her moccasins and dipped her toes alongside pebbles in a shallow stream. A hint of her ankles peeked from just below her pale brown skirt hem.

"Miss Whitfield—" Butler began.

"Yes?" she replied innocently, drying her toes.

He licked his mouth. "I fear you might catch a chill from that wind advancing from the mountains."

"A valid concern, Mr. Butler. What do you suggest I do about the situation?"

With legs spread wide, he dangled his fists from his leather belt. "Wrap yourself up tight in your blanket. For the entire night. On the far side of the fire."

"But Mr. Butler! You've been entrusted with my care. Should I not sleep on the same side of the fire, that you might keep better watch over me? Something malevolent might . . . might *snatch* me."

He scowled at her. "Sleep wherever you feel safest, woman." He unrolled his own blanket and stretched out his raw-boned frame.

Rachel set out her blanket near his. She snuggled down atop its soft folds. "Good night, Mr. Butler."

"'Night," he muttered, rolling onto his side, away from her.

Tentatively, she reached toward Butler. Fingers shaking, in a featherlight gesture, she touched his back. Barely. A scant touch. He could easily choose to ignore it if he wished.

"Rachel," he growled.

"Yes?"

A hesitation. "Good night, Miss Whitfield."

She swallowed hard. "I . . . I'm cold, Jonah." She watched his chest rise and fall.

"Your blanket—"

"Does not stave off the chill night air. I shiver from the cold."

Oh, the cursed demon inside her drove her relentlessly on, casting out all of Old Eliza's cautions. The demon demanded warm male arms to enfold her against the night. Not just any arms. It had to be Jonah Butler's muscular embrace.

He rolled back to face her. He studied her silently. His intense gaze spoke of his own inner struggle as he drank in her petulant face and cascading hair. With one hand, he reached to stroke those curls of creamy fire.

"Come here, Rachel. Let me warm you."

Fetching her blanket with her, Rachel wriggled inside Butler's outstretched arms.

He scowled at her shining face. "This is purely an arrangement of convenience, Miss Whitfield, to stave off your death of cold."

"Oh, quite, Mr. Butler." She squirmed against his lanky body and yanked her blanket over the two of them.

"There shall be no kissing."

"Of course not, Mr. Butler. I understand perfectly."

"And no . . . What's that you're doing?"

"Just trying to borrow some extra warmth from you, Mr. Butler," she replied innocently. "The night grows cold."

He tucked the top blanket around her throat. Uneasily, he draped his arm over her petite frame. "There shall be no hugging. This . . . this is not an embrace."

Eyes shining as she lay beside him, Rachel looked up at his solemn face. "Of course not, Mr. Butler." Her hands probed the folds of his leather wamus for warmth as her legs pressed against his thighs.

His Adam's apple shifted.

"Are you warming yet, Miss Whitfield?"

She blinked at him. "Yes, Mr. Butler. Are you?"

Sweat beads formed along his brow. "Indeed, ma'am."

Reaching up to pat his jaw, she played with his stubble. "You need a shave, Mr. Butler."

He repositioned his legs.

"God, woman! I need . . ." He found her mouth and covered it with his own.

She slipped deeper inside his arms.

He pulled her tight against his work-hardened body.

The demon inside Rachel would not release her. It drove her on with bewitching urges. Try as she might, she could not summon up Old Eliza's cautionary words. With every ounce of her energy, she needed to feel all the roping curves of Jonah Butler's body.

She needed to taste him.

She kissed him back.

When his tongue probed inside her own mouth like an aggressive serpent in search of a victim, oh Lord, she welcomed the advance! Her tongue mated with his. A vibrant experience, new and exhilarating! She needed to share this sizzling new explosion of senses with only one man. The man she'd grown to love.

Jonah Butler.

Kissing her throat, he reached for the curve of her breast. His mouth delved below her kerchief, deep inside her shift, till he found her aroused nipples.

Her sighing moans drove him on. Clutching her tightly in his arms, he suckled her.

"Jonah, my darling!" she cried, frantic with joy at the feel of him touching her in new and exhilarating ways.

"From that first kiss, Rachel, back in Venango, I knew I had to kiss you again." He teased her earlobe with warm whispers. "Do you know, sweet Rachel, how difficult it was for me to keep my hands off you on this tortuous journey?"

She reveled in the feel of his mouth and tongue over her lobes, her face, her throat.

"Beast," she replied, kissing him back. "You showed me only your rope, not your desire."

He grinned. "I shall have to resurrect that rope, if only to keep you near my side for—"

She blinked innocently. "For what, Jonah?"

"This, my love."

Still fully clothed, he pulled her beneath him and pressed his bulk against her body.

She wove her fingers through his black hair and clawed at him in a frenzy of need. What could Old Eliza possibly have meant about pain from men? Rachel felt ready to explode with demand and ecstasy. The warm muscular feel of Jonah Butler's male body atop hers thrilled her more than she could ever have imagined.

"Rachel," he whispered, his mouth tasting her breasts, "sweet Rachel. Have you never had a man?"

She stroked his shoulders and clung to his neck. "Never. You shall have to teach me, dear Jonah."

Rolling off her and lying on his side, Butler propped his head on his fist. "A man grows hard for the woman he loves." He trailed her hand down his chest and belly.

She felt the emboldened bulge at his groin. Her fingers explored the leather-covered protrusion. "You mean this?"

He groaned at her gentle touch.

The wail of wolves echoed from the distant Blue Mountains. Pines rustled and bent low under assaulting night winds.

Ears cocked, Butler sat upright on the blanket and let out a long breath. "Lovely, innocent Rachel. 'Tis time for you to sleep."

She sat up beside him and stroked his stubbled face. "Jonah, I feel something strong and good for you."

He laughed harshly. "And I feel . . . ah, Rachel, the desire I have for you could crush mountains. But you were entrusted to my care."

"And so you have, Jonah! No man could have guarded my safety more diligently than you."

The noisy shimmer of trees stirred horses to

whinny. Their bells chimed softly, adding to the night symphony.

"More miles lay ahead before we reach Lancaster, sweet Rachel. Your pa relies on me to get you there safely, without wolves gobbling you up. Two-legged wolves as well as four-legged ones. Without any man—French or English—ripping off your clothes. Including myself."

Seated on the ground beside Rachel, Butler lit his pipe and drew deeply on the stem.

She watched the moon glow subtly illuminate his firm jaw profile. To argue with Jonah Butler was futile. To cross him was dangerous. To love him?

Ah, to love the brawny drover seemed most hazardous of all.

Eighteen

"Three horses need reshod, Miss Whitfield," Butler announced in Carlisle next morning, well before the morning sun topped an embracing arc of oaks and hickories. "Have a look around if you like, but don't stray far."

Rachel strolled the valley settlement, rimmed both north and south by mountains. Four main streets joined a center square, where a lime kiln fronted a stone quarry. A dozen English soldiers lounged about the blacksmith shop. Beyond crumbling ruins of a stockade, clustered Delaware and Shawnee Indians gestured animatedly with a handful of Tuscaroras.

Rachel sauntered past Carlisle's five houses and a log cabin courthouse, when a female voice chimed out.

"Alone on the trail with such a . . . a vigorous man?" A squat white-haired woman with an ample bosom frowned at Butler's robust figure propped against the doorway of Carlisle's smithy.

"You . . . you know Mr. Butler, ma'am?"

"Everyone hereabouts knows of Jonah Butler's reputation."

"His reputation?" Rachel gulped. She wanted to hear the woman's words. Yet didn't.

"Best Indian translator in the province, so the men tell me. You can stake a trade on Jonah Butler's word, so they say. No one else can bridge the gap between politicians in Philadelphia and backwoods Indians quite so well. But a hard-living man, no doubt about it, missy. And . . . you travel alone with him?"

Rachel nervously tidied her thick, honey-colored plaits. " 'Twas not my idea, madam, I can assure you. My pa gave me no choice in the matter of traveling with Mr. Butler."

"You poor dear!" she exclaimed, seizing Rachel by the elbow. "My name is Lizzy Nichols. Come inside my kitchen for a cup of tea and tell me all about your tribulations. Every sordid, er, trying detail."

"So you see, Mrs. Nichols," Rachel summarized, a short while later after divulging an edited version of her travel experiences, "Mr. Butler, being an old friend of my pa's, was a perfect gentleman on our journey."

"Yes," Lizzie Nichols replied, disbelieving. "So it would seem. Dreadfully unfortunate about your young Mr. Blaine. And having to leave your sweet little horse in Shippensburg."

Rachel paced the kitchen's naked wood floor. "Tom shall recover. He must! His sweetheart in Lancaster awaits him."

Lizzy offered Rachel a warmed tea biscuit. "I only hope your Mr. Blaine does not encounter a sinister threat in the area. We hear from the Shawnee that the Fox prowls somewhere in this valley, even as we speak. Though why, no one knows."

"The Fox!"

"Indeed, my dear. A vicious Frenchman who kills for his own cruel amusement. For no apparent reason. You know of him, then?"

"Only too well, I fear. He and his men assaulted my family at Venango."

"I daresay the wretch will not enter Carlisle." Lizzie puffed out her chest with pride. "We are the county seat, you know, of the new Cumberland County. We even hold court in the log building next door to my house!" She lowered her voice. "Except, that is, when Indians surge on the warpath."

"Warpath? Here?"

"I fear so, my dear. Carlisle lies directly on the *Great Trail*. Runs from Harris's Ferry to the Potomac. 'Tis a favored path of the Iroquois when they venture into the Carolinas to attack Cherokee and Catawba. And, I might add, when the Carolina Indians return the favor by dashing north to attack the Iroquois." Lizzie sighed. "A lovely town, all the same, my dear. Truly."

A two-year-old boy with a mop of unruly dark curls darted into the kitchen.

"Grandma!" he shouted to Lizzie, presenting her with a handful of goldenrod wands grown limp from his tight-fisted grasp.

"Lovely indeed, Daniel. Thank you, my pet," she cooed.

"A beautiful child, Mrs. Nichols," Rachel commented. "May I hold him?"

"Oh, indeed. He would love nothing more. If you're willing to tote him around, Daniel will give you a most amusing tour of Carlisle."

Enchanted, Rachel held out her hands to receive the boy. "Such an agreeable child. Daniel, how would you like to help me locate my guide, Mr. Butler?"

Clutching a pinch of gingerbread offered by his grandmother, the child nodded.

Lizzie Nichols faced her guests. "I suggest we search the stables first, Miss Whitfield. Unless your

Mr. Butler has gone someplace to slake his thirst, as men are wont to do."

Her Mr. Butler? Rachel liked the sound of those words more than she cared to admit. It could never be, of course. Jonah Butler belonged to no woman, least of all Rachel Whitfield. Shortly, they'd reach the Susquehanna River, where Rachel would launch her dash north . . . never to see the burly drover again.

Crossing Carlisle's town square, the three found Butler listening intently to a pair of Shawnee travelers. He saw the child cuddled in Rachel's arms and appeared to flinch. His tanned face grew somber.

"The horses are reshod, Miss Whitfield," he announced, his gruff voice sinking to a near growl. "In order to reach the Susquehanna by nightfall, we must ride at once."

An enigma was Jonah Butler, Rachel decided as she rode the pack train's end horse that afternoon. A womanizing brute who behaved as a gentleman alone with Rachel when he had every opportunity of acting otherwise. A brash, fierce man who treated humans and animals with tender compassion. A nonmarrying sort whose eyes misted when he beheld cherubic, cake-clutching little Daniel Nichols.

"I shall never understand you, Jonah Butler," she whispered, riding far behind him. "But after tonight, it matters not. I shall never see you again."

Munching one of Lizzie Nichols's cold biscuits on a rest stop, Rachel swung her gaze from flame-kissed September foliage on low hills . . . to Butler.

"Do you not like children, Mr. Butler?" she asked point-blank.

He scowled. "Why do you ask?"

"When you saw Daniel Nichols, the tyke in

Carlisle, you became almost . . . harsh. I thought perhaps you—"

He cut her off. "You were wrong, Miss Whitfield." He turned aside to retie a loosened bundle.

"You do not abhor small children?"

"I harbor no opinions one way or another regarding children." Dodging her questions, he worked at repairing a frayed leather strap.

Rachel gently stroked the white blaze on her horse's forehead. "You know, Mr. Butler, in Carlisle they spoke knowingly of the Fox. They suspect he currently lurks in these hills with his men. Why, they cannot imagine."

A small muscle in Butler's jaw tensed. He locked eyes with Rachel. "The Fox destroys women and children, Miss Whitfield. And slaughters men."

She fidgeted under his persistent gaze. "Why are you reminding me of this?"

He slid his arms around her waist and kissed her.

"Because, my dear Miss Whitfield, you must not entertain the notion that you can barter with this man for Zeb's life. You will surely lose your own in the process."

Silently she lingered against the warm, hard curves of Butler's lanky frame.

He nuzzled her throat. "Rachel?" An implied question. Butler stared unflinchingly at her. "The reason, Miss Whitfield, why you schemed to rescue Zeb."

"He's my bro—"

"The *reason,* Miss Whitfield. Try the truth this time."

Rachel's eyelids fluttered anxiously. "I owe Zeb a favor, Mr. Butler, just as you owed Pa one. Zeb saved my life when we were children. He nearly lost his own in the process. Foolishly, years ago, I disobeyed

Pa and went swimming in a deep and dangerous water hole."

"Zeb rescued you?"

"Yes. And near got swept away himself. I feared Pa might switch my behind if he knew. In return for Zeb's promise of silence, I told him if he ever needed my help, I would be there for him. I promised, Mr. Butler."

Avoiding the drover's stare and eluding his embrace, Rachel knelt to pluck a handful of purple asters. "A more delightful September afternoon I cannot imagine, Mr. Butler. The brilliant blue sky, music shared by a cheerful lark beneath swaying scarlet leaves, the scent of pale violet gentians."

He adjusted Rachel's saddle. "By tomorrow you shall have more time to enjoy the flowers."

"Why, sir?"

He directed her to mount up. "The blacksmith in Carlisle felt certain I could secure a new assistant at Harris's Ferry once we cross the river."

Their last day together alone. Likely their last night alone together, one way or another.

Feeling the easy sway of her horse beneath her, Rachel plotted her strategy. Tonight she would drug Jonah Butler with the last of her vine stem and leaves. She would slip north along the sprawling Susquehanna's west bank. And finally fulfill her promise to Zeb.

But never see Jonah Butler again?

Rachel squeezed her eyes shut. Tears slipped between her lids and spilled onto her cheeks. Pain caused by a man? *Emotional* pain? Was this what Old Eliza meant? The agony of a broken heart as a woman was torn from her sweetheart forever?

"God willing, Miss Whitfield," Butler proclaimed late that afternoon, "our last halt before the river."

"I was a child the last time I crossed the Susquehanna. We were all together then. Even Momma." Her gaze dropped to her hands. "Sometimes I feel so alone."

He stooped to pick a tattered daisy and presented it to her. "You are not alone now, Rachel. I shall watch over you till you rejoin your sister in Lancaster." He gently massaged her shoulder.

"You never speak of your own mother, Jonah. Or your father."

A thin veil crossed Butler's swarthy features. "Nothing to tell." He turned aside.

There was, of course. She knew it intuitively.

She placed a cautious arm on his leather sleeve. "In those handsome, shining dark eyes of yours, Jonah, lies a measure of sorrow."

He scoffed. "Your fertile imagination at work again, Miss Whitfield."

Her hand slid down to linger at his lean waist. "I am not easily fooled, Mr. Butler. Did your parents, whom you do not seem eager to rejoin, cause that hurt?"

His mouth twisted into a faint, crooked grin. "Persistent wench, are you not? Let us merely say that, in the past, my parents and I differed over several important life choices for me."

"Such as?"

He stroked her cheek. "Did I ever tell you that I struggle to discern whether your beautiful large eyes are predominantly green, or blue?"

He kept a great deal to himself, this brawny Pennsylvania fur trader, Rachel realized. If she stayed at his side beyond this day, she might learn more of his concealed past. But she could not. Must not. To live, Zeb Whitfield needed her assistance.

– And Jonah Butler was not the marrying sort.

He leaned close to her. His large hands cupped her face as he kissed her cheek.

Her fingers glided from Butler's waist to rest on his wide leather belt. The same belt that held his lethal weapons. Her fingers caught on a tiny pouch made of remarkably soft, thin leather tied to his belt.

"How exquisite!" she commented. "Never have I seen such finely worked leather. From afar I once saw you admire the pouch's contents."

Butler released Rachel and turned aside to busy himself with an unbalanced fur bundle.

On that last leg of their journey before the river, Rachel smelled the exhilarating nearness of water. Sedges and cattails lined side streams. Billowing clouds capped low hills. Pintail ducks quacked nervously under the watchful eyes of a peregrine falcon.

The Susquehanna River . . . this very night!

" 'Tis the point where I must drug you and flee north, Mr. Butler," she murmured as she rode. Her fingers probed inside her pocket for those last precious vine leaves. Hopefully, just enough herb to do the deed.

If she fled, she would never see Jonah Butler again.

"Fie!" she whispered, seeing river hills come into view. She'd fallen unexpectedly in love with the brash trader, knowing all the while that Zeb might die without her help. Indecision bound Rachel tighter than any rope ever could.

She glimpsed tantalizing hints of the broad river through breaks in blue hills. Butler gave a hand signal to halt.

"This is it, then," she whispered, dismounting with

a rustle to the ground. Her body quivered. Her hands shook. She nervously probed her pocket to affirm the presence of those ominous dried leaves.

After dark she would offer Jonah Butler the sinister tea.

Her fingers worked quickly to hobble each horse and loosen their bell clappers.

Butler curried the animals. "A respite from your labors tomorrow, Miss Whitfield," he called out.

Could the husky trader read her thoughts? "Why do you say that, Mr. Butler?"

"Tomorrow I'll hire a new assistant at Harris's post. Doubtless a young lad eager to earn a few coins."

She would never be alone with Jonah Butler again. Never.

Ladling steaming rabbit stew into wooden bowls, Rachel felt her entire body pulse. Her hands shook. She spilled soup in her trembling haste.

Butler caught at her hands. "You seem out of sorts tonight, Miss Whitfield. Have you unmentioned concerns?"

"'Tis nothing, sir."

"Nothing? Your hands tremble as if you'd seen a ghost. I shall do what I can to resolve whatever troubles you."

"You cannot!" she burst out. "That is—"

"Is it Tom's welfare that concerns you?"

"Yes! 'Tis it! Indeed, yes. I cannot bear the thought of poor Tom's suffering. Not knowing whether he lives or dies a miserable death."

"Dear Miss Whitfield, heart so full of tender compassion." He rubbed her palms.

Compassion? Ah, fie! If Butler only knew. Her intent was to drug him into a stupor this very night. Merciful heavens, this *very night!*

"A-and my poor little Sara. I miss her amusing little ways so. Her sweet, amiable shyness."

Butler's large hands slid further up Rachel's arms. "I shall do what I can, Miss Whitfield. Once across the river, I shall hire a runner to return to Carlisle. If Tom and your horse are healthy once more, they will be brought to you in Lancaster."

"Truly, Jonah? Oh, think how Tom's sweetheart will rejoice at the sight of him!"

"You must gird yourself for the possibility that neither Tom nor Sara . . . will have survived."

She nodded.

He kissed her in the dusky autumn evening, when soft breezes spoke of sedges and moist earth and rustling leaves. She watched him spin away to calm a restive gelding. Only a few more precious hours with Jonah Butler. The thought of never seeing him again tortured Rachel.

Where lay her duty? To her imprisoned brother? Or to the drover who'd stolen her heart?

At the sight of Butler, Rachel's eyes welled with tears of farewell. A towering urge rose inside her. She swallowed hard to contain that sense of urgency. She must not reach for Jonah Butler. *Must not!* Yet something fierce and driving throbbed an insistent message.

Touch him, it begged. *Kiss him. Have him! This very night!*

Rachel dabbed tears from her dampened cheeks. For one long moment of hesitation, she hugged herself hard and stared at the gently lapping Susquehanna.

Listening to water splash against earthen banks, she shuffled toward Jonah Butler.

She slid her arms around his waist and leaned her

head against his back, as she'd done when they rode together.

"I shall never forget you, Jonah Butler," she murmured.

"Nor I, you, sweet, lovely Rachel. When I return from Philadelphia—should I survive the mauling from those hostile politicians I am sure to receive—I shall attempt to visit you at your sister's home."

"Perhaps." Closing her eyes, she felt misty night air sweep across her face. "Kiss me, Jonah."

Surprised at her invitation, he turned around and reached for Rachel. His lengthy kiss stirred them both. He paused long enough to study her sparkling eyes.

"Seems like I best sleep on the opposite side of the fire from you tonight, Miss Whitfield."

"Much too lovely a night to sleep just yet, Jonah. Do you not agree? Come sit by the fire with me just for a while." She slapped at persistent insects. "Surely the flames will keep insects at bay . . . while we talk."

Talk quickly led to touch. And to lengthy kisses. Butler's tongue parted her lips. And probed. And tasted the silk of her cheek, the curve of her lobe, the angle of her throat.

Butler drew away. "Rachel, this cannot go on." His deep breaths sliced through the autumn night.

She traced the curve of his stubbled jaw with her sensitive fingertips, then trailed her hands down over the buckskin lacing of his shirt.

"No?"

"No, my beautiful temptress."

She planted a delicate kiss on Butler's mouth. "I love you, Jonah."

He seized her by the arms. "Rachel, there are things you do not yet understand about a man."

Enchanted by the moon, the river breezes, the velvet call of an owl, Rachel snuggled closer to Butler. "Tell me about them, Jonah."

He coughed. "In the interest of protecting you from your own impulses, Rachel, I shall attempt to do so. You see, when a man sees a beautiful woman such as yourself, he . . . that is, he becomes—"

"Yes?" Toying with tangled fringes on his shirt, she stroked Butler's arm.

He began again. "When a woman touches a man, as you're doing now, Rachel, he grows—"

Her eyelashes fluttered. "Yes, Jonah? Pray continue. I find this conversation most intriguing."

He bent down and kissed her mouth. His hands edged around her back, drawing her tight against him. When he broke off the kiss, her large misty-green eyes and saucy dimples undid his composure.

"Damn it, Rachel, when a beautiful woman plays with a man, he grows aroused."

"Aroused? Mercy, Jonah. What happens then?" Awaiting his reply, she slid her hands up over his shoulders.

He kissed her again, this time longer. He clasped her more tightly. His breathing grew uneven. "He kisses the woman, Rachel. Until he cannot stop."

"Cannot stop? How distressing, Jonah." Her fingers explored the tanned creases along Butler's jaw. "What does he do then?"

Nuzzling her ear, he playfully tugged the lobe with his teeth. "Sometimes he does things he later regrets."

Huddling beside the fire, she wriggled in his arms to eliminate all space separating Butler from her inquisitive body. "How positively dreadful, Mr. Butler. Such as what?"

She ruffled her fingers through his hair.

"Such as this."

Leaving no doubt of his intentions, Butler kissed her. This time he deepened the kiss with his tongue. Never removing his mouth from Rachel, he kissed her cheeks, then her throat. His forceful tongue probed and tasted below the edge of her shoulder scarf.

Moaning, Rachel sagged against Butler's chest. "'Tis not dreadful, Mr. Butler. 'Tis unharnessed joy."

He tipped her back till she reclined on her blanket. He lay beside her. "But an aroused man does other things as well, Miss Whitfield."

"More?"

"Much more." He leaned over her.

Reaching up for him, she framed his face with her cool hands. "I cannot imagine what else there might be, Mr. Butler."

Kissing Rachel, he liberated her from her scarf. And freed her breasts from her constraining corset and chemise. His strong hands warmed her nipples into rosy blooms. When he drew her onto her side and suckled lavishly, she gripped his shoulders.

"Oh, my dear Jonah!" she cried, clutching at his shirt. Frightening contractions, hot and sweet and insistent, tormented Rachel's belly. When his fingers found her pulsating moist cleft, she washed away on waves of ecstasy.

Her unrestrained sighs enflamed Butler. He guided her hand to the covered bulge at his groin.

"The difference between a man and a woman," she murmured, feeling the ridge of his hardened organ. Her curious fingers explored up and down its protruding length.

Butler groaned. "My dear Rachel, a man can only stand so much torment."

Wide-eyed, she watched him. "Does my touch bring you pleasure, Jonah?"

"Rachel, my love, your slightest touch rouses me to perilous heights." He rolled from her side and sat upright. He pulled a long, deep breath.

"Jonah?" she called softly, holding out her hand to him. "What is it?"

"You're a virgin, Rachel. And in my protective custody. 'Tis not right that I take you here and now."

Her eyes shone in the dark. "This night, out here under an autumn moon with breezes sighing through buttonwood trees? Jonah, my darling, this night is the most perfect night of all for you to teach me about love."

"I do love you, Rachel. That's the problem. I care what happens to you. Remember, my girl, I'm not the marrying sort. I don't want to hurt you."

Music to her ears, even if she never saw him again after tonight. "This night we shall remember for the rest of our lives, Jonah. Come to me, my darling." Still lying on her back, she reached up her arms to receive him.

His muscles rippled as he eased his body over hers.

Demanding what only Jonah Butler could give her, Rachel clawed at his broad neck and shoulders. His kisses, his warm precious touch, the weight of his rugged body atop hers scorched Rachel's senses to maddening heights. When he filled her with his stiffened manhood, she cried with delectable pleasure and pain all at the same time. Gently he stroked in . . . and out, till she shouted his name in sweet ecstasy.

When his warm release spilled inside her, Butler groaned in pleasure under the shadow of blue river hills.

She watched him sleep, late that night, as hickories

and hemlocks swayed in September gusts. She fingered the dried leaves concealed in her hip pocket.

Tomorrow at dawn she would drug Jonah Butler, before his river crossing.

Her glance returned to his sleeping form, then north in the hilly darkness.

Zeb Whitfield needed her help . . . the assistance she once promised him. But Zeb was a large, strong-fisted man. Perhaps he would find a way to free himself. Or had already done so. Rachel loved two men, in different ways. Which one, more than the other?

Staring at the crackling fire beneath an open sky, Rachel struggled between thoughts of her brother . . . and the man she'd grown to love.

Nineteen

Crisp morning rays pierced low-lying white mists near Chabert Michaux's failed campfire. He nudged his brother and their two Ottawa companions awake.

"Not a cloud in the sky, Philippe. A perfect day for us to claim our rightful treasure—the finest furs ever yielded by creatures of the Ohio Valley."

"Our rightful treasure? Some might dispute your words, Chabert."

"'Tis ours, I tell you! Jonah Butler owes me that, and a great deal more. He stole Collette, my woman, Philippe. Now I shall seize his furs . . . *and* his new woman. A fair trade, with interest, I should say."

Rubbing sleep from his eyes, Philippe seized a pumice stone and grinned. "I shall sharpen my weapon till it can fair slice through Jonah Butler's unsavory gut."

"Not too fast, however, *mon frère.* I should like his lovely lady to witness his slow disembowelment. The miserable wretch made love to Miss Whitfield last night, you know. Perhaps after wounding him, I shall cut off his prized member. In front of her."

Chabert tipped back his head and laughed, then abruptly muffled his outburst to avoid detection by his prey.

Philippe Michaux fingered his freshly honed knife.

" 'Twas fortunate that a rattlesnake waylaid Butler's assistant. Careless fool. That should make our takeover much easier."

"Oui. From the looks of Monsieur Blaine when we left him at Carlisle, he has not long to live. Such a pity." Flushed with a sense of imminent gain, Chabert Michaux chuckled.

"We have only Butler and his woman with which to contend. And she will be useless in his defense. Only Butler stands between us and those magnificent furs." Eager to set off, Philippe anxiously flexed his fists.

Chabert massaged the ache in his twisted hooked nose. "A reminder, Philippe. Everyone knows you are lethal with your knife. But do be careful around the woman. I want no harm to befall Miss Whitfield. Not yet, anyway." Chabert's fleshy tongue traced the sharp edges along his chipped front teeth.

"Whatever plans you devise for the woman, Chabert, make certain I get a turn with her as well."

"We both shall, *mon frère.* And every Indian who desires a turn with the wench. After all, we are generous men, Philippe, are we not?" He guffawed. "Then after we finish with her, we shall demand a king's ransom from her stubborn father."

"Magnifique, Chabert! You know, when Eli Whitfield's back was turned, I stole enough quick glances to know his warehouse overflows with crockery, iron, powder, salt, cloth—"

Chabert angrily silenced his brother with a wave. "Not merely an abundance of trade items, Philippe. *Quality* items. All due to those blasted British naval ships, I tell you! English traders can supply Indians with better trade offers than can the French for their furs. Damn them all! *Damn* them!" Angry red blotches enflamed the elder Michaux's cheeks.

"Calm yourself, Chabert. We are about to seize what is rightfully ours." Philippe rubbed the pumice stone one last time over his glistening knife edge— his weapon of choice.

"Oui, mon frère." Chabert pulled at his groin in eager anticipation. "Ahead of us shall soon lie one very dead English trader, one lively wench . . . and a wealth of the finest Ohio pelts."

Dousing the remnants of their fire, Chabert signaled to his Ottawa companions.

" 'Tis low, Jonah. I can tell by the tree line along the banks."

From beneath the brim of his rumpled hat, Butler glowered at the Susquehanna River. Exposed boulders revealed clear indications of recent drought. Shielding his eyes with his opened hand, he scanned the river's width. "No sign of Harris's ferry boat yet this morning."

With a consoling gesture at Butler's sleeve, Rachel stood in his shadow. "What if . . . what if he is not able to cross the river because of the drought?"

"We have no choice, Rachel. We wait here until he does come."

Gazing east across the river, Rachel's sharp eyes caught a flutter of movement far in the distance. "Jonah! See? Could it be . . . ?"

Butler grimaced. His equally sharp vision told him the truth. " 'Tis only heron fishing over the water."

"Have faith, Jonah. Such a glorious autumn morning! 'Twill be an auspicious day, I feel it in my bones."

He kissed the tip of her nose. "Do you now, luv? I am to trust your intuition?"

"Always, Jonah."

"Then I shall not need to tie my spare gun to your saddle?"

She laughed. "Now that we approach civilization, I shall have no need of your gun. Lizzy Nichols assured me that we would see many pack trains lining the river banks, especially on the east side."

"None here at present, though I see a cloud of dust farther down the Blue Mountains that likely signifies one is on its way from Ohio." He massaged her arm. "No regrets that we spent the night away from any settlers last night?"

"Regrets?" Rachel stood on tiptoe and kissed his mouth. "My only regret, Mr. Butler, is that the night ended so soon."

"Ah, woman, I have work to do. And your kisses divert my concentration."

"To what, Jonah?" she asked, feigning innocence.

He patted her bottom. "To recollections of a rousing night I shall never forget. I'm a man, luv. I need to forget you ride with me. Otherwise I ache to undo that corset of yours and—"

"Yes?" Smiling at Butler, she moistened her lips.

He shook his head. "Nay, you vixen. One more look at your saucy dimples and I shall forget my resolve. Best to check on those new horseshoes immediately before my hands rove to your soft white skin."

She watched him stride toward the restless horses. And silently cursed her fluid goals. Her love for Jonah Butler exploded all her objectives like tree pollen on a windy day.

"Very well, my darling Mr. Butler," she murmured

half aloud, out of his earshot. "I shall stay with you only until we cross the river. Then we shall part ways forever. You will have the assistance you need with the pack train. And I? Oh, Mr. Butler! I shall finally flee north as I intended all along."

The thought of leaving Butler for good after their passionate night together made Rachel cringe. Every fiber in her trembling body squeezed agonizingly tight.

Was *this* the pain Old Eliza alluded to?

"I shall miss you, my darling Mr. Butler, with all my heart and soul," she whispered, choking back tears.

She trudged toward her tail-swatting mount to adjust its bit. The beauty of that lush September morning made Rachel scan the Cumberland Valley, stretching to the west and south, for signs of approaching travelers.

None appeared.

Absentmindedly Rachel shifted her gaze north to a long ridge of the Blue Mountains bordering the valley. A flutter of color and movement caught her eye.

Another bird?

No creature in nature ever wore that precise shade of crimson, best as she could recall. Except man.

Tiny hairs on Rachel's neck stood on end. If only she still had her silver pendant! She clutched futilely at her naked throat where Old Eliza's protective necklace had once dangled.

"I'm being silly for naught," she chided herself.

If men approached, surely they were just friendly settlers. Or convivial traders. Or welcoming Indian acquaintances of Butler's.

"Yes. Surely 'tis all they are," she whispered, to comfort herself.

Still, she watched for further indications of human approach.

Some inexplicable urge made her reach for Tom Blaine's Pennsylvania rifle, still tied to her saddle. "I'm being foolish, I know," she murmured. Butler would be back within sight momentarily. Seeing his reassuring presence, she would laugh about her consternation and—

A gleam of silver mirrored on the ridge caught Rachel's eye.

Suddenly, a flash of fire erupted from that same wooded ridge. A shot!

Before Rachel could scream, she heard Butler's horse squeal. Furiously she grabbed black powder and ball, loaded her long rifle, then returned the ramrod to its place under the gun stock.

Shouldering the gun, she dashed toward Butler.

A crimson stain oozed from the back of his shirt as he ducked low and loaded his rifle.

Two more shots rang out from the wooded ridge.

No time, now, for Rachel to ask why anyone would want to shoot Butler. Or both of them. *Why* was unimportant when guns continued firing at them. Butler needed her help!

Despite her rifle's weight and her professed lack of skill, Rachel hoisted the heavy gun into position and fired in the attacker's direction.

Branches rustled in a flurry of activity up on that hostile ridge. As if men scurried, perhaps even battled one another. While she struggled to reload, Butler squeezed off a shot.

"Hold your fire, Jonah!" A voice called out.

Butler blinked in disbelief. "'Tis . . . 'tis Swift Otter!" he bellowed.

Waving his arms, the half-breed Indian emerged

from a tree line into the open valley. "They fled, Jonah. My friends chased them off. A blotch of blood signified that you wounded at least one of them."

Butler lowered his smoking rifle. "You saved my life, friend."

Swift Otter smiled. "A fair turn, Jonah, for all you've done for me and my family."

"Then you followed us all the way from Ohio?"

"Not you. We followed the Fox, to see what he intended this far east."

"The Fox?" Rachel's hand flew to her gaping mouth. "Was it he who attacked us?"

Swift Otter nodded. "Yes."

"And he fled?"

"With his men."

"Oh, mercy! How I wish I could have spoken with him. 'Twas he, that same evil man, who seized my poor brother!"

"You may yet be given that chance, Miss Whitfield," Swift Otter replied. "The Fox never gives up. Unless he's now dead, he will not rest till he comes after you again."

"Jonah!" Rachel cried suddenly, catching sight of the spreading crimson ooze on Butler's shirt. "We must tend you at once." She raced to his side.

Swift Otter watched her tug off Butler's bullet-torn garment. "The coward's way." He spat out his words. "Shooting a man in the back. You never had a chance, Jonah."

"He meant to kill you, Mr. Butler," Rachel murmured, kneeling on bent grass beside Butler to dress his fresh wound. "Not just wound you. But why? Why would a Frenchman want to destroy you? Would he go to all this trouble just to keep you from reaching Philadelphia?"

Swift Otter's gaze shifted from Butler's eyes to Rachel's confused, upturned face. At a nod from Butler, he remained silent.

"I suspect so, Miss Whitfield," Butler solemnly commented, wincing as Rachel probed his wound.

Finished cleansing, she bound his naked shoulder with torn strips of her apron. "Heaven has seen fit to spare you once more, Mr. Butler. The bullet seems to have deflected off the angle of your shoulder. Apparently you shall live to become a moving target once again."

Rachel's jovial tone belied her true concern. She frowned at Butler's pallor.

"Can you ride, Jonah?" Swift Otter asked.

Butler snorted. "The only time I shall not be able to ride is when I lie cold and dead."

"Which may happen sooner than you think, Mr. Butler, at the rate you're going!" Rachel exclaimed. "I shall shortly have no apron left with which to bind your numerous wounds."

Swift Otter pointed east across the shallow, sprawling Susquehanna. "Prepare to ride then, friend, for the ferry is on its way."

"Hallelujah!" Rachel cried, whirling to see for herself.

"My friends shall watch over you till your pack train is safely across the river."

Butler reached to shake the Lenape's hand. "I am indebted to you. When I return, I shall have gifts for you."

"Many times have we protected one another's backs, Jonah. I look forward to your return. You know where to find me."

"Please," Rachel begged of Swift Otter. "I, too, am

immensely grateful for your help. But I have one additional favor to ask of you."

"Ma'am?"

Rachel nervously twisted her fingers. "I beg of you, sir, in your travels, have you heard any news of Zeb Whitfield, my brother?"

The half-breed shook his head.

"He was captured by the Fox in May of this year. Zeb might be dead. But I choose to believe he's being held in some French prison, possibly in Montreal."

Again, Swift Otter shook his head.

Rachel's shoulders sagged. "Thank you all the same, Swift Otter."

"I have heard nothing of Zeb Whitfield's whereabouts, ma'am. But the woods have ears. I shall listen for news of your brother."

She brightened. "Thank you, indeed!"

On the Susquehanna's knobby-hilled eastern shore, a cacophony of noise, commotion, and dust greeted Rachel and Butler. More than two dozen pack trains shuffled along deeply rutted mud trails. Men shouted at yapping dogs and frisky horses. Women fretted over children and uncertain futures. And tiny black gnats made victims of them all.

Rachel found a brief moment alone with the trader. "Forever after, I shall keep a gun at my side, Jonah Butler," she declared.

He smiled at her fortitude. "I tremble at the thought, ma'am."

"Jest if you like, sir, but I feel I must join your legion of protectors and watch over you. Binding your wounds has become something of a habit for me."

"I need you for more pressing urgencies, Miss

Whitfield," he whispered for her ears alone. His knuckle gently nudged her chin.

"Jonah, by tomorrow at the latest we shall part in Lancaster. H-how will I know you have properly healed?" She toyed with the remnants of her apron.

"Thanks to your tender ministrations, I shall heal perfectly."

His words failed to convey the meaning she sought.

"But I shall not know, you see, Mr. Butler. Your present pallor alarms me. Will you . . . revisit Lancaster upon your return from Philadelphia? Solely, of course, to inform my family of your rejuvenated health and success upon completion of your mission?"

She longed to slip inside Butler's strong arms. Not possible, of course, with numerous drovers and settlers bustling around them. Just then, Butler's boisterous new assistant, Will, pumped Butler's hand and introduced himself.

Riding southeast toward Lancaster, Rachel's head spun with confusion. Nothing about this journey had evolved as she'd expected. Nothing at all. Leaving her pa back in Turtle Creek, she had instantly despised Jonah Butler for his audacity. And feared his touch at the same time.

She had even feared Tom Blaine—yet the lad could not have been kinder to her. Now Blaine lay near death. Or gone, poor soul, without ever saying farewell to his sweetheart.

Somewhere in their perilous trek across those Endless Mountains, Rachel had fallen desperately in love with burly Jonah Butler. And at every turn, at every opportunity to dash toward her brother, Rachel had chosen the brash trader instead of Zeb. What sort of madness had swept over her?

Would Butler ever return to her lonely arms?

Someone in addition to his parents awaited Butler in Philadelphia. A woman, no doubt, given Butler's illustrious history of bedding women. A woman he appeared reluctant to see. Given the chance, however, that same woman might work at dazzling Butler with her affection. She would offer him kisses. Warm embraces. Perhaps even naked passion between sheets.

Riding one horse behind Butler now, as their pack train hugged the Susquehanna, Rachel marveled at his lovemaking the previous night. He'd carried her to the heights of bliss. Now, he was about to ride out of her life. Perhaps forever.

A dreadful sorrow constricted Rachel's throat. The pain that men caused? 'Twas *heartbreak*. Reaching for her missing silver pendant, Rachel began to understand the wisdom of Old Eliza's words.

Coarse, dark-brown hair dangled loose over Chabert Michaux's forehead as he shoveled the last scoop of earth over his brother's grave.

"Farewell, Philippe," he growled, moist-eyed. Chabert gulped a fiery shot of Monongahela whiskey before slumping to the ground.

His two Ottawa companions held out their hands for a drink.

"A short one, only!" he bellowed at them. "We cannot afford to become drunk. We have work to do."

"You said we would return to the Ohio after attacking Butler."

Michaux's head jerked up. "Fools! I thought the outcome would be far different. Now Butler rides off with only a slight wound, and Philippe lies dead in his grave, poor bastard. I have added reason to kill that rogue trader."

The shorter Indian braced the air with his hand. "But Butler's gun did not kill Philippe."

Michaux's eyes widened as he contemplated the shaven-headed Indian. "What do you mean, monsieur?"

"I saw it clearly. The woman fired the lethal shot. The one that hit Philippe. He was down before Butler even fired."

"You mean . . . Mademoiselle Whitfield killed my brother?"

Both Indians nodded.

Michaux's eyelids formed harsh slits. "Bitch!" He uncoiled himself from the ground and paced between two inclines matted with trampled cohosh. "I shall add this to her torment. When I finally get my hands on that woman, she will pay in too many ways to count."

"Do as you like. We shall return to Presque Isle."

"But you cannot, *mon ami!* I shall need your assistance. I can make it worth your while to stay with me."

"How? You lost Butler's furs."

Michaux stroked his grizzled chin, then reached for the silver pendant dangling from his throat. "I have other means. When we capture the Whitfield woman, one of her relatives will pay a costly ransom for her return. Or perhaps Butler will pay himself." Michaux managed a flinty smile at the thought.

"To attempt seizing her amid all those pack trains between Harris's Ferry and Lancaster is madness," the taller Ottawa asserted.

"We are not mad, messieurs. We are clever. We

shall calmly wait till Mademoiselle Whitfield reaches Lancaster. Then we shall trick her into leaving town with us. I know just the way to do it. Oh, by God, that little bitch will pay exorbitantly for her sins!"

Twenty

Dust clouds swirled above pack trains passing one another along the Susquehanna's eastern bank. Dogs yipped and darted among countless horse legs. Leather whips cracked, horses reared, babies squalled, men shouted. The damp smell of river air pungent with hints of decayed fish and sodden vegetation settled along the riverbank.

After long days on lonely mountain trails, Rachel goggled at all the noisy clamor.

Riding south and east, just one horse behind Butler as he followed the river, she watched the drover forlornly. "I shall never be alone with you again, my darling," she murmured under her breath.

Plodding horses splashed diamonds of water as Butler's pack train rode across Swatara Creek. At a boisterous roadside inn, aromas of fried bacon and warm coffee hung on the air. Butler paused to rest the horses.

Gusts tore at Rachel's apron and pale brown skirt as she dismounted. "The clouds, Mr. Butler," she commented, pointing overhead. "A fair storm brews."

They ate deer and wild duck at the inn. Out by the dooryard, a young boy played his violin while a grizzled old wheelwright blew on a dented harmonica.

Sharp whip cracks and noisy male curses caused

Butler to glance up from his mug of cider. Pulling in
to the roadside inn, a half dozen horses flinched at the
impatient whip hand of their driver.

Disgusted, Butler spat on the ground.

"Sad, indeed," Rachel whispered to Butler. "Those
poor animals wince at the crack of his whip. They
fear their driver."

"Aye. 'Tis no credit to a man when his animals
cower before him." He glared at the drover, who disappeared inside the inn.

Swallowing the last of his cider, Butler strode toward the quivering lead horse. He stroked the
animal's shoulder and spoke in low tones. Instantly,
the horse calmed.

Butler's new young assistant, Will Groff, leaned toward Rachel. "Mr. Butler has a way with animals,
miss, does he not?"

Contemplating horses munch their corn and oats,
Rachel tried not to smile. "Indeed. And with people
as well."

When Butler ambled back to Rachel's side, a tiny
boy with thick dark hair stumbled past the trader. Butler paused. He stared hard at the child.

Rachel caught sight of Butler's haunted expression.

His breathing seemed to shift. His sizable hands
opened and clenched as he watched the giggling child
toddle away from its mother. Butler's thumb massaged the small leather pouch dangling from his belt.

Rachel found his reaction puzzling. "Beautiful
child," she commented to the drover when he reached
for another mug of cider.

He nodded. "Aye."

"Healthy and bouncing, so like little Daniel, back
at Carlisle." She studied Butler's inscrutable mien.

"He shall not remain healthy for long if he toddles

before onrushing teams," he growled. Butler scooped up the child from the dust-choked road as another team galloped toward them.

The gleeful boy nestled against Butler's sturdy shoulders. For one long moment the two leisurely contemplated one another.

Rachel approached them with a smile. " 'Twould seem, Mr. Butler, that you not only have a way with horses but with children as well."

He quickly handed the child off to its mother. "An amiable child, 'tis all," he replied, brushing off his words with a cough.

Three friendly drovers circled Butler.

"You shall have need for all your charms shortly, Jonah," one declared. "Convincing those bloody Philadelphia politicians to send guns and men out to the Ohio? A chore indeed."

"Aye," a second agreed, puffing on his charred clay pipe. "They close their ears when it comes time to arming frontiersmen."

A third clapped his beefy chapped hand on Butler's back, forcing the wounded trader to wince. "But if any man can make 'em sit up and listen in Philadelphia, 'twould be Jonah Butler, eh, men?"

Dark crimson oozed over the shoulder of Butler's linen shirt.

"Bloody hell, Jonah!" the first bellowed. "What in Gawd's name happened to ye?"

"The Fox shot Mr. Butler," Rachel offered. "In the back, mind you." She tightened Butler's dressing to staunch the fresh bleeding.

"Bastard!" the second drover exclaimed. "Meant to kill ye, he did, Jonah. Lucky ye survived. That damned varmint sneaks through the mountains at will. We shall all have to watch our backs from now on, I fear."

Will Groff, Butler's gangly new hire, dashed up to the group. "Mr. Butler! The smith said your horses have been reshod, sir."

Eyeing the impending storm, Butler upended his pipe. "Time to move on, then."

Rachel sidestepped several free-ranging chickens. "While you men recheck the loads, Mr. Butler, I shall barter for some venison and bread for the last leg of our journey." She hastened along the worn mud path leading to the inn's front door.

The second drover drew hard on his pipe. "Fine-looking woman, that," he said in Rachel's direction. "You thinkin' of marryin' her, Jonah?"

Butler scowled. "Do I look like the marrying sort?"

"You were at one time."

"No more. A woman needs a man to watch over her. I don't stay in one place long enough for that."

"Hell, Jonah, we all have wives back east. No reason you can't too. Unless you've grown buck-shy." He winked at Butler. "Or unless the lady won't have you." He cackled mischievously.

"She's the daughter of Eli Whitfield, you old nosy fart, and even less interested in marriage than I. My job is to guide her to her sister's home in Lancaster."

"Nothin' more?"

"Nothing!" Butler insisted.

"Eli? Fine man, yessir. Good bloodlines, there, Jonah. And your job was just to . . . guide her over the mountains?" The drover laughed, then spat on a grass mound. "You're blind as a bat, Jonah. That little filly looks at you with a special twinkle in her eyes. Maybe it's time you rethink your marryin' ways."

"Maybe it's time you tend your horses, you pathetic old goat, and stop bleating about romance where there is none." Butler's teasing was good-humored but firm.

He strapped food supplies to Rachel's horse and offered her a lift to remount.

"Your wound, Mr. Butler—" she fretted.

"Shall be fine, Miss Whitfield. With you riding immediately behind me, I know my back will be well guarded."

She lowered her voice. "Please, Jonah, do let Will handle most of the lifting. At least till your wound stops oozing."

Managing a crooked grin, he evaded her query and mounted his own lead horse.

With a crisp autumn wind at his back and a storm confronting him, Butler thanked providence he could not see Rachel Whitfield as he rode. In warm breezes of daylight and chill darkness of night, she lingered in his mind. Tart, shapely, determined Rachel. No woman had ever aroused all his senses like saucy Rachel Whitfield, with her eyes the color of a forest mountain, her hair shining and full of fire, her skin softer than a lamb at birth.

Even poor Collette had never roused him to this height of agitation.

But marriage?

Lord, no! Not until Butler built up a solid trading empire that ran from Lake Erie all the way out to Illinois. Not until he settled his personal score with sinister Chabert Michaux. Not until . . . until he could outrun the sorrow that stalked him day and night.

Butler fingered the small, finely worked leather pouch dangling from his belt.

To accomplish all those things, he first had to convince Philadelphia politicians of the French menace creeping down the Allegheny River.

Marriage? Bound to one lone woman with an invisible rope thicker than any man-made hemp? Butler could not allow such an encumbrance.

Furious winds clawed at the fringed wamus he wore over a linen shirt. He glanced overhead at boiling navy blue clouds.

In a few short hours, he would deposit Rachel Whitfield with her sister and never see her tormenting smile again.

"How strange, Jonah, to finally be free of the pack animals."

Rachel tied her horse's reins to a hitching post in front of the three-storied Boot and Crown Inn, next midday, and circled her gaze around Lancaster's center square.

"A good deal," Butler commented, regarding the sale of his fur and ginseng packs at a Lancaster warehouse. "Now, some warm food, Miss Whitfield. Then we shall locate your sister."

She dabbed at her rain-soaked, muddy clothes. "The town has changed so, since I was a child. So many more people and buildings! And do look at the mix of dwellings."

On four main streets, story-and-a-half chinked log buildings predominated. A few half-timbered log dwellings, built in the Germanic style, stood out with their steeply pitched roofs and attractive angled beams. An occasional brick or stone dwelling broke the monotony.

"Your sister might not recognize you," Butler commented, biting into hot corn and chicken pie at a small table fronting the inn's fireplace.

"Nor I, her, Jonah. Eight years ago she married George Howard, a wealthy businessman here in town. She's a fine lady now. Oh, Jonah, perhaps she will not want me to stay with her! Pa insisted I come, but mayhap—"

He placed a calming finger to her lips. "All will be well. But whether you continue at your sister's house or not, promise me, fair Rachel, that you will remain here in town."

Her eyes peeped over her cider mug at Butler. "Whatever do you mean, Jonah?"

"I know you all too well, my girl. That feigned innocence may fool others, but not I. No dressing as a boy and slipping north to Montreal. Or dressed as a girl, for that matter, with your fetching appearance."

"Why, Jonah! I blush at your insinuations. Truly I do. I shall amuse myself within the confines of my sister's elegant drawing room. If she'll have me, that is."

Rachel picked nervously at the pie's flaky top crust.

He enveloped her two hands in his own. "No man alive knows Pennsylvania's back hills better than Swift Otter. If there's any news about Zeb, he'll learn of it."

She evaded his questioning stare.

"Rachel?"

She turned aside to inquire of the innkeeper directions to Sukey's house.

With Jonah Butler at her side, Rachel hesitated before a finely built two-story brick house with sash windows. She raised her tense fist to tap on the carved oak door.

A servant girl, wiping her hands on a long white linen apron, whipped open the door. She blocked access to a polished central hallway. "Yes?" she asked, appraising the unrefined, mud-streaked couple standing before her.

"Might this be the home of George Howard?" Rachel inquired.

"Yes."

Rachel choked back an exuberant shout. "Please, miss, tell Mrs. Howard that her sister, Rachel, has arrived all the way from our father's Turtle Creek trading post to visit her."

The skeptical maid hesitated. "Please wait outside, ma'am. I shall inform Mrs. Howard of your arrival." She closed the door firmly in Rachel's face.

Curtains fluttered inside tall front windows apparently pried open to admit warm September breezes.

After what seemed an eternity, Rachel heard stiff skirts rustle through a hallway. Then an impatient yank on the front door, which flew open under the barrage.

"Rachel! Merciful heavens! I scarcely believe my eyes!" Susannah Howard swept her younger sister into her arms and squealed with delight. "Come in at once. You and your husband must be exhausted from such an arduous journey."

She drew back to view her visitors.

"Sukey, Mr. Butler is not my husband."

Sukey Howard smiled mischievously. "No?"

"No. I am not married. Mr. Butler is a frontier trader with his own packhorses. Pa collared him to escort me east, to you. You know how bothersome Pa can be."

"Indeed! You must come sit down and tell me why Pa would insist on such a thing. Anna?" Sukey

Howard clapped her hands for the maid's attention. "Kindly fetch refreshments into the drawing room for my sister and Mr. Butler."

"But, Sukey, we have labored on the trail for days. We shall soil your lovely—"

Sukey clasped her sister's hands. "I shall hear none of it, Rachel, dear heart. You simply cannot imagine how overjoyed I am to have you here with me."

Situating her two guests around a dainty piecrust table, Sukey Howard poured tea and sliced apple cake for them. "Forgive me, Mr. Butler. I have chattered on without giving you a chance to speak. Perhaps you could tell me why Pa felt it so urgent for Rachel to leave the frontier."

"To save her life, Mrs. Howard." Butler swallowed tea from a creamware cup.

"You make it sound so dire. Why ever so?"

Rachel set down her teacup. "Surely you heard the news that Frenchmen captured Zeb?"

"Well, yes, we received word of that assault. But that happened farther up the Allegheny River, did it not? At Pa's old Venango post?" Sukey Howard dabbed at her mouth with an ivory-colored linen napkin.

"The French army is pushing south along the Allegheny River, Mrs. Howard."

Sukey blanched. "South, Mr. Butler? Toward Pa, you mean? Whatever for?" She tipped a silver teapot to refill Rachel's cup.

"Toward the Ohio Valley, Mrs. Howard. Though they tell the Indians otherwise, they mean to seize control of the river clear to the Mississippi."

"They secretly plan to build a French fort at the Ohio forks, Sukey."

"But how dreadful! What of the British traders out

there?" A slow measure of ominous comprehension flooded Sukey's rouged cheeks.

Butler shifted his long legs. "I feel certain the French mean to drive them east, Mrs. Howard. Or kill every English trader they encounter."

"Mr. Butler is headed directly to Philadelphia to alert the governor and the Pennsylvania Assembly, Sukey. As for me, Pa distrusted the way Frenchmen . . . contemplated me."

"I see. So he convinced you to ride east with Mr. Butler."

Rachel giggled. "In a manner of speaking, Sukey. You know how backwoods-brusque Pa can be, especially since I did not want this particular journey."

"Indeed. I owe my marriage to Pa's implacable determination. Let me guess." Sukey folded her hands on the lap of her floral-print silk gown and chuckled at her guests. "He shackled you to Mr. Butler's side."

She surveyed her guests' embarrassment. Her chin sagged. "You . . . you mean he did?"

Rachel nodded. "Precisely, I fear."

"But how did you tolerate this affliction, my dears?" Through narrowed lids, Sukey Howard dragged her gaze from her demure sister to the broad-chested figure of Jonah Butler.

"I confess, Sukey, those first few days I longed to kill Mr. Butler."

"And . . . you, Mr. Butler?"

"I fear my sentiments toward Miss Whitfield were much the same. At first."

"And later? After you had traveled together for several days?"

Rachel coughed quietly. "We . . . we managed to work out our differences. We reached an equitable arrangement."

At those words Butler eased his burly frame to a standing position. "Thank you for your kindness, Mrs. Howard. I have imposed on your hospitality long enough, ma'am. Now that Miss Whitfield is safely in your hands, I shall find lodging for the night and seek a fresh horse for tomorrow's ride."

Sukey Howard looked aghast. "But Mr. Butler, you cannot! Indeed, not after your long, arduous journey with my sister. To leave now . . . it simply would not be proper."

"Ma'am?"

The front door opened and banged shut. Male footsteps clattered through the hallway toward Sukey Howard's elegant front parlor.

Twenty-one

"My dear Mrs. Howard, where are you? Have you everything in readiness for tonight?" Shuffling foot noises followed a bang of the front door.

"In the parlor, Mr. Howard," Sukey replied, lowering a silver fork onto her creamware plate. Ecru lace on her white lawn cap shimmered as she rose stiffly to greet her husband. "We have guests, sir."

"Guests? Already?" George Howard scuttled into the parlor.

Slight, pale, and wearing an enormous cadogan wig above a fine-tailored silk suit, Howard frowned at the hulking frontiersman and mud-speckled maiden in tattered clothes lounging in his home.

Sukey extended her arm by way of introduction. "My dear sister, Rachel, has been escorted all the way across the Endless Mountains by the kindness of Mr. Jonah Butler. Such wonderful news, do you not agree, sir?"

Howard pondered his two casually dressed guests. His nose wrinkled, as though he had been forced into the presence of foul-smelling social inferiors. "Charming," he commented in clipped, dry tones.

"So I am insisting that they both attend our soirée tonight."

George Howard's head jerked up. His eyes bulged.

"But is that wise, my dear? Surely their journey tired them."

"We shall of course forgive them if they retire early, Mr. Howard. But they will enjoy greeting your business associates. And certainly the townsmen will relish hearing all their tales of French intrigue along the frontier, for they have news to impart, Mr. Howard, that will impact your business."

At those words, Howard hesitated.

"Anna?" Summoning her maid, Sukey reached for her sister. "Anna will help you bathe and dress for tonight, Rachel. You can wear one of my gowns. And I imagine Mr. Butler—"

"I must immediately visit the livery stable, ma'am, to secure a suitable horse for tomorrow," he replied.

Sukey nodded. "After that, I highly recommend the Black Swan Inn, on the square. Smythe, the proprietor, will provide you with comfortable lodging."

"And assist you in purging yourself of road dust, I might add." Eyebrow upraised, George Howard dabbed at an imaginary lint speck on his fastidious garments as he contemplated the burly packhorse drover standing in his immaculate parlor.

"But I must insist, Mr. Butler," Sukey continued, following him to the door, "that you return and let us properly thank you for protecting my sister. Dinner at six o'clock, sir, followed by an evening of music and conversation."

Pausing at the front door, Butler silently glanced over his shoulder at Rachel.

She saw reflections of rich brown earth and moonless, love-filled nights in his dark eyes. Feeling as though her soul had been wrenched from her body, Rachel watched Butler mount his weary horse and ride off.

Sukey clapped her hands together jubilantly, before leading her sister toward the hall stairs. "Oh, Rachel! You could not have picked a finer day to arrive. We shall have an exciting evening party."

"Have you not a multitude of tasks in preparation?"

"Indeed, Rachel. But you can help me. After we get you changed, that is. Then tomorrow, I want to hear all about your exciting adventures."

Upstairs, Anna scrubbed Rachel's back while Sukey Howard disappeared into another room. A wardrobe door opened and closed. Shortly, a noisy rustle of fabric signaled her return.

"I think this green silk will be perfect for Rachel. What do you think, Anna?" Sukey held up an emerald silk gown with pleated sleeve cuffs of pale yellow-on-green brocade.

"Oh, yes, ma'am! Perfect with her eyes and hair."

"Mm-hmm. This gown should certainly catch your Mr. Butler's eye. And you shall have pearls. And a painted fan for flirting, of course."

Rachel endured Anna's dressing assistance. "Sukey! You misunderstand! He is not my Mr. Butler."

"No? Well, he will be, Rachel, dear, after he sees you in this gown."

"He leaves for Philadelphia tomorrow, Sukey. Likely I shall never see Jonah Butler again."

Sukey Howard blocked her hands on her slender hips and laughed. "Oh, my dear little sister! I saw that amorous expression in Mr. Butler's eyes when he bid you farewell this afternoon. A look that cannot be mistaken."

"Bosh! His eyes spoke only of a man concerned about obtaining a fresh horse and a soft bed."

"A horse and a bed? Dear sister! 'Tis clearly time

for a lecture from your married sister on a man's intentions. Though I have not sufficient time to educate you the same day as Mr. Howard's party, we shall definitely schedule some women's talk for tomorrow."

Rachel contemplated her outspoken sister. "Sukey, you will not embarrass me tonight with such comments in front of Mr. Butler?"

Experimenting with a new hairdo, Sukey lifted several locks of Rachel's freshly washed hair. "I shall restrain my forthright nature tonight, dear. I would never do anything to embarrass you. But I tell you of a certainty, if ever a couple seemed more in love than you and Jonah Butler, I have yet to meet them."

"Sukey!"

"And when the two of you are ready, you will indeed marry one another."

"Sister! You grow more outrageous by the minute. Jonah Butler, a rogue with no inclination to settle for one woman, leaves town tomorrow. And I shall—"

"Yes?"

Rachel bit her tongue. She could not tell Sukey of her own plan to bolt north the minute Butler left town. For now, that audacious scheme must remain a well-kept secret.

"And I shall . . . be so busy listening to your countless absurd tales that I shall have no time, or interest, in any man."

Sukey tipped back her well-coiffed head and laughed heartily. "Ah, what an evening we are about to have!"

A tall case clock chimed the hour in a downstairs hallway.

Sukey whirled from the guest bedchamber. "I must attend to some details, Rachel. When you finish dressing, Anna will do your hair."

Staring in a Philadelphia Chippendale mirror, Rachel watched Anna labor over her hair and felt strangely bereft. Aching. Dreadfully lonely.

And Rachel knew why.

Her pain was caused by a man, as Old Eliza had warned. The pain of loving one man with every particle of her being and watching him walk out of her life. Even for one afternoon.

Rachel studied her mirrored reflection as Anna finished lacing several ribbons through her new hairstyle. Against Rachel's better judgment, she reached for a tiny rouge pot and dabbed pink onto her cheeks. A ridiculous gesture. Butler would not notice her appearance. His mind dwelt on politics. On reaching Philadelphia with ominous news of French aggression. On obtaining the best price for his pelts.

He would not notice.

"Still . . ." Rachel murmured. She dabbed another sweep of rouge on her cheeks.

Violin music played softly in the background that evening as platters of veal and ham and chicken in red wine sauce magically appeared from the kitchen.

Rachel watched impatiently for Butler's arrival, as if she had not seen him in a dozen years. Peeking out the Howards' front window, she scanned Orange Street.

"Look at her, Anna," Sukey teased, at her sister's back. "Anxiously awaiting her sweetheart."

"Sukey, you are impossible!" Rachel blustered. "And indeed you err. All this traffic is a novelty for me, 'tis all."

"Traffic, eh? Indeed, Rachel, dear." Sukey's laughter pealed down the center hallway as she darted off to inspect food preparations.

In the midst of guest arrivals, Rachel nearly overlooked Butler's approach, so altered was his appearance.

He wore a dark blue silk suit with a tan waistcoat and breeches, over a white shirt and stockings. Gold buttons and trim edged his fine garments. Clean-shaven, wearing a powdered wig caught back with a black silk tie, Butler scarcely resembled the primitive pack drover of a few hours ago.

Rachel quickly turned aside from the window and pretended indifference to Butler's arrival. She feared betraying herself. If she gazed on his handsome, resolute figure, he might detect her profound longing for him. Worse, she might beg him to stay.

Jonah Butler. Not the marrying sort. Not a man capable of abiding with only one woman.

"Good evening, Miss Whitfield."

Hearing that deep, rusted voice at her back, Rachel squeezed her eyes closed and trembled. She drew a long breath, then turned to face him.

She blinked at the sight of his polished, elegant figure. "Good evening, Mr. Butler. You look so . . . different. Never since I met you have you looked so much the gentleman."

"'Tis a merry charade, ma'am. You know me better than most. A rogue scoundrel is what you called me. A rogue scoundrel is what I am." Contemplating Rachel's refined appearance, Butler's dark eyes sparkled. A crimson glow ascended his throat.

"A scoundrel does not show compassion for his animals, or for children, as you've consistently done, Mr. Butler. A scoundrel does not minister so kindly to his apprentices, as you've done."

He scanned her beauty with obvious appreciation. "But a scoundrel does tie up his comely hostage and not permit her ever to escape."

Rachel vigorously exercised Sukey's painted fan. "Jonah, at some point, I realized I—"

"Attention, everyone!" Sukey Howard shouted above the commotion. "Dinner is ready. Kindly find your seat, please."

By a strange coincidence, Rachel found herself seated next to Jonah Butler at Sukey's long dinner table—obviously one of Sukey's ploys.

A prominent Lancaster merchant, across the table, peered above his spectacles. "Mr. Butler, a pleasure to finally meet you, sir. Only yesterday I returned from a business trip to Philadelphia. Your name is revered in trading houses there as a man capable of linking Philadelphia with the Indians of the frontier."

George Howard's eyebrow quirked as he swung his gaze peevishly at the backwoods trader. "'Twould seem your reputation precedes you, Mr. Butler."

"Only the good parts, I should hope. Sir," Butler continued, turning to the merchant, "thank you for your kind assessment."

"You bring us news of excellent economic opportunities on the Allegheny frontier, sir?"

"Unfortunately, sir, I bring you news of French aggression. Their army is at this precise moment inching its way toward the Ohio forks."

"Sir!" The merchant nearly lost his spectacles.

"They mean to dominate the Ohio River by erecting a French fort at the forks."

"But that will mean—"

"Precisely," Butler responded. "If we allow that to happen, France will control the fur trade all the way from Canada to New Orleans."

A squat Lancaster banker lowered his fork. "Then you must ride to Philadelphia and alert the governor.

Tell him what you know. Describe to the Assembly what you have seen!"

"Precisely what Mr. Butler intends doing first thing tomorrow morning." Sukey's interruption broke the train of conversation. "Now, gentlemen, I see your tense brows furrow at these matters. Talk of armies and war will only roil your digestion. I pray you continue your discussion of these concerns over brandy and tobacco after dinner."

Butler's silk-clad arm pressed against Rachel's own. She relished the feel of him at every moment throughout dinner.

He bent down to whisper in her ear. "I thought you lovely from the first moment I saw you, Miss Whitfield. But never have I seen you so beautiful as tonight. It seems your glamour radiates through both tattered homespun and elegant silk."

She blushed at his compliments. Her gaze drank in the noise and proximity of a polite social gathering. "'Tis grand here, indeed, Jonah. But I am a country girl at heart. I was happiest of all out on those mountains. Listening to the birds sing, watching the sunset with you each night, sleeping under the stars—"

His voice low, he whispered, "I shall miss you tonight, Rachel. Might you consider joining me at the inn for our usual bedtime banter?"

She looked aghast. "Certainly not, sir! What would the townspeople think?"

"I suspected that might be your response. Then we shall not see one another after tonight, Rachel. I leave at dawn."

At the close of dinner, Butler immediately was drawn into a circle of businessmen anxious for every shred of frontier information. News that would directly affect their livelihood. Perhaps even their families' safety.

Rachel ached at leaving Butler to that tight cluster of men. He looked devilishly handsome in his sophisticated city attire. Occasionally he flashed her fiery glances that spoke of moonlight and restless bodies intertwined on soft blankets.

Stirring with a hollow longing, Rachel forced herself to make polite conversation with town matrons.

Later in the evening, Sukey seized Rachel by the arm and glided her toward Butler. "Rachel, dear, I so counted on showing Mr. Butler my impressive herb garden but find I am consumed by hostess duties. I would hate to think he'd leave town tomorrow without seeing my endeavors. Would you kindly do me that favor?"

"Your . . . herb garden?" Rachel had no idea where it lay, especially in the enveloping dusk.

"Yes. You recall, Rachel, the garden I pointed out to you this afternoon." Sukey gave her sister a wink and eased her out a back door.

Butler took the hint at once. "Most kind of you, Mrs. Howard. I should be most eager to see the clever manner in which you designed your kitchen garden."

Head held high and aloof in stiff-lipped propriety, he steered Rachel by the elbow into the garden till they passed a row of tall clipped hemlocks. When he was alone with Rachel in the dusk, he released her arm and faced her with a grin.

"I do swear, Mr. Butler, I have no idea which of you is quite the naughtier—my sister or you."

He opened his arms to her. "Come here, my sweet."

In the dark, Butler's eyes shone, his white teeth sparkled, his hair gleamed under a thin crescent moon. Garden breezes hinted of spicy rosemary and sage as somewhere a rusted gate creaked back and forth on its hinges.

She flew into his outstretched arms.

He pulled her close and kissed her. "I shall miss you, Rachel, luv," he whispered into her ear. He nuzzled her lobe till she groaned. His hand warmed the curve of her breast. " 'Twill seem strange, not checking on you in the night."

"Poor Jonah!" she teased. "No one to scold and lash with a rope."

He kissed Rachel again, pressing her firmly against his own hard body. His arms tightened around her waist. He deepened the kiss, probing the soft recesses of her honeyed mouth. "Stay with me tonight, Rachel. One last night."

"I cannot, Jonah. You well know I would be pilloried in the town square if I should be discovered."

Kissing away her objections, he lavished affection on her cheeks, her throat, her shoulder. "I shall sleep with my door ajar, Rachel. My room is at the top of the Black Swan's stairway, the second floor. And I shall pray that you come to me."

Twenty-two

Sleep evaded Rachel that night . . . the first of many without Jonah Butler.

His image tormented her. Thrashing fitfully in her canopied bed, she struggled to blot memories of the handsome trader from her thoughts. Jonah, tall and fierce on horseback. Jonah, compassionate to his assistants and small children. Jonah, making delicious, passionate love to her out on mountain trails beneath the stars.

"Jonah!" she murmured, fighting back tears of desire.

Unable to sleep, Rachel tiptoed to a six-over-six window and raised the sash. She stared in the direction of the Black Swan Inn, where Butler doubtless lay sprawled on some narrow bed awaiting her. Lonely in his room, as she was lonely in hers.

"Never did I dream, my darling Jonah," she whispered, "that our journey would end as it has." Her rage had evolved into love for the only man ever to conquer her passions. Butler had taught her how to love a man.

Now he would vanish from her life forever.

The ache in Rachel's gut threatened to tear her apart. *Pain?* Oh, Old Eliza had told it well! Men wreaked painful havoc on the women who loved them. Rachel's fingers edged to her naked throat. If only she still had her precious silver locket—the necklace known to save its wearer's life. Perhaps, magically, she could have kept Jonah Butler at her side if she still possessed it.

In the dark of night, Rachel might possibly slip undetected by townspeople down Orange and Queen streets to the Black Swan Inn . . . and Butler's waiting arms.

But he would know.

Butler, the self-described nonmarrying sort. She'd merely be another wench to warm his empty bed. Another toss in the hay.

In the end, he would still vanish.

Rachel crept silently back into her feather bed and pulled the woven coverlet up to her chin.

A rooster's strident crow woke her at first light next morning. "Jonah . . . my darling . . . about to leave!" she whispered.

In haste, Rachel pulled a striped cotton dress over her chemise and petticoat, laced up her corset, and hurried toward the Black Swan. Might there still be time? She could tell Jonah she loved him. She could—

But when she reached the oak doorway of the inn, there was no sign of Butler or his horse. Her calfskin shoes pattered against a narrow brick path.

"M-Mr. and Mrs. Howard insisted that I convey a message to Jonah Butler," she lied to the inn's proprietor.

"Too late, ma'am. He's already gone."

"Gone?" Rachel's shoulders sagged as she trudged back toward Orange Street to the Howard home.

She learned, that day, how dreadfully empty a house could be without Butler inside it. How desolate an entire town could be, in fact. Despite the presence of countless other people.

At breakfast, Sukey insisted on hearing all the details of her frontier family, and Rachel's journey.

"A tragedy, indeed, about poor Tom Blaine," she lamented afterward. "This very morning we shall both pay a call on Miss Lily Martin. She will be comforted to learn of Blaine's great love for her."

But the visit was scant comfort for Rachel, despite Lily's fond welcome.

"My poor darling Tom!" Lily exclaimed. Her blue eyes misted. "Pray, Miss Whitfield, might there still be hope that he lives?"

Sukey patted the girl's hand. "Always hope, my dear. Hold the good thought."

"'Twas kind of Mr. Butler to settle Tom in at Carlisle before he departed. A more thoughtful man does not live. Except my dear, sweet Tom, of course. Tom often mentioned that Mr. Butler was equally kind to his wife."

Rachel's spine stiffened. "His . . . his wife?"

"Yes. He called her that, anyway, though I'm uncertain whether the marriage was ever solemnized. She lives somewhere near Presque Isle, I think."

"P-Pre—" The unfinished word stuck in Rachel's throat like a chipped bone.

Sukey eyed her stricken sister. "Rachel, dear, you look a bit peaked. Too much activity in one day's time, I expect."

Back in her own home, Sukey settled her younger sister in a Windsor chair and pressed for more details. "What is this all about, Rachel?"

Tears spilled onto Rachel's cheeks. "I had no idea he had a wife, Sukey. None at all. I even asked him once if he was married."

"And his reply?"

"That he was not the marrying sort."

Emitting a huge sigh, Sukey offered her sister an embroidered linen handkerchief. "Altogether puzzling, I must say. 'Tis quite obvious to me that you two are madly in love with one another."

Those words brought a fresh spate of tears to Rachel's eyes. "But it can never be, Sukey! Not only does he have a wife, but the ogre *lied* to me about her existence."

Sukey paced the tongue and groove floor. "There must be an explanation for this confusion, Rachel. Give Mr. Butler a chance to—"

"A chance? I shall never see the wretch again! Even if he returns to Lancaster someday, I shall never speak to him again."

"Ah, the treacherous course of love." Sukey shook her head. "Why is it love can never flow smoothly?"

Ten days later, as Rachel quietly plotted her trek north, she crossed Lancaster's center square toward an open-air market. And spotted Jonah Butler riding into town. At the sight of his rugged charm, she felt as though she were melting into the earth.

"Damn his soul!" she muttered under her breath. "I shall on no account be his mindless plaything."

Pivoting, Rachel scurried up narrow Grant Street. She ignored the sound of hooves clattering behind her.

"Miss Whitfield!"

She would not turn around, she would not turn, she would not . . . Closing her eyes, Rachel prayed for strength and the proper selection of words.

A quick rustle, and suddenly Butler's horse blocked her path. "Miss Whitfield, a pleasure to see you once more. Might I offer you a ride to your sister's home?"

She exhaled long and hard. "No, sir, you may not. 'Twould not be proper. Besides, 'tis only a short walk to the house." Rachel walked as fast as her legs would transport her.

"Then I shall ride alongside you."

Her chin jerked upward. "Do as you like, sir. You usually do anyhow."

He contemplated her hostile response. "Not even a 'Did you have a safe journey, Jonah?'"

She sniffed. "You are back, Mr. Butler. Therefore I can assume your journey was safe."

"And you do not care to survey my assorted wounds, as you always did on the trail?"

Her gaze shot anxiously to his rugged figure riding tall in the saddle. "Were you hurt again, Jonah?"

His mouth shifted into a mirthless grin. "Well, as expected, I was excoriated for my news by most Philadelphia politicians. But I am hurt most of all by your frigid and puzzling response."

"Nonsense. You can be shot or torn to pieces, Jonah Butler, but nothing ever *really* hurts you."

In front of the Howard house, Butler dismounted and tied his reins to a log post. "Rachel, I missed you more than I can tell. May I come inside and hear why you've turned so against me?"

"You may not. You are a—"

"Mr. Butler!" Sukey Howard stood in her doorway surveying the sparring couple. "How wonderful to see you again! Do come inside and regale us with news of Philadelphia's pomposity."

"But Sukey . . . ?" Rachel spun from Butler to her sister.

"Thank you, Mrs. Howard. I should like that very much."

Gritting her teeth, Rachel hated him. Hated her sister for putting her in this awkward situation. And hated life for ever transplanting her to Lancaster. She would escape the first minute she could. From Butler, from this house, from this town. No man would ever seduce her again to drool foolishly over him as she had done over Jonah Butler.

Sheer weakness. And Rachel Whitfield was *not* weak.

Face contorted into a sulk, she endured Sukey's wretchedly polite tea ceremony in the brocade-draped front parlor with Butler.

"Oh, mercy!" Sukey suddenly exclaimed, glancing from Rachel's taciturn pout to Butler's glowering features. "Frost appears imminent tonight, and I so longed to harvest my rosemary and sage before sundown today. While Anna and I work on dinner, I wonder if you two might do me the great favor of gathering herbs from my kitchen garden?"

Rachel glared at her obviously conniving sister.

"I would so appreciate it, my dears," Sukey pleaded, brooking no argument. "Mr. Butler can carry the basket for you, Rachel, while you pick." She wedged a straw basket into Rachel's hands and shoved then both out her kitchen door into the garden.

Lower lip jutting forward, Rachel scuttled down a smooth mud path. Butler followed till they passed a line of blackberry bushes.

Suddenly he seized her by the arm.

"Release me!" she demanded.

"Not till you tell me what this is all about."

Enflamed by pain and anger, Rachel could scarcely speak. Her bosom heaved and fell. Glaring up at Butler, she shook a finger in his face. "Sir, you vilely misrepresented yourself."

"In what manner?"

"You told me you were not the marrying sort."

He swallowed hard. "I meant it, Rachel."

"Did you, now? How dreadfully convenient. I wonder, Jonah, have you neglected to inform your wife of this attitude?"

"My . . . wife?" Chill afternoon breezes rustled lavender and dill as a cardinal warbled from a neighboring oak.

"Yes, Jonah. The wife you occasionally trouble yourself over in Presque Isle."

Butler crumpled onto a wooden garden bench. "How did you learn of this matter, Rachel?"

"From Lily Martin. She . . . mentioned your kindness to your wife. I rejoice at least, Jonah, that you are kind to your wife."

"Sit down, Rachel." Eyes downcast, Butler patted the bench beside him. "I need to tell you about Collette."

Her lips quivered. She fought back tears. "I'm not certain I can bear to listen. I lost my heart to you on the trail, Jonah. Even freely gave you my maidenhead. But never . . . never did I guess you were this duplicitous a cad."

"Sit, damn it, or I shall tie you to this cursed bench."

She sat. But on the bench's opposite end. Hands gripped tightly together in the lap of her cotton print dress, Rachel stared straight ahead. She heard Butler draw a long, ragged breath.

"I once had a wife, Rachel."

Aghast, she squirmed to face him. "You cast her aside?"

"No. I'm not that kind of man, Rachel. Collette was a sweet-natured woman who followed her kin as they fur-trapped along Lake Erie."

"Was?"

He nodded. "Collette is dead, Rachel. And so is our child."

"Jonah!"

He rose and leaned against a split-rail fence. "I rarely speak of them."

"Why? Because of your anguish?" Her eyes followed his broad shoulders as Butler hunched over the fence.

"My rage, my anguish, my fear of unraveling as a man if I mention them."

Still seated, she reached for his hand. He backed away from her. His stricken face tore her heart in two.

"Tell me about them, Jonah. Please. I need to hear their story. And you need to tell it."

He hesitated. "Collette was half-French, half-Huron. Not beautiful in the classic sense, but lovely and warm and sweet all the same. Despite living with her Huron mother's people, Collette defied tradition and used the name her French father gave her. We became man and wife in the eyes of God, and most men."

"Did you love her, Jonah?"

"Yes."

"The boy, Jonah. Your child was a little boy, was he not?"

Eyes misting, he nodded.

"I guessed as much. Several times I saw you soften greatly when you beheld tiny boys. First, Daniel at Carlisle. Then the toddler along the Susquehanna. Tykes with dark eyes and wavy hair such as your own. What was the boy's name?"

"Marcel."

"Marcel. A beautiful name, Jonah. How did he . . . did they die?"

Butler's face flushed with fury. His fists balled at his sides. "They were killed by one man's jealous hatred. And a tumultuous night of snow."

"A man's jealousy? Did another man love Collette, Jonah?"

"Yes. I shall kill him one day, but in my own time, my own way. You know this man, Rachel."

"I?"

"Unfortunately so."

"Then tell me his identity at once, Jonah!"

" 'Tis none other than Chabert Michaux. The Fox."

She shot up from the bench and yanked Butler's arm. "You mean Chabert Michaux and the Fox are one and the same? The man responsible for my brother's capture . . . is the same man guilty of killing your wife and child?"

Rachel could scarcely comprehend Butler's words. She sagged back down onto the bench.

"Tell me how he did this, Jonah! How did he kill your family?"

"Chabert Michaux fancied Collette. Was obsessed with her, in fact. She wanted no part of him. When Collette married me, Michaux vowed revenge. One night, as a monstrous snowstorm rose near Niagara, Chabert told her I was badly hurt by a bear and calling for her."

"An untruth?"

"A cruel lie. I was safe and warm by the fire in a trapper's hut. That dreadful night, Collette carried the boy as she plunged into the howling storm in search of me. Somehow she became disoriented. They found her next morning, frozen to death and clutching our cold, blue son."

Rachel eased toward Butler. She laid a gentle hand on his back as he shuddered.

" 'Twas only recently that I learned of Michaux's role in their deaths. Swift Otter told me on this journey."

"Forgive my foolish behavior today, Jonah. I did not know. I love you, my darling. More than I have ever loved any man on earth. Please, let me help you." Tears moistened Rachel's cheeks.

In that late afternoon air rich with the scent of silvery lavender, Butler turned by degrees to face her.

Twenty-three

Unsmiling, Jonah Butler regarded Rachel's shining upturned face. "Never have I encountered such a stubborn, wily, tenacious woman." His hands remained at his sides.

She blinked at him. "And those are my good traits." One honey-colored tendril, eluding Rachel's elaborate hairdo, dangled against her throat.

With one finger, he lifted that errant strand. "You ignore all my advice. You ride over the mountains like a raucous pack drover. You wield a gun with the ferocity of a backwoodsman. And when you wake in the morning, with those green eyes and hair of golden fire, you look more beautiful than an Allegheny sunrise."

"Is . . . is that good, Jonah? Or bad?"

One hand still clutching the fence rail, Butler leaned closer. "'Tis very good, Rachel Whitfield."

She breathed in the comforting luxury of his clean male scent. His warm nearness. "When you first brought me to Sukey's house, then left, I felt . . . felt dreadfully lonely, Jonah."

"No rope, no attackers, no Mr. Butler. Very serene." His wry smile faded to one side.

"'Tis difficult for me to confess, Jonah, but I liked going to sleep each night and waking every morning to find you close by my side."

His large hands reached slightly for her waist. "With or without the rope?"

Rachel felt her heartbeat speed as Butler's mouth neared her cheek. "Love is the tie that binds two lovers, Jonah, more surely than any hempen knots."

He planted a gentle kiss on her hair. "I fought loving you, Rachel. Hard. More fiercely than a fish out of water, or a drunken pirate crazed by gold, I fought against your tantalizing charms."

"You never wanted to love a woman again?"

"Never."

"And . . . and were you successful?" She closed her eyes as Butler nuzzled her ear.

"When I rode to Philadelphia, I sensed I had abandoned half myself in Lancaster. It seems I need saucy, impertinent, sensuous Rachel Whitfield at my side to be complete."

His arms tightened around her waist. His mouth sought the upturned curve of her throat as she slid her cool fingers over his chest.

"Tsk. A dreadful predicament for a big, strong bear of a man such as yourself, Mr. Butler. What will you do about this dilemma?"

Soft raindrops moistened the silken air and pattered against their sophisticated attire.

He kissed her mouth lightly. "I have not yet decided."

She threaded her fingers through his wind-tossed hair and kissed him back. "Perhaps we should discuss it over tea." She kissed his chin. "Or over a high ridge splashed with sunset." She kissed his shaven cheek.

"Rachel," he warned.

"Or . . . " Her moistened lips parted, Rachel kissed his mouth again as escalating rain pelted them both.

He buried her in his arms and devoured her with a kiss that left her legs trembling.

"Rachel, my love," he began. "I—"

"Mr. Butler? Rachel!" Sukey Howard cried from her kitchen door. "Pray, finish harvesting herbs tomorrow. I fear you might catch your death of cold in this rain."

Huddled by Sukey's cavernous kitchen fireplace, Butler winked at Rachel. "Remember, Miss Whitfield, that day we warmed ourselves before your father's fireplace at Turtle Creek?"

At the recollection, she giggled into her palm. "Ah, yes, Mr. Butler. You leered at my ankles and I despised you with a passion," she whispered back.

Mirth vanished from his face. "And now?"

Within earshot of Sukey and Anna, she dared not pour out her heart to him. That she loved him with a devotion too intense to describe. Her eyes locked with his dark solemn gaze.

Anna peered out the Howard's back door. "Rain seems to have abated," she called out.

"Then I must return to the inn, Miss Whitfield."

Rachel tugged at his coat sleeve. "Just in case you are interested, Mr. Butler," she whispered, rolling her eyes impishly, "that window at the back of Sukey's house is mine."

"That one?" He lowered his voice. "Up there? On the second floor?"

"Yes. Right beside that sturdy maple tree with numerous stout limbs." She smiled sweetly at him. "Not that I am issuing you an invitation, Mr. Butler. Indeed, that would not be proper, and I am ever a proper lady."

"Quite." He glanced from the ground up to her window. "You are, of course, prepared to bandage my wounds, Miss Whitfield, should I attempt such a moonlit folly as a climb?"

"Indeed, Mr. Butler. I shall bandage your hurts. And kiss them all as well."

He groaned. "Ah, Rachel, my love, 'tis you now who have me tethered by a rope of madness."

Waving Butler off, Rachel strolled back inside in time to overhear an angry conversation emanating from the Howard parlor.

"George, will you—?"

"Oh, do not bother me with your trifling annoyances, Mrs. Howard. You are well provided for. Should I care to dine with you tomorrow, I shall do so. Most likely I shall be . . . elsewhere." At that, George Howard huffed off to his own bedroom and slammed the door.

Rachel comforted her stoic-faced elder sister with a light touch to the arm.

"You've been so kind to me, Sukey. I only wish I could put the light of happiness back in your eyes. The way you were as a child."

Sukey covered Rachel's hand with her own. "You must not mind my situation, Rachel. I do what a woman is meant to do. Care for my husband. Manage affairs of the household. Entertain his business associates."

"Does Mr. Howard . . . love you?"

"Yes. I think so. At least, I thought he did when we first married."

"You have no children, Sukey. Does he . . . ?"

"Ma'am?" Anna burst in. "Pardon, ma'am, but Mrs. Postlethwaite, from the church, is at the door and begs a word with you, if you please."

Turning aside, Sukey clasped Rachel's hand. "You must not trouble yourself over me, Rachel. Ponder, instead, how you will manage that tall, handsome trader who clearly is besotted with you, as you are him."

"Message for you, Mr. Butler, sir." The Black Swan's proprietor handed Butler a folded paper sealed with a red wax blotch.

Tearing the missive open, Butler scanned its scrawled contents, then frowned. "Damn!" he muttered.

"Trouble, sir?" The innkeeper paused from whisking clumped mud out his front door.

"A summons to Philadelphia for another session of talks."

"The governor, sir?"

Butler nodded. "But I have no choice. The Assembly must be convinced that if they fail to send guns and soldiers to the Ohio . . ."

"Lancaster might become a French town?"

Angry sparks ignited Butler's face. "I must leave for Philadelphia at dawn, Mr. Smythe."

The proprietor swallowed hard. "I shall have a fresh horse ready for you, then, sir."

Rachel blew out a squat tallow candle and finished undressing by the light of her bedroom fireplace. Loosening brown twill front lacing, she dropped her corset on a chintz wing chair. Combing out her hair, she stared out the bedroom window at stars glittering between crisp golden leaves of a huge old sugar maple.

Even a few hours away from Jonah Butler agonized her. Sweet love. Was that the pain Old Eliza spoke of?

A slight smile curved Rachel's mouth.

The slivered moon formed an enticing arc. 'Twas madness to even think that Butler would approach her bedroom at night . . . by climbing the tree, of all things!

Rachel laughed aloud.

Even so, Butler was a brash mountain man. No telling what he might attempt. Even in the dark. She nudged her window sash up a few inches, then with a sigh crept into bed beneath her feather quilt.

Shortly afterward, she heard dogs barking somewhere in the direction of Queen Street. Leaves rustled excessively, unnaturally, outside Rachel's window. She tiptoed across the hooked rug to have a look. And gasped.

Jonah Butler had climbed the maple tree and eased his bulk onto a branch leading directly to Rachel's window.

She feared his weight might send the limb crashing to the ground. Rachel clasped one hand over her mouth, lest she cry out. With the other hand, she eased her window open farther.

By inches, Butler crept along the quivering limb. At last, he squatted face-to-face with Rachel, who leaned with outstretched arms toward him.

Studying the window's size, he put a silencing finger to his lips and gestured for her to move back. Carefully, he eased one leg across the sill, then bent low to accommodate his long frame. And could not move.

"I'm stuck, luv," he whispered.

"Wait!" She shoved the window up to its full

height. And pressed a quick kiss to his contorted mouth.

He warmed. "Ah, luv, now you've created a whole new predicament." He grunted, and labored. At last, clearing the window, he stood firmly planted inside Rachel's bedroom.

"I tell you, Rachel," he muttered, brushing bark splinters and window dust from his shirtsleeve, "facing down raging bears and screaming panthers and howling wolves on the trail is far easier than reaching you in a civilized bedroom."

She giggled.

Standing on tiptoe, she glided her hands up over his shoulders and leaned against his hard-muscled frame. "But Jonah, luv," she asked coyly, "which do you find more pleasurable?"

In answer, he pulled her tight into his arms. He buried his face against her throat. "Panthers are less troublesome," he growled, nuzzling her ear. "Bears are less ferocious." He covered her mouth with his own in a lingering kiss.

"And wolves?" she asked sweetly when he paused.

Unbuckling his weapon-laden leather belt, he grinned. "Wolves, my love, do not tear into me with your same vigor."

At those words, she leaped back into his arms. "'Tis a cool evening, Jonah Butler. Come warm my bed and continue your sweet lessons of love."

When they lay naked and intertwined under the feather quilt, she stroked his stubbled cheeks. "My darling Jonah, how strange to think that when I first beheld you, I feared you."

He kissed her bare shoulder. "And I, you, luv."

"Why?"

"You held such sway over me, I knew before long

I would have to confront my past . . . and forever alter my future." He cradled her breast in his warm palm. "I love you, darling Rachel. With all my heart."

The words she'd been waiting to hear!

She felt his engorged flesh harden against her belly. His hands and mouth gently massaged and teased Rachel's body till she whimpered. His eager tongue tasted all of her. Her earlobe, her searching mouth, her nipples, her belly, her . . . ! "Oh, Jonah!" she whispered as he tasted her in ways she'd never experienced.

She begged, she clawed at him, she ripped at his long dark hair. Still, he would not relent.

"Not yet, luv," he rasped, kissing her breasts.

Thrashing in honeyed urgency, she seized him in her hands and massaged till at last he eased inside her slick depths. "Oh, my darling," she wailed. "Oh, my . . . my . . . !" She floated away on an ambrosial cloud.

She crumpled into his arms just as she felt his masculine release deep within her.

Cradled in soft down, they clung to one another.

His callused thumb toyed with her chin. "I shall have to leave again tomorrow, luv."

"West?" She snuggled against his furry chest.

"Nay. Philadelphia." He told her of the governor's urgent summons.

"Your parents, Jonah. Do they wish you to remain in Philadelphia?"

"Ardently." He stroked her flowing hair. "They envision me as a citified dandy dressed in fine silks and blissfully negotiating trade arrangements from within Philadelphia counting houses."

She looked up into his eyes. "And conveniently married to a demure Philadelphia woman?"

"Precisely. They never understood my need to live and deal on the frontier. Or my friendship with 'the savages,' as Momma and Pa are prone to call Indians."

"Did they know of Collette . . . and Marcel?"

Butler's face hardened. "They knew. And refused to accept her. Another reason they press me to lodge and marry inside Philadelphia's borders. They wish such a 'fiasco' never to happen in our family again."

Her slender fingers followed the angle of his broad neck. "How long will you stay with me tonight, Jonah?"

"As long as you like, luv."

"How will you . . . escape?"

"The same way I entered."

"And if you get stuck again?"

"I shall simply wave to the townspeople and shout that I came here at night to make love to my sweet Rachel."

Her mouth gaped. "You monster! You would not!"

"Well, then, that I have switched trades, that I now repair broken windows at midnight."

"You are frightfully naughty, Jonah Butler. Will you come back to me after your sojourn in Philadelphia?"

"Would you like me to?" Butler kissed her splayed hair.

"More than a garden needs warm spring or parched lips crave water, Jonah, I should like you to come back to me."

He kissed her. "I need you, Rachel. To continue my life, I need you."

Savoring his hair-sprinkled, naked, masculine hardness, she wriggled seductively in his arms. " 'Tis a cool September night, Mr. Butler. And I need warming in, oh, so many ways."

He rolled Rachel, taunting and laughing, onto her back and kissed her wriggling body into eager submission.

When the rooster crowed next morning, Sukey Howard encountered Jonah Butler dismounting from the crotch of a huge maple tree in her backyard.

"Morning, sir," she said, studying the red-faced trader.

"Good morning to you, Mrs. Howard. I . . . had early business today on Orange Street. On passing, I took time to note what a fine specimen of a maple you have here." He stroked the coarse, furrowed bark.

Sukey nodded. "A fine tree, indeed, Mr. Butler, though I note that some of the upper branches seem harshly abused. Perhaps some wild creature has been climbing up there." Her eyes danced in the slanted morning light.

Butler avoided her stare.

With a wave to Rachel, peeking from her upstairs window, Sukey lowered her voice. "Next time, Mr. Butler, consider using the front door. 'Twould be far easier." She laughed merrily and, waving him off, went inside.

At Lancaster's open-air market that morning, Rachel inspected fresh-killed chickens and tried not to think about Jonah Butler's Philadelphia family. They wished him to remain in the city. They would work at persuading him to stay. To marry a Philadelphia woman.

"Will he return to me?" she murmured under her breath as she strolled the market.

And what of his promise to locate Zeb Whitfield? Had he forgotten? Was Butler merely a rogue of the highway? Surely he was more than a lecher bent on carelessly debauching women on his travels. Surely!

For Jonah Butler, Rachel had broken down all her reserves. She'd fallen in love with him. And it left her vulnerable to a broken heart.

Traipsing back to the Howard house, Rachel brightened at her sister's cheery greeting.

"Rachel, my dear, I have a pleasant surprise for you."

"Yes?" Rachel slipped off her hooded cloak.

"An old friend of yours and Pa's, from Turtle Creek, is here to see you with some *wondrous* news!"

Rachel clapped her hands together. "Mary Hutchings! Or Tom. Is it Tom Blaine?"

"No, dear. 'Tis—"

"'Tis I, Mademoiselle Whitfield." Chabert Michaux, attired in Indian-style leggings and a fringed leather wamus, bowed low before Rachel. "With a most excellent *communiqué*."

Through narrowed eyes, Rachel grimly contemplated the Fox. "Yes, monsieur?"

"First, mademoiselle, I wish to return something of value to you." He held out Rachel's sparkling silver locket.

"My necklace! Wherever did you find it, monsieur?"

"Regrettably, you dropped it on a mountain trail, mademoiselle. I recalled having seen it earlier on your lovely throat. May I now assist you by placing the pendant around your neck?"

"You may not, monsieur. I am quite capable of affixing it myself." Ah! She relished the feel of that protective amulet around her throat once more. Safe, at last! Old Eliza had assured her that the silver pendant saved the life of its wearer at least once.

Sukey poured tea for them. "Dear Monsieur Michaux assured me he has news of Zeb's whereabouts, Rachel."

"Amazing." Rachel sipped tea and cautiously eyed Michaux. "Tell us more, monsieur."

"A fine English gentleman, Monsieur Hoffman, awaits us at the Episcopal Church, Mademoiselle Whitfield. He assured me that he can tell us precisely where Monsieur Whitfield is being held. I felt certain you would wish to speak with him directly, so I asked him to wait there at the church for us."

Rachel fingered the silver pendant. She sensed great danger. Yet this was precisely what she longed to hear.

"I shall fetch my cloak at once, monsieur. The church is only a short walk from here. Sukey, come along with us to hear the good news."

"How I wish I could, Rachel. But, alas, George insisted that I discuss family accounts with him. When you return from the church, dear, you must relate every single word of this exciting news to me!"

Rachel's glance swung from her cheerful older sister to Chabert Michaux's chipped tooth and blotchy countenance. The Frenchman's invitation had brought her to a critical juncture. Either it was a means to finally locate Zeb Whitfield.

Or an open trap.

Either way, Rachel could not afford to neglect the opportunity. She drew her cloak tight around her shoulders and followed Chabert Michaux out Sukey's front door.

Twenty-four

Michaux nudged Rachel by the elbow toward St. James Episcopal Church on Duke Street. "I knew you would be thrilled with Monsieur, er, Hoffman's news, Mademoiselle Whitfield. I came to you as soon as I heard."

She despised Michaux's touch. "Could he not have come to my sister's house as well?"

Michaux's eyes flared. "Oh, but Monsieur Hoffman is a most pious man, mademoiselle. After his arduous journey to Lancaster, he insisted on kneeling at the church to give thanks for a safe arrival."

Long purple shadows stretched like grasping fingers from the small stone church. Something about those shadows made Rachel shiver. Surely other worshipers would be in the vicinity. She would seek their—

Suddenly Rachel's world went dark.

Girding himself for the long ride ahead of him, Jonah Butler with a companion rode east of Lancaster. He crossed Shippen Street just as a young boy, breathless from running at top speed, called to him.

"Mr. Butler! Wait, sir! I have a message for you!"

Pulling back on the reins, Butler halted. "Who from, boy?"

The youth handed Butler a scrawled note. "An Indian, sir. Gave me a groat to fetch this to you at once."

Butler unfolded the paper. His eyes narrowed as he read the note in his hand. He flipped a shilling at the boy. "Good lad. Is this Indian messenger still in center square?"

"Thank you, sir!" the boy cried, eyes ablaze at Butler's reward. "He rode off soon's he gave me this."

"Which way?"

"North, sir. Directly up Queen Street."

Butler unfolded the paper and reread the terse note:

I have Mademoiselle Whitfield. If you wish to ever see her alive again, come at once to the first hill north of Lancaster. Do not delay. I have not much patience.

Chabert Michaux

Butler grimaced. His gut tightened into a painful knot. He *had* to ride at once to Philadelphia. Thousands of lives likely depended on his urgent plea for backwoods weapons. But must he make this vital trip at the cost of abandoning Rachel Whitfield to some cruel fate designed by a madman? The same madman responsible for the deaths of his wife and son?

"Michaux, you bastard!" he muttered. "I shall not let you do it again."

Torn by his twin responsibilities, Butler clenched his jaw. He quickly jotted several imperatives on paper, then handed the paper, along with a sheaf of notes retrieved from his saddlebag, to his companion.

" 'Tis a matter of life or death," he told the older man. "God help me, I must follow my conscience. You, sir, shall ride to Philadelphia in my place." After giving instructions, Butler switched directions and headed north on Queen Street.

Two dark-complexioned riders suddenly galloped toward him.

Lying supine on hard ground, Rachel awoke to a harsh male guffaw as a blindfold was yanked from her face.

"Monsieur . . . I do not understand," she told Michaux. She wrenched against the bonds that pinned her arms behind her back and lashed her ankles together.

He laughed again. "Of course you do not, mademoiselle. The Fox is far too clever for you. And your sly American lover. I have just outwitted both of you."

Michaux inspected the flintlock mechanism of his long rifle. He carefully measured black powder and poured it into the rifle's muzzle.

Her heartbeat raced. "What do you mean?"

"I mean, my seductive little treasure, that your lover is riding straight into my trap. And you . . ." He languidly stroked her bosom. "You, my dear, are the bait. After I dispose of the offensive Monsieur Butler, you and I will spend a long lovely night together, mademoiselle. A *very* long night."

He retrieved a lead ball from his pouch and centered it on a leather patch over the muzzle.

"You wretch! What do you know of my brother's welfare?"

"Your brother? Ah, yes. Travel with me, Mademoiselle Whitfield, and I feel certain we shall locate your brother . . . *some day.*" Michaux laughed uproariously.

He shoved the ball and patch deep into the barrel with a ramrod, then turned to one of his Ottawa cohorts. "Guard her closely, Lone Wolf. She's clever, this one. Though not so clever as the Fox! Black Eagle, you come with me."

Clutching his long rifle and powder horn, Michaux slipped through tangled wild grapevines to a concealed rock some forty yards away.

Rachel studied her Indian guard, busy gnawing on deer jerky. "Are you a brave man in battle, Lone Wolf?"

The Indian blinked at her. "Very brave indeed."

She smiled sweetly. "I possess medicine that would make you even braver still. Nay, even invincible to bullets!"

He eyed her skeptically. "You?"

She nodded. "A dried herb, which must be conveyed by my hands only to the recipient. The medicine lies concealed inside my silver locket. Untie my hands—gently, you understand—and I shall bestow the medicine upon you."

Lone Wolf hesitated. He glanced at Michaux's distant crouching figure, then back at Rachel. Discreetly, he slit open the rope binding her hands.

Flexing circulation back into her blanched fingers, Rachel opened Old Eliza's locket and dumped the last precious remnants of her cached dried soporific herb into her palm.

"Your water mug, sir," she demanded. She sprinkled the dried concentrated herb in his wooden mug. "You must drink it all at once for the medicine to be effective, sir. Do not hesitate."

Lone Wolf gulped it down.

"Excellent, sir. Now, sit down and close your eyes. That's it! Relax, and allow this powerful medicine to enter your body."

She watched closely as Lone Wolf soon sagged flat on the ground. Crawling to his side, she delicately retrieved the smaller of his two knives from his belt and slit the rope binding her ankles.

Crouching low to avoid detection, Rachel scanned the low hills north of Lancaster. Fruit trees speckled fields of corn and buckwheat. Cows, oxen, and bleating sheep grazed on sprawling pasture lands. Rachel's gaze came to rest on the hunched forms of Chabert Michaux and Black Eagle.

Both men sat concealed within a cove of vines. They faced south. On their shoulders, loaded and cocked rifles were aimed at the figures of three men approaching on horseback.

Rachel's hand flew toward her heart. The lead man was none other than Jonah Butler . . . riding straight into Chabert Michaux's line of fire!

To save Butler's life, Rachel had to do something at once. If she alerted Butler, the Fox would surely kill her. No matter. For Jonah Butler's sake, she had to take that risk.

Facing Butler's approaching form a hundred yards away, Rachel waved her arms and screamed with all her energy.

The sparkle of her necklace caught Butler's eye.

"Bitch!" Michaux snarled. "Black Eagle, dispatch that vixen. I shall finish off Butler." He squeezed off a shot at the trader.

Dashing down a hillside toward Butler, Rachel heard the shot. "Please, God, please! Not Jonah!" she cried.

Smoke emerged from Butler's rifle. Chabert Michaux crumpled onto the ground. Butler quickly reloaded. This time he aimed for the assailant who stood with his gun trained on Rachel.

And fired too late.

After Black Eagle fired, Rachel sank to her knees.

Another puff of smoke rose from Butler's gun, and the Ottawa dropped.

Scanning the horizon from horseback for other assailants, Butler and his two companions reloaded.

"Rachel!" he bellowed, searching for her fallen form till he saw silver sparkle again in the sunlight. He galloped to her side and leaped from his horse.

"Jonah," she murmured, nestled in the tall grass. "Thank God you were spared!"

Sweeping her into his arms, he quickly examined her wound. "Darling girl, you risked your life to save mine."

"I love you, Jonah. I would die for you if need be." Her weak voice trembled as she studied a curiously dressed Indian who'd ridden up immediately behind Butler.

"Rachel!" The Indian suddenly exclaimed upon seeing her.

"Quick!" Butler shouted. "We must get her out of here in case more of Michaux's men linger."

Rachel's vision blurred as she looked from the Indian's muddied face to Butler's. "I . . . cannot understand. This Indian looks—Jonah? Am I dreaming?"

Lifting her onto his horse, Butler clamped a handkerchief on Rachel's wound and held her close till they reached Sukey Howard's house.

"Lay her on the sofa, Mr. Butler!" Sukey directed, hovering over her sister with fresh water and clean muslin for dressings. When she finished dressing Rachel's wound, Sukey offered her sister sips of water. "Feeling any better?" she asked.

Rachel managed a slight laugh. " 'Tis my turn to be wounded, it would seem. Mr. Butler and I take turns, you know."

Kneeling at her side, Butler reached for Rachel's hand. "It would seem, Rachel, that you and I were put on this earth to watch over one another."

With one hand she patted his stubbled cheek and smiled. "I cherish that mission, Jonah Butler, without the compulsion of any rope."

He kissed her hand. "To uphold my end of the bargain, luv, I have no recourse left but to marry you. Then I can guard you day and night."

"Oh, yes, Jonah!"

"Careful what you promise, luv. Your sister and brother witness your words."

"Brother? You mean . . . George Howard?"

Butler's dusky Indian companion, with his arm around Sukey's waist, stepped forward. "He means me, Rachel. Zeb Whitfield in the flesh."

"Zeb!" she cried. "But . . . how? Oh, my head aches and I understand nothing."

Zeb reached for Rachel's hand. "You and I both have Jonah Butler to thank for our lives, Rachel. Jonah's Seneca friends, including Little Elk here, found me in a foul Montreal prison. They dressed me as one of their own, and brought me safely down the Susquehanna to Lancaster."

"So you see, Rachel," Sukey chimed in, "nothing left now but for you to rest up for your wedding. Oh, how merry! We have much to celebrate indeed. I shall begin planning for the occasion at once." Sukey clapped her hands together with excitement. "Anna? Anna! We have food to prepare."

Two days later, in the Howard garden, Rachel sat on a wooden bench with Zeb on her left side and Jonah Butler on her right. "Jonah, my darling, we agree not to be separated anymore," she said, "but where are we to live?"

"Zeb and I have a proposition for you, luv."

"'Tis a dangerous one, Rachel," her brother agreed. "But we would all face it together."

"Well?" she begged, looking from Zeb to her future husband. "You rogues have both aroused my curiosity. I have not shrunk from danger heretofore. What is it?"

"The three of us would return to the Ohio Valley," Butler explained. "That is, to your father at Turtle Creek. Together, we shall expand my network of pack trains and frontier warehouses."

"And the French? How are we to deal with French soldiers swarming toward the Ohio?" Rachel glanced from one man to the other.

A crooked smile caught at Butler's mouth. "Carefully, m'dear. *Very* carefully. The Assembly in Philadelphia has been amply alerted to French aggression. When they finally begin to converge forces on the Ohio, we'll be there to assist them in a dozen different ways."

"High adventure!" Rachel commented, gleefully clapping her hands together. "Oh, Pa will love it all!"

Crisp maroon and beige leaves drifted lazily onto their shoulders under a brilliant September sky.

The sudden approach of a man wearing a slouch-brimmed hat startled Rachel. He strode directly toward the threesome.

"We meet again," a male voice announced.

Rachel's hands flew to her mouth. "Tom!" she cried, suddenly recognizing Blaine. "Dear Tom!" She leaped from her garden bench and embraced the youth. "Praise be, you bested the rattlesnake!"

Blaine shook hands with Jonah and Zeb, then gestured in the direction of Vine Street. "I'm off to find Lily Martin. But first I want to show Miss Whitfield—"

"Sara! Tom, dear boy! You brought Sara back to me!" She clasped her hands and beamed.

The wedding occurred on short notice. A double wedding, followed by bride cakes covered with almond icing and washed down with sweet punch. Jonah and Rachel Butler greeted guests alongside Tom and Lily Blaine. Clutching Zeb Whitfield's arm, Sukey Howard smiled over them all.

"My silver pendant," Rachel commented to her new husband, as she basked in the love of her family and friends. "Old Eliza said it saves the life of its wearer once, then must be passed on. I've had my turn. But I puzzle over who ought to receive the necklace next."

He patted her hand, laced round his elbow. "When the time is right, luv, you will know."

"Just as I knew you were the only man for me?"

"'Tis forever, luv," Jonah whispered. "We shall bandage one another's wounds forever."

Rachel pinked with joy. "Darling Jonah. I shall need all of eternity to show you how much I love you."

"Without benefit of a rope?"

Rachel slid her hand tighter round his arm. "Do save the rope, Jonah. Hang it on a wall in our new home. 'Twill serve as a reminder of when we first fell in love."

His eyes crinkled in merriment. "I have better ways of reminding you, luv."

"You *scoundrel,*" she whispered, laughing back at her new husband. "I can scarcely wait!"

AUTHOR'S NOTE

Marilyn Herr writes both contemporary and historical fiction. She's happiest when immersed in nature. Gardening is a joy so long as she can contemplate flowers, listen to songbirds, and ignore weeds. A former nurse, she finds that writing is a magic door leading to a surprise kingdom where her imagination can roam freely. She loves hearing from readers at: mherr@ccis.net.

Put a Little Romance in Your Life With
Melanie George

__**Devil May Care**
0-8217-7008-X $5.99US/$7.99CAN

__**Handsome Devil**
0-8217-7009-8   5.99US/$7.99CAN

__**Devil's Due**
0-8217-7010-1 $5.99US/$7.99CAN

__**The Mating Game**
0-8217-7120-5 $5.99US/$7.99CAN

Call toll free **1-888-345-BOOK** to order by phone or use this coupon to order by mail, or order online at **www.kensingtonbooks.com**.
Name_____
Address_____
City _____State_____Zip_____
Please send me the books I have checked above.
I am enclosing $_____
Plus postage and handling* $_____
Sales Tax (in New York and Tennessee only) $_____
Total amount enclosed $_____
*Add $2.50 for the first book and $.50 for each additional book.
Send check or money order (no cash or CODs) to:
Kensington Publishing Corp., Dept. C.O., 850 Third Avenue, New York, NY 10022
Prices and numbers subject to change without notice. All orders subject to availability.

Visit our website at **www.kensingtonbooks.com**.